Ed Perez wants the simple things in life: a mass of riches through any means possible, a new and mysterious mistress, and unquestioning adoration from the mainstream media. Since he's the new U.S. president, that shouldn't be a big thing to ask for ...

Or, it wouldn't be if people stopped getting in the way of his ruthless schemes. A wronged head of security; a beautiful Brazilian woman hiding a tragic secret; and a rich CEO pulling Ed's strings behind the scenes are the least of his worries.

He's also got to worry about his brain-dead trophy wife; a slightly unhinged and thoroughly eccentric dictator; and his gay son, Diego, whose environmental activism won't allow him to stand by and watch his father profit from the decimation of the earth— even though it means Diego's putting his own life and the life of the people he loves most in danger.

Centered around a colorful and diverse group of characters, Jon McDonald's *The Seed* is a tangled tale of politics, greed, murder and the struggle for power.

I0544006

This is a work of fiction. All characters, places and events are from the author's imagination and should not be confused with fact. Any resemblance to persons, living or dead, events or places is purely coincidental.

Copyright 2016 by Jon McDonald

All rights reserved, including the right of reproduction in whole or in part in any form.

Published by
NineStar Press
PO Box 91792
Albuquerque, New Mexico, 87199
www.ninestarpress.com

Print ISBN # 978-1-911153-89-4
Original Cover Art by Aria Tan
Print Cover by Natasha Snow
Edited by Erica Mills

No part of this publication may be reproduced in any material form, whether by printing, photocopying, scanning or otherwise without the written permission of the publisher, NineStar Press, LLC

THE SEED

An Ironic Political Thriller

Jon McDonald

Dedication

To the McDonald's Farm gang
Mike and Barbara

Prologue

The Planting

Tous tightly clutched the tattered leather pouch to his side. After being torn from his mother at the age of fourteen, it was all he had left from his family. The bag was almost empty; it held little more than some rough sacred stones to ward off the evil eye, and a stash of fruit from the Monkey Bread tree that had sustained him on the journey across the Atlantic. The fruit was now almost depleted.

Slaves were regularly fed yams, and oat stew—hardly a substantial diet. But Tous's Monkey Bread fruit, which his people considered a whole food, had kept him in better health than most of the other slaves. He'd concealed his pouch from the masters, but doing so meant sequestering himself in the foulest part of the ship to avoid detection during the horrendous trip over from Africa to the shores of Brazil.

Once they arrived, the ship's master, eager to be rid of his stinking cargo, forced the slaves—at least those who were still alive—from the bowels of the ship's hold. They were herded by the crew onto flat-bottomed boats and transported up a wide river valley where the rain forest came down to the edge of the river. As Tous crouched in the bottom of the boat, he noticed how different the fecund forest smelled—of mulchy damp—and tasted—of copper and salt—from the dry hill region of Africa where he'd been born and raised.

Once situated in their new home, it was the slaves' job to clear away the forest and prepare the soil for the planting of sugar cane. But the cemetery was growing faster than the cane fields. Many of his fellow slaves came down with fever in this hellish mosquito-ridden climate, and as there was little that could be done for them, many of them died.

How ugly the clear-cut fields were in this strange and forbidding

1

land. The animals and birds grieved and fled. The waste from the burned slash clouded the river. The rains created flooding and erosion. But slowly the land was forced to yield, and the sugar cane fields were established. Barns, sheds, and a sugar mill were built. The master's house rose on the high ground, and finally, simple shacks were erected for the slaves.

When Tous turned sixteen he was baptized and given the last name of Braga—after the master's home district in Portugal. He was given a wife, Graça. On their wedding day, having bribed the overseer with a pencil he'd found behind the Master's house while gardening, he was allowed to take her up to his favorite spot on a high rise just downriver from the plantation. It was drier there and reminded him of his home. He gave her the very last remnant of his homeland as a wedding present—a seed from the Monkey Bread fruit that had sustained him on his journey across the Atlantic, his sacred stones having been stolen from him not long after he first settled on the plantation. It was his most precious possession, but as she held it in her hand she appeared puzzled. She looked up at him with questioning eyes.

Tous smiled and took the seed from her hand. He put it in his mouth. The seed had dried during the two years he'd been in Brazil, and he wanted to moisten it. He leaned in toward her, and as he kissed Graça, he transferred the seed to her mouth. She was startled, but also aroused. As they kissed, they played a game of "pass the seed," the game moving them to seek a bed of grass to consummate their nuptials.

At the exact moment their baby was conceived, establishing a new line on a new continent, Graça pushed the moistened seed into the soft earth at the margin of the grasses. It marked the spot where history would play out in ways that could not yet be foreseen. Just as the seed germinated in her, the seed of the tree sprouted and began to grow into a tall and majestic sentinel that would oversee this land for centuries to come.

PART I: A NEW DAWN FOR AMERICA

The President-Elect

Mid-November after the presidential elections

Edward Perez, President-Elect of the United States of America, sat at his desk at Perez Petroleum, in the heart of downtown Chicago, clearing out his office. It had been a long and grueling election campaign. While he was elated at his personal victory, he was also exhausted. He desperately needed a week or two without the media pounding after him every waking moment. Elena, his new, thirty-eight-year-old, campaign-perfect wife, was nagging him to take a Caribbean cruise, but the Secret Service had nixed that idea immediately. As the new president-to-be, they told him, he would be way too exposed and vulnerable. Elena would just need to get used to this new way of living—restricted and under constant Secret Service supervision.

Edward's family had a summer estate on the Michigan Upper Peninsula right on the lake, surrounded by vast acres of unspoiled mixed conifer and maple forest. It was the perfect location for the peace and quiet he craved. Once he was inaugurated, Edward could take Marine One and, in no time at all, be at Milwaukee's General Mitchell International Airport if he needed to catch Air Force One to get back to Washington in a hurry. So, instead of a cruise, it would have to be a working vacation at the summer house in Michigan—though, because it was now late autumn, there was always the danger they might become snowed in.

Elena's fantasy of a tropical paradise vacation had to be put aside, he'd decided, as pressure was now on for him to select his cabinet, and not even Elena's pouty pleading could dissuade him.

Today it was time to turn Perez Petroleum over to his Board of Directors and consign the Chicago house to his son, Diego, and/or his daughter, Carmella, for caretaking for at least the next four or eight years.

It was not an easy task for him to relinquish control of the business he'd founded in a parched Texas town over forty years ago. He had started out with nothing but a rusted Ford pickup, a few hired hands, and his native smarts—building Perez Petroleum into the second largest, privately held, gas and oil exploration company in the United States, with many domestic and overseas contracts.

But Ed had been a hard worker, and while his hair was thinning, he had maintained his shape and macho Latin good looks. He inspired confidence on a campaign poster or on the cover of *Time Magazine*. By leveraging his humble beginnings and the exploding worldwide energy crisis, and with the help of major Republican backing and corporate money, he had overcome all opposition to his candidacy—despite heroic efforts to defeat him by the environmentalists, and (what Ed called) the dippity-do liberals.

"Mr. President-Elect, AmVista's Chairman, Terrance Geiger, is on line one," Ed's secretary announced, poking his head through the office door.

"Kevin, you know I'm not taking any more calls here. I'm done. My transition team is now handling all my communications."

"I explained that, sir, but he says it's very urgent. He asks as a personal favor."

Ed pondered for a moment.

"I guess it won't hurt just this once." Ed picked up the phone. "Terrance, you old dog, what's up?"

"Ed...sorry...I mean, Mr. President-Elect..." Terrance laughed. "This is going to take some getting used to."

"Ed's fine."

"I know this is probably not the way these things should be handled now, but I need you to know something very important that might well affect your presidency."

That got Ed's full attention.

"Just a moment." Ed went to the office door and closed it so no one could listen in—neither his business staff, nor his presidential team. "Go ahead, Terrance. What is it?"

"My sources in Venezuela tell me there's a major military buildup about to take place that could adversely affect the global energy markets."

"Really? I've not been briefed on any such activity."

"My source is very reliable, and we both know Casados is such a wild card. I'm sorry that we ever had to use him to help us with that Brightway business. And, Ed—" he paused, unsure if he needed to say this—"But I just wanted to remind you to erase any trace of your involvement with Brightway."

"I'm aware of that Terrance, believe me. I've taken all the necessary precautions."

"Good. And Ed, I just want to be sure you understand, this Venezuelan situation could potentially escalate into a major conflict. Please keep an eye on Casados. He's a wily critter."

Ed was silent for a moment. So this was what it was going to be like to be president, he realized in a brief moment of panic. He'd need to surround himself with the very best people as close advisors.

"Terrance, let me have some of my people get back to you for a briefing on the Venezuelan details. I'll give your report my fullest attention. Thanks for the heads-up." Ed made a mental note to consider Terrance Geiger as his energy secretary.

☆☆☆

Diego steadfastly refused to use a dictionary when he was doing the Chicago Tribune crossword puzzle in bed on Sunday mornings. Brandon, on the other hand, had no such qualms. Diego told Brandon he was cheating whenever Brandon consulted the dictionary he kept surreptitiously tucked under his pillow, but Brandon shrugged the accusation off. Chiquita couldn't care less. The Chihuahua scratched an urgent itch behind her left ear, curled up again between the two of them on the bed, and immediately dozed off again.

"What are we going to do about the apartment when we have to move into your dad's place?" Brandon asked, contemplatively, after he got stuck on forty-nine down.

Diego responded with a combination of an "Um" and a cough.

That was not a satisfactory answer for Brandon. "What?"

Diego shook out the sports section in annoyance. "I've already told you we can't discuss that just yet. I don't have all the details about the house. I don't know what Carmella's plans are. I don't know what Dad's plans are. And I need to have this fucking Secret Service briefing before we have any idea about what we can or cannot do."

Brandon grinned. "Am I gonna have a Secret Service detail too? That would be so cool."

Diego shook his head. "I doubt it. I can just see my dad's Nazi supporters having a shit fit over his gay son using taxpayer dollars to coddle his male lover."

"Hey, that's it," Brandon yelled suddenly, grabbing his puzzle page. "What's it?"

"Forty-nine down—coddle. Perfect. There's my last word."

"Yeah, but you cheated."

"I don't think so."

Diego looked nothing like what you might expect a president-elect's son to look like. At age thirty-two, with his long black hair, his scruffy beard, and his dark piercing eyes he looked more like a mountain man than a president's son. That was partly due to the fact that he had just returned from a two month trip to Bhutan. He hadn't reacclimated yet to the wilds of urban Chicago after the rigors of meditating in a monastery. He needed a haircut and a shave to be all spiffy and presentable tomorrow morning when he returned to work at Gardner, Chappell, and Banks—a leading Chicago law firm that had taken on Diego as a junior associate, but only after his mother's urgent and insistent pleading. She was one of their top billed clients and had clout with the brass. Not that he wasn't bright and well qualified for the position. But his rebellious reputation in the legal community preceded him: he was considered fiercely anti-establishment and too politically ambitious.

He identified himself as a *Terraist*—a term derived from the word Terra meaning "Earth." Diego had worked for several years with a number of different mainstream environmental groups, but their inability to accomplish anything of significance only frustrated him. So he'd decided he needed to work from within the system, closer to the heart of darkness—where he could subvert corrupt power structures like a Trojan virus growing stealthily inside an infernal machine. That's why he'd pleaded with his mother to help him find the right firm to take him on. He relished the idea of being a wolf in sheep's clothing. His saucy renegade mother, long divorced from his father, happily complied.

Brandon stared at his wild-man boyfriend. "I'll be very pleased when I can see your face again. You look like a wilderness wolf-man right now."

"I'll shave the beard if you cut my hair. I have to be bright and shiny as a new penny when I go back to work tomorrow."

"Well, maybe." Brandon hesitated. "But I'm not at all sure I like you going out there again to work for The Man."

Diego threw his hands up in the air. "But how else can I subvert the system? I have to do something to counteract my father's dastardly deeds."

"You are *too* much. But I still don't understand how you two can get along as well as you do. He must hate what you do."

"He does, and I certainly hate what he stands for too, but it doesn't get in the way of our personal relationship. And he does accept that I live with a crummy, lowlife homo, so he can't be all that bad."

Brandon threw the arts section at Diego and bounded out of bed to be the first in the shower. Chiquita sprang from her sleep in shock and consternation at the disturbance and charged out of the room to her supper bowl, seeking solace after the rude interruption of her nap.

☆☆☆

At three a.m. on a bitterly cold morning near Columbia University, along the upper west side of Central Park in New York City, a solitary figure stalked the almost deserted street. Only the occasional cab or solitary car cruised by. The androgynous figure, rushing along the park, was wrapped in a down coat, knit cap, and muffler—hiding all but their eyes and nose—frantic breath gushing forth like ghostly blossoms. The person waved their arms wildly in the air as they carried on an inner monologue. A casual observer might be inclined to cross the street to

9

avoid such a person, assuming it was some unstable crazy who might pose a threat. There was no way to guess the depth of their anger, or realize the insipient danger the figure posed—a danger that could reach even to the highest levels of the land.

It's What's Best for the Country

Six Months Earlier

The AmVista Center in downtown Houston was an ostentatious gem on the Houston skyline, funded by the rapidly expanding price of oil. The corporate offices were popularly called the eggplant—not unfairly, given its appearance. The main office tower was rounded at the top while its tinted windows reflected a faint aubergine hue.

The stepped plaza around the building consisted of a series of ponds, each sporting its own fountain. Anyone walking into the building when it was windy was refreshed with a cooling spray on a hot Houston summer's day. And while the office tower claimed a quarter of the block, the rest of the block was filled by the AmVista Sports Center—a complex of hockey, basketball, tennis, and racquetball facilities, with, of course, ample underground parking.

The AmVista boardroom took up the whole top floor of the office tower. Terrance Geiger sat at one end of the board table. His back was to the table; he faced the floor-to-ceiling windows, his legs stretched out before him, as he leaned back in his chair, gazing across the shimmering pollution that is the Houston skyline. He was thinking.

One would hardly take Terrance for an oil man at first look. He had none of the sun-burned, rough-skin look of an oil man who had worked his way up the corporate ladder from the oil fields. No—Terrance was more of the Harvard MBA type. In his mid-fifties, he was trim, athletic, and sharp of mind and instinct. He had directed a number of diverse corporations over the years—ruthlessly—and always with his eye on the next conquest—to be master of a corporation who climbed ever higher up the list of the Forbes top 100 companies.

Deborah Salcido knew better than to interrupt Terrance's thought process. Instead, she waited patiently for him to return his attention back to her. A woman in her forties, she was Texas blond and tough and lean as a hungry coyote. Despite the tough demeanor, Deborah didn't look like a typical head of corporate security either. The position was usually filled by ex-military types—guys with chiseled jaws, washed-out blond crew cuts, and previously broken noses. What Deborah did possess, though, was something most of these other guys didn't— ruthless cunning. She had started her career in her father's security and alarm business in Corpus Christi. Her brothers—wimps, as she saw them—had no interest in the family business. But Deborah did. Within two years of starting at the family firm, she had taken over the business and built it into a thriving statewide enterprise. She was as ruthless with her competitors as she was in every other aspect of her life. Rumors flew about how she might *really* have eliminated some of her competition. Rumors that caught Terrance Geiger's attention when it came time to fill the head position of AmVista corporate security. He'd recruited her eagerly and had given her the job on the spot before her first interview was even over.

Finally, Terrance returned his attention to Deborah, his face lighting up with a satisfied smile. "It certainly looks like Perez has this election thing in the bag. Barring some unforeseeable revelation, our energy PACs, along with Drugs, Chem, and Wall Street have managed to control the media and the message very much in his favor."

"Money talks," Deborah said with a smirk.

"Yes, it does," Terrance said. "And I have every reason to believe that the onerous restrictions and regulations on our industry will soon begin to tumble in our favor. The enviros don't stand a chance with a Perez White House."

"But none of it would have happened without the oil shortage. I don't suppose you might know how that came about do you?" Deborah smiled a conspiratorial smile. Terrance returned her smile, but wagged his finger at her in a subtle warning.

"I have no idea what you're talking about," he said coyly. "But now, down to today's business." He placed his hands on the table and was ready to move on.

He called his assistant. "Will you please send Ben in now?" He turned back to Deborah. "I want you here when we get this guy's report. There are some issues we need to discuss when he's finished."

"Ben Folinari?" Deborah asked.

"Yes. He's just returned from northern Brazil. He and his team have confirmed a huge new oil field just south of the Guyana border. But we're having some difficulty getting access to the land we need."

A couple of minutes later, Ben was shown into the conference room.

"Please take a seat, Mr. Folinari." Terrance directed Ben to a seat on his left and across the table from Deborah.

"Ben, how did the negotiations go?" Terrance asked anxiously.

"Not great. They absolutely won't sell. The land's been in their family for generations. It's a matter of pride for them. They insist that money is no incentive for them at all." Ben sat back in his chair.

"There must be alternative drilling sites," Terrance said with an edge to his voice. "There are certain to be other locals you could approach who would be delighted to do business with us and our rich supply of Yankee dollars. No?"

Ben squirmed in his chair. "I wish I could say there were, but the geological configuration there is such that to drill in any other location than at that particular spot would cost us literally millions more. And access to transportation would be another huge problem. I'm afraid if we want to access this oil we need that land."

"Did you offer to buy only the mineral rights? There's no reason we need the land as well, is there?" Terrance asked.

"Of course, I offered," Ben answered. "But it's not quite as simple as that. Look, we need their land for headquartering our operation for the petroleum extraction. We also need to build service roads around the area, and we would need to construct a pipeline to the river across their land and a lot of the neighboring properties as well. We can ship the crude out by river, but it's a shallow draft there. The big tankers can't access it, so we need to ship the oil downriver in smaller boats to the nearest port where the super tankers can dock. All of that has got to be considered. But these people say they want nothing at all to do with us. They've got this humongous ugly, big, old tree smack dab in the middle of their property. They say that it, as well as their land, are sacred or some such crap."

"And you're certain of the quality of the find?"

"Oh man, like you can't believe. An ocean of sweet, sweet crude." Ben shook his head. "You've looked at my report, right?"

Terrance nodded, then sat back in his chair and thought for a moment, a smile finally flickering, his eyes crinkling. "Money always talks—eventually. You just didn't go high enough with your offer."

Ben shook his head. "I wouldn't count on it. You had to be there."

"We'll see, we'll see," Terrance said confidently. "And, of course, there are always other means of persuasion as well." Terrance gave a quick, but meaningful glace to Deborah.

"Is there anything else, sir? My team's ready to go back out."

Terrance shook his head. "Thank you for your report. We'll inform you as soon as we work out our next steps. And I promise you we will succeed."

Ben stood, nodded, and left the room.

Terrance turned to Deborah as the door shut behind Ben.

"So you see what we're up against."

"Yes." Deborah sharpened her gaze.

"Any thoughts?"

"Of course. But it depends on the parameters and restrictions."

Terrance nodded. "I would ask you to consider this problem and bring me some suggestions for action—without *any* parameters or restrictions."

She nodded. "I can certainly do that."

"And for now, it is to be just between the two of us, you understand?"

"Of course. You can always count on my complete and absolute discretion."

☆☆☆

Lia Braga was a petite but powerful young woman. She dressed casually in African-inspired clothing. Her skin was the color of caramel, and she wore her dark hair close cropped, almost like a boy, because she didn't like to fuss with it. And her simple, natural beauty was more than enough to inspire admiring glances from both men and women alike. She spoke beautiful English, with just a hint of the Samba dancing playfully through her speech.

She wore little makeup, but her large brown eyes were bright and captivating. Tonight Lia stared glassy-eyed at her computer screen. She had been communicating with a company in California that was interested in developing products made from the Baobab fruit, but she was struggling to understand the spreadsheet they'd submitted for her consideration.

For Lia's graduate thesis, she was exploring the nutritional benefits of the Monkey Fruit, which came from the Baobab tree. The fruit tasted like a cross between grapefruit, pear, and vanilla; could be a sustainable food that would benefit the producers in Africa; and would provide a new high powered super food to a starving world.

☆

Lia's boyfriend, Cran, who was standing behind her, put his hands on her shoulders.

"Are you ever coming to bed?" he asked. "It's after three, you know."

She let out a sigh and looked up at him. "It is late, isn't it?"

"You are *not* going to solve all the world's ills at three a.m. You need to get some rest. You have that tutorial tomorrow, remember?"

"I know. Just five more minutes." She stared at the computer screen once again with absolutely no comprehension as to what she was looking at. "I have no idea what attenuated annuities are, and how they relate to super-foods entirely baffles me."

"I'm not sure you're even reading that correctly. But that doesn't matter right now." Cran picked her up from her chair and carried her to their bedroom. Her head rested sleepily on his shoulder. He had already pulled back the covers, and he laid her gently on the bed, then pulled the covers up snugly around her neck. She watched him return to the computer and shut it down so she would not be tempted to return to its seductive siren song. He returned and crawled back into bed beside her. She rested her head on his shoulder as she swiftly drifted off to sleep.

And that night she once again dreamed of her home and family in Brazil.

Lia was the very first in her family of seven generations to go to college—and she'd worked hard to make her family's dreams for her a reality. She'd graduated with honors from her Brazilian university, a feat that ensured she was accepted on full scholarship to study for her masters at The Earth Institute, Columbia University in New York City.

A lot was riding on her making a success of her studies. Her family, though humble, was proud of its heritage. She dreamt often of the rambling farm her ancestors had established in the gentle highland above the river, just down from the sugar plantation where the family had been forced to work as slaves for nearly a hundred years.

Looming high and majestic in most of her dreams, was the Baobab—or Monkey Bread tree—her great-great-grandmother had planted in a location that was blessed with fertile soil and an abundance of spring water. The tree had served as a talisman for the family—a hope for a better future. And by the time they acquired the land, the tree was already thirty feet in diameter—a monster trunk with a strange scruff of leaves and branches at the top. It looked like a giant carrot sticking out of the ground with a green toupee.

And then, as tired as she was, she drifted on into an even deeper and dreamless sleep.

☆☆☆

The Perez campaign headquarters was bustling with activity after the recent positive poll numbers were released. New media requests were pouring in, and the volunteers were frantic with requests for campaign buttons and bumper stickers. The new polls showed the candidate leading by a few percentage points nationally, but there were still far too many states leaning toward the Democrats, and Perez did not have enough electoral votes locked up to clinch the election. Still, they were five months from Election Day, and a lot could happen in that time.

"We're taking a hit with the evangelicals," Martin Buckley, the overweight, frazzled, and hard-nosed Perez campaign manager said, sliding a paper across the table to Ed.

"Why is that? I stand for everything they could possibly want." Ed scoffed, tossing the paper aside.

Martin proceeded cautiously. "Well, to be honest, it has partly to do with Elena."

"Oh Christ, what has she got to do with any fucking thing?"

"Well, if you scan that report you'll see a lot has to do with her age— so much younger than you are. And then there's your divorce from Milly. There's a perception out there that you, ah...dumped Milly because of the breast cancer, and that it was way too soon after the divorce when you hitched up with Elena... See where I'm going with this?"

"I dumped Milly 'cause she was a fucking radical bitch. Jumpin' hell," Ed wadded up the report and tossed it across the room at the poster of his Democratic opponent that the staff used as a dart board. "Well, what can we do about it?"

"Look, your polls are nice and high with the Hispanics, and you've got business solidly behind you, but you are sucking with the evangelicals and the independents. The independents are almost always a toss-up anyway, but the evangelicals—we should be able to lock them up—if we play it just right."

"Okay, okay. How do we fix it?"

"And then there are the rumors of your affairs..."

"Oh..." Ed paced the room, lighting up one of his smuggled Cuban Cohibas.

"You know the Dems are working full tilt trying to dig up those fine ladies."

"Can't we just kill 'em?" There was a stunned silence. Ed looked up and waved his cigar. "Joke, joke. God, you guys are just *wa-a-ay* too serious. You gotta get a life."

Martin was not amused. "Maybe after the election—unless you would like us all to take an extended vacation right now."

"Sorry..."

"And then there's your son... You know..."

"The fag. Yeah. Well, that's just off limits. We are not gonna go anywhere near that bullshit." Ed paused and smiled. "Well, maybe we could recruit a boyfriend for our little pudgy Carmella and have a big white wedding in August. That could help. All that squishy family stuff—great press, right?"

Martin nodded, but was not satisfied. "But the evangelicals—we still need to get together a solid strategy to wrap them up."

"What about if I get baptized again?" Ed scoffed. "I could do it each day for a week across the south. That might do it?"

"Come on... You are *not* helping."

"Isn't there some goddammed conference coming up. Some stadium bullshit... Couldn't I go there and spill my guts about how much I lo-o-o-o-v-e Je-e-e-s-s-s-u-s, and I could grovel and puke and make 'em all weepy. That should do it."

Martin rose from the table and moved toward the door as though to leave. "Well, I can see that you are not going to take this at all seriously. So if you lose this election please don't come crying to me afterwards."

Ed was thoughtful. "Can't we make some kind of a deal with somebody? Find some top preacher guy and offer him a cabinet post or something, and then he can rally all his troops behind me?"

Martin chuckled. "Hey, you might just be onto something there. Let me make a few calls."

☆☆☆

The conference hall was crammed with a mix of boisterous roughnecks fresh off the oil rigs and suave corporate executives anxious to get back to their thousand-dollar escorts waiting in expense-account hotel rooms.

All of them were packed in to attend the US Oil and Gas Producers Association's annual meeting, which was being held in Chicago at the McCormick Place convention center. Terrance Geiger was seated at a table up at the front of the conference room near the speaker's table. Ed Perez was seated next to him.

Ed kept his eyes firmly on his phone, texting his way through the presentation speech. He smiled weakly at Terrance and apologized, "Running a campaign, you know..." Terrance nodded.

After his speech, the speaker paused and pointed his finger at the table with Terrance and Ed. Ed was still too preoccupied with his phone to notice; Terrance nudged him. "Now as a non-profit trade association, I am sure you all understand that we cannot officially endorse any candidate for president." There was a roar of laughter from the audience. "However, it does not take a stretch of the imagination to understand who the next president of the United States is going to be." A spotlight picked out Ed at the front table. He put on his biggest candidate grin. "I would like to take just a minute to call your attention to a very special guest here this afternoon, a close friend of our current member Terrance Geiger—and himself a past member of our organization. I think you all know our guest's name."

The crowd roared and shot to their feet in a standing ovation. Ed stood modestly and waved his hand. He leaned into Terrance and whispered, "Thanks for letting me attend. It's been a great honor, but I've got a dozen other stops in Chicago this afternoon."

Terrance stood, slapped Ed on the back and held his hand up high in the air like a referee announcing the winning championship boxer. "Keep up the good work, old buddy," Terrance whispered as Ed disengaged from him. He strode toward the exit waving to the assembly, the spotlight following and embracing him all the way until he disappeared through the exit doors.

☆☆☆

Diego was struggling with his head. It was hot and itchy, and he could barely see out of the eye holes. He hadn't thought about the sweltering heat when he'd volunteered to be a dancing polar bear for the GreenPAC demonstration. Now he felt like a fool in this ridiculous costume. But despite his discomfort, he couldn't help but laugh at the thought of what his father would think of all this. His father's new role as a presidential candidate had thrust Diego into the unlikely role of being a spokesperson for everything his father was against.

Of course, he didn't regret it—this was his calling—but it put tremendous pressure on him to stand up and be on the mark every single time he was out in front of a crowd. He was not just some dedicated protester. He was a symbol—a potent weapon against his father—an embarrassment and a nascent political force of his own. But, just now, he was struggling to get a breath of fresh air, and as he yanked the skanky bear head off the costume, he saw Terrance Geiger standing directly in front of him. Terrance immediately recognized Diego.

"Diego?" a surprised Terrance queried.

"Mr. Geiger?" Diego responded, equally surprised.

"I was just with your father at the convention. Did you know he was in town?"

"Of course."

"And you chose to dress like this and prance around with this radical group when you know how important it is right now that we all support your father's candidacy?"

"You and *your* group can support him all you want, but you can count out all of us in this group." A cheer went up from the fifty or so committed environmentalists that Diego worked with, as they waved their signs of protest.

Terrance studied Diego for a moment, before a faint smile appeared, and his eyes crinkled. "Tell me, son, how exactly did you get here?"

"I live here."

"No, I mean how did you get to this demonstration? Did you drive? Did you take the bus—the El?"

Diego smiled back. "I walked. No, I didn't use any of your global warming products to protest your global warming products." Others in the demonstration laughed and cheered again.

Terrance smiled a self-satisfied grin. "Very well, I admire that. Now tell me where do you live? Do you live in a hole in the ground? Do you hunt your food with a pointed stick? How do you really think this world runs? How exactly do you live your lives—all of you—without energy? How many of you use iPods, iPhones, iPads? Do you Google and Tweet and look for friends on Facebook?" The crowd was silent." His grin twisted into a superior smirk. "And what do you suppose they run on— squirrels in a cage? Do you listen to music at home? Run computers, watch TV? Do you cook on a stove, keep your food in a refrigerator, mow the lawn, take the bus or the train to school or work?

"Energy. Energy. Energy. This whole fucking world devours energy. And if someone doesn't have it, they want it. Now why don't the whole lot of you grow up and get a life? Examine this world a little more closely and with just a dash of reality."

Diego was not going to be intimidated by Terrance, and he moved closer to stare directly in his face. "And that is exactly why we are here. Of course energy is important. We're not morons. But we need to put our minds, resources, and dreams into alternative energy. We need to work together to harness the sun, the wind, the ocean. We need better and newer technology. But every time some new and promising technology comes along, you guys buy it up, bury it, and claim that only fossil fuels can save our lifestyles and, of course, protect your profits."

The protestors cheered Diego and pressed around him, jeering at Terrance.

Terrance reached into his pocket and pulled out a wad of cash. He peeled off five hundred-dollar bills and thrust them into the neck of Diego's bear costume. "Here. My donation to your oh-so-worthy cause." He turned to leave, but then swiveled back. "And be sure to record my donation as a gift from AmVista Gas and Oil...and send me the receipt."

☆☆☆

Lia was bustling around her bedroom, packing. She was excited to be going home to visit her family for an extended vacation, but she wasn't going just to enjoy her family. The trip was necessary in order to continue her research on the Baobab tree. She was progressing on her thesis, and her negotiations were heating up with the California company interested in using the monkey bread fruit as a new nutritional product. They had perfected a technique to dehydrate the fruit into a powder without the need for excessive processing and had discovered it contained six times the amount of Vitamin C as oranges, twice the amount of calcium as milk, and had a lower glycemic index with more fiber than bananas, apples, apricots, or peaches. They predicted a vast potential for profit.

Cran stood in the doorway watching Lia pack.

Lia had met Cran, an MBA major, in a thesis management seminar and was immediately attracted to him. While he was not tall, he was compact, muscular, and his long, dark hair fell forward over his face in a winning, boyish way. He was an assistant coach on the swim team. Within a week of their meeting, he'd invited Lia to the Columbia-Yale competition. The sight of him in his Speedos, with his coaching jacket, and cute little whistle had enchanted Lia, and within just a few months they'd moved in together.

Cran came up behind Lia, and she felt him put his arms around her from behind. "I'm really going to miss you," he sighed. "I'll be thinking of you every day I'll be working alone on my thesis."

She turned around in his arms and kissed him tenderly. "Me, too. But it will be good for both of us. Just think how fresh it will be for us when I return."

Cran hesitated a brief moment. "Baby, I've been thinking about us. And with you being gone most of the summer, I want you to have something to look forward to while you are deep in the wilds of the jungle."

Lia laughed. "Oh Cran... I think you have a gross misconception of where my family lives. We are hardly deep in the jungle."

Cran shook his head. "That's not important. What I'm trying to say is, I want us to marry when you get back. I was thinking of an autumn wedding at my family's place upstate. It will be so pretty in the fall. The trees will all be so beautiful then..."

Lia put her hand up to Cran's cheek. "Oh baby, that is so sweet, but you know how I feel about marriage." She shook her head. "I love us just the way we are. I don't need a marriage contract to be true and loving to you. And I hope you feel the same about me. And if it ever comes time for us to part, then we can just walk away."

"But what if we have children?" Cran responded.

"Then we will love them unconditionally."

"But..."

"No buts." Lia flashed him a smile and settled the discussion for the moment by planting a warm, wet kiss on his mouth. Within moments they had toppled onto the bed to execute a more passionate farewell. Cran would have to be content with this arrangement for the time being.

But he didn't seem to mind all that much.

☆☆☆

Carmella was so pissed. She'd been looking forward to her junior year abroad in Indonesia. Her plan was to spend part of her time exploring Balinese mask-making, her new passion after her trip to Bali last summer. But now that her father had decided he was running for president, he'd said it was impractical and unsafe for her to go to Indonesia alone. He'd said that until he became president (he was very sure of himself), there would be no Secret Service protection for his family. The extended tantrum she'd thrown had no effect: her father had insisted that she would spend her junior year back at Columbia. He'd promised her a trip abroad once the election was over, but told her she'd just have to make the best of it until then.

Everyone said Carmella had a sweet face. Which usually meant everyone thought she was fat. True, she was a *little* overweight, she admitted. She'd struggled with her weight all through her teen years, even flirting with bulimia until her mother took her in hand.

Then she'd discovered fencing in her freshman year at Columbia, and quickly became a major threat in epée on the women's fencing team. She was Ivy League woman's champion in her sophomore year, and there was even talk of her qualifying for the Olympics. And though her weight was still a concern, she believed she'd turned a corner in her quest for health and beauty.

But now that she was being denied her year abroad, she needed to search for a compensating passion, something besides fencing and her usual roster of undergraduate classes.

Today, since she was summering at the family retreat on Lake Michigan, she combined this search with the opportunity to lounge— sitting on the end of the pier, her feet splashing lazily in the lake. The sun was warm, but a refreshing light breeze blew across the cooler water and kept her comfortable as she flipped through the Columbia course catalogue looking for an interesting elective. Diego had suggested that she look at the Earth Institute to see if it might be offering any undergrad courses as it was considered a major player in environmental research.

23

Carmella adored her older brother. He was funny, and always accepted and encouraged her, even during her awkward years. She had been the first one he had come out to. And she totally supported him in his renegade environmental causes. She'd taken his suggestion: Now her search brought up a course in sustainability management which caught her eye. Reading the course description, she became more interested. It involved not only classroom study, but also some interesting sounding field trips and hands-on research. The instructor was a female teaching assistant, Lia Braga.

Hmm, that sounded promising. Carmella marked it in the catalogue and jotted it down on her list of classes to sign up for.

Just then her phone gave out a loud burp ringtone—a fact that annoyed her mother no end—signaling an incoming text. Her friends from down the shore, siblings Skip and Louise Mellon, texted her—did Carmella want to come sailing? Oh yeah! And she dashed back to the house. College courses would just have to wait.

☆☆☆

"The big problem we have, as I see it, is going to be the Brazilian government," Deborah Salcido said, as she sat alone with Terrance Geiger in his elegant and expertly decorated office—as cold and intimidating as he was with its cold marble surfaces and cool blue-gray fabrics. "We can't just instigate this kind of operation without legal repercussions. I'm sure you can appreciate that."

Terrance pursed his lips, unwilling to accept her conclusion. "Brazil is a very big country. Lots of wilderness. Lots of resources. Lots of corrupt officials. I don't believe we will have any problem with the Brazilian government. They know which side their bread is buttered on." Deborah smiled. Terrance leaned forward, "And you have exhausted all other avenues of persuasion with these peasants?"

"I'm afraid they are completely intractable."

"Too bad. It's always preferable to ease the way with money. Violence can often be a little messy. And the press doesn't like it very much."

"Of course."

"So you're prepared to proceed? Everything is ready?"

"It is."

"And there really is no other way to persuade these people?"

"I honestly don't believe they are open to any reasonable offer."

"And what about an unreasonable offer? Compliance is always preferable to force, even at a steep price." Deborah shook her head. Terrance hesitated but a brief moment. "Then let's go forward with your proposal."

"You won't be disappointed, I promise."

"And no slipups."

"Nothing can go wrong. It's well planned. All contingencies have been accounted for."

"Very well, you have my permission to proceed."

☆☆☆

Diego tugged at the stiff collar of his shirt. He hadn't worn a shirt and tie—except around his father—for years. But now that he was just about to enter Harold Chappell's office for his first day at his new job, he had to look the part. In his previous roles, working for environmental groups, casual dress had been the norm. He suddenly had a moment of panic as he contemplated the impending change in his life. But he took a deep breath and pushed through the office door with purpose and resolve. He knew Mr. Chappell would expect that from a new associate.

"Sit," Chappell barked, his back turned toward Diego, as he studied a brief. Harold was the senior partner, a man of heft and presence—his manner and corpulence reminding Diego of a scowling Supreme Court justice. There was an extended silence as Diego waited for Mr. Chappell's attention to turn to him.

Finally Mr. Chappell faced Diego. "So, you're a mama's boy?"

"I beg your pardon, sir?" Diego managed, in a controlled but slightly flustered response.

"Your mother got you this position; is that not correct?"

"Well, I believe she contacted your firm and enquired if there were any available positions. That was my understanding."

Harold smiled. "So that's your understanding, is it? I see.

Well...such a pleasant misinterpretation of the facts. Actually, your mother begged for us to take you on. She seemed to believe you were almost unhirable in the open market with your rebellious reputation and your leftist political ambitions." Chappell took out a cigar and took his time lighting it. "But she was finally persuasive when she threatened to take her very substantial business elsewhere unless we found a cozy place for you here in this firm. And as we greatly value her continued patronage, we decided to give you a try—on a trial basis, of course. You will have six months to prove yourself."

"I will do my very best for you, sir."

Chappell turned toward his office window as he puffed on his cigar. "And now I understand you are planning to take a two-month leave of absence in just six weeks. Is that correct?"

"I explained when I interviewed that I had a prior commitment. I booked a spiritual retreat in Bhutan months ago," Diego said, with just the slightest twitch of his left eye.

Chappell smirked, "A spiritual retreat? Really? How charming. And what exactly does your father think about all this nonsense?"

"We don't often see eye to eye on a lot of issues, sir. But to be honest, his opinion is not really of any concern to me. I certainly don't seek his approval for my actions. We often have to agree to mutually disagree on many issues—his as well as mine."

Harold smiled slightly. "Good, got some spunk, I see. Very well. You are on a trial basis for six months, including the two you will be absent. And as we at G, C & B are toying with the idea of opening a department of environmental law, you might just find your place here after all. But I am keeping a keen eye on you, young man." He extended his hand to Diego. "Good luck."

"Thank you, sir."

☆

"Wuf Moskowitz," the lanky young man with a straggly beard in the cubicle next to Diego's offered his hand. "Well, Jerome really, but everyone just calls me Wuf."

"And why is that?" Diego asked, shaking hands.

"You know, see a hot broad and I go woof, woof. Just sorta stuck."

Diego laughed. "Yeah, I do that a lot too, only with me it's hot guys."

"Gotcha. Let me know if you need any help—you being the newbie and all."

"Thanks, appreciate that."

Diego's desk phone rang. It was his first call at his new job, and it startled him. "Hello, Diego Perez," he answered tentatively—quite unsure as to who might be calling him so soon.

"Darling, how *are* you getting on in your new position?" a woman's voice crooned.

"Mother?" Diego was surprised to hear from her so soon.

"You have no *idea* what I had to do to get you that little job. They are a tough bunch, that lot. That's why I like them. But don't tell them that. I like it when they come groveling for my business. Keeps them honest and alert. How's your new office?"

"Mother, I don't have an office. I have a cubicle in the middle of a room large enough to house a basketball court with at least twenty million other cubicles."

"Well, you can't have everything right away, I guess. You have to earn a few things in life, don't you?"

"Yes mother, as you so often make abundantly clear."

"Well, I just wanted to say hello on your first day. And please do give a big raspberry from me to your father and that child bride of his. I sincerely hope he gets some nauseating social disease from her and gets trounced in the election. I just can't imagine having *him* as our president. I mean, I have seen him *far too many times* sitting on the john to ever take him seriously as commander in chief and leader of the free world."

"Mother..."

"Oh, and do save Saturday next for me—won't you my darling? I have an event at the museum, and I need you to escort me."

"I'll certainly try."

"Oh no, my dear—not try. You know how I hate that word. Just say, 'Yes, Mother.'"

"Yes, Mother."

"You are all the sweetness and light in the whole wide world. Bye, darling."

☆

Brandon was already seated at a window table at Drew's when Diego rushed in to join him for lunch. It was supposed to be in celebration of Diego's first day of employment but Diego wasn't exactly in the mood to celebrate.

"Oh...," Diego exclaimed, as he collapsed into the chair across from Brandon.

Brandon leaned across the table and gave Diego a quick kiss. "So how's the first day going so far? Save any forests yet?"

Diego banged his head on the table, rattling the silverware. "I don't know if I can do this, Brandon."

"Of course you can. What about all those grand plans to subvert the system from within?"

"Did I really say that?"

"I'm afraid you did, sweetie."

"Can I take it all back? Can I go home now?"

"No-o-o. Come on, get a grip. Have a nice salad. The Niçoise is well respected here."

"No, no, no. I need some real man food, something from a carcass. I need to gnaw on bones."

"Well, you could always join your father's presidential campaign if this job is just too much for you."

"You don't prize your life very highly, do you?"

Brandon attempted to divert the conversation. "You look very nice in a tie. I hope you have more than just one of those in your closet. Do we need to go shopping?"

Diego took a deep breath and leaned back in his chair with both hands on the table. "Okay, I get it. Gotta suck it up and get on with my plan to rule the world." He sighed. He motioned to the waiter. "Let me have the Ruben with extra spicy mustard and a very, very...very dry martini."

✩✩✩

Lia realized all too quickly how comfortable she had become with her new life in America. While her apartment in New York was considered modest by NYC standards, in Brazil it seemed extravagantly palatial. Here, her bed consisted of a frame with ropes crisscrossing to support an exceptionally ratty old mattress. The windows were plastic, and running water was considered the luxury of luxuries in this impoverished area. Her father was so proud of his primitive plumbing job that had brought water into the house. But the faucet dripped constantly, and it drove Lia crazy. Had he never heard of changing out a washer?

After her first day at home, Lia went into town with her father in his beat up old Ford pickup and surprised him by buying the family a generator so they could also have electricity a few hours in the evening—not completely unselfishly, though, as Lia needed electricity for her laptop to do her research.

The next day her father, with the help of five nearby neighbor men and boys, worked through the day and into the evening to install basic wiring and lights. It was simple and primitive work but it would serve. And the neighbors and family celebrated with a feast and cheered when Lia was able to plug in and turn on her laptop—a device few of the locals had ever seen before.

Lia's four brothers and two sisters, ages six to nineteen, had been thrilled to see her when she first arrived and thronged around her asking endless questions and demanding her attention all at the same time. Lia, as the eldest, had always been looked up to by the others. The fact that she had gone to college and lived in the United States only added glamor to her considerable stature within the family. Lia loved her brothers and sisters, but secretly she had a favorite. Scruffy little Cala, at six, with her short-cropped hair and quirky smile, had captured Lia's heart. She was shy and preferred to play by herself—except when Lia was at home. Then she followed Lia everywhere. Cala even curled up at the foot of Lia's bed on a mat to sleep at night, no matter how often Lia urged Cala to sleep in her own bed in the children's room.

But Lia had serious business to do while she was at home; she needed to spend time with her studies and research on the Baobab tree. Of course, the original specimen planted by her ancestor was the focal point on the family land, but Lia was primarily interested in the propagation of the tree on a mass scale. If her project was to be commercially viable, she needed to know how to create forests of these trees in the Americas as well as importing the fruit from Africa and perhaps even creating plantations here in Brazil. When she had last visited, she had experimented with propagation through grafting, and it was one of her prime tasks this visit to see how well the grafted trees had done. She also wanted to see just how long it took for the seeds to germinate, so she set up a small experiment to measure that soon after she arrived. In the heat of the scorching Brazilian sun, she constructed a plastic greenhouse with hoops of rebar and PVC piping—and covered them with a long row of plastic sheeting to protect the new seedlings.

And then every evening, after she had helped her mother with the dinner preparation, Lia would slip away from the house and walk barefoot over to her tree. Or, more accurately, the family tree—but to her it was *her* tree. As the sun set behind the trees down by the river she would either sit beneath the tree, her back up against the solid trunk, and think, or she would walk around its circumference, touching the bark with her hands, caressing it like a lover's back. The trunk was still warm from the heat of the day, and as the air cooled for the evening, the tree felt warm and comforting like a mother in winter. These were the moments that lived deeply in Lia, and drove her to pursue the laborious and exacting technical work for her thesis.

Little Cala had always wanted a tree house, and she had finally persuaded her father, when she turned six, to construct her a simple platform out of spare boards in the gallito tree behind the house. She guarded it fiercely from the other children as she considered it her own special redoubt.

Lia had only been home a few weeks when Cala came to her as she was working on her computer.

"When will you come play with me in my tree house?" Little Cala asked as she stared up at Lia with her large brown eyes.

"Um. Soon I promise."

"Tomorrow morning?" Cala pleaded.

"Okay."

"You promise?" Cala held up one of her dolls—made from knotted rags with a large nut for a head. "You can help me name all my dollies."

"Yes, I promise."

☆

That evening Cala was already asleep on her mat at the foot of Lia's bed while Lia worked on her computer. She was thinking about bed, when Tomas, her father, came over and sat across from her at the table. She thought he looked much older than his fifty years. His face was lined and leathery from working so many years in the Brazilian sun. He managed a faint smile, running his hands through his hair and then just looked at Lia for a long moment before speaking.

"Did you want to ask me something, Papa?"

"I don't want to disturb you," he said, but kept his gaze on her.

Lia leaned forward, keeping his gaze. "Is something troubling you?"

"I don't read so good you know," he said, as he fumbled with a paper he kept in his back pocket. He brought it out. He unfolded it and smoothed it open on the table in front of Lia. "Do you mind taking a look at this? I think I understand, but you might explain it to me in simple words. I'm not sure I know everything it's saying."

Lia took the paper from him. It was an officially stamped state document. She began studying it. "Dad, when did you get this?" she asked.

"'Bout a month ago, more or less."

"And have you done anything about it?"

"Well, I showed it to your mother."

"Oh Dad... Why didn't you let me know about this sooner? You know what this is, don't you?"

He bowed his head and spoke softly. "The government wants to take our farm."

"Yes, and the time for you to appeal is already past. Didn't you consult with an attorney or at least somebody at your bank? They could have advised you."

"I wanted to wait and see what you would say. You have all that education. I thought..."

She shook her head as she thought about what could be done. "Well, this is really serious. We have to do something about this first thing in the morning. This can't wait."

"Yeah. Officials have been out here several times telling us we have to leave. I just tell them to go away, they ain't getting our land for nothing."

"Oh, Papa..."

"I know... Thanks. Don't know what we would do without you." And with sorrowful eyes, he reached across the table and took Lia's hand.

☆

Lia was suddenly awake. What was it? It was totally silent except for a few morning birds and the soft rustle of the wind through the dried palm fronds outside the bedroom window. There was just the faintest dawn light. Lia was only half awake, but alert enough to listen. No one else was up and about yet. Her mother would be the first one stirring, lighting the kitchen fire and starting breakfast, but Lia could tell it wasn't her.

Then Lia realized what it was. It wasn't what she heard, but what she *didn't* hear. The drip from the kitchen sink had stopped. She thought for a moment. Had her father been up early to fix the washer? She doubted that. No, it must be something else. She got out of bed and, in her bare feet, carefully went to the front window that looked out across the farm toward the Baobab tree. She couldn't see anything in that direction. She went to a side window that looked out toward the road. Nothing in that direction either.

Then she noticed that a man with a toolbox came quickly out of the family well house. He looked briefly back at the house and then disappeared through a bamboo grove that hid the road at that point. Her first thought was that there were probably others out there hidden by the trees. She rushed to the sink and turned on the water, but nothing came out. She then ran to her parents' bedroom.

"Dad, Mom—get up!"

"What?" Her mother asked, her voice thick with sleep.

"Someone's shut off the water. And there may be others out there. I think they are coming to take the farm today."

Her father shot out of bed. Her mother followed, struggling to put on her bathrobe. Tomas rushed to the armoire, reached deep into the back, and pulled out a shotgun.

"Papa, no! That is not how you want to handle this," Lia pleaded. But he paid her no attention.

"Get the kids out back," Papa shouted, his face contorted in anger as he raced to the front of the house and out the door, shooting a round of shot in the air as a warning.

Mother and Lia gathered the kids together, who were terrified and crying, and headed out the back of the house.

"To the barn," Mother called to Lia. "There's a cellar. We should be safe."

But Cala pulled at Lia's hand and pointed to her tree house. Lia hesitated—they really should all stick together—but Cala pulled at her again, more insistent this time, and Lia followed, watching the others retreat to the barn. As she climbed up the tree, Lia realized this could be good; it would afford her a view of her father and whoever else might be out there.

Lia held Cala tightly as they lay flat on the floor of the platform. Lia could see well from this height, but the branches and leaves hid them mostly from sight, unless someone looked directly up toward them, as it was almost full light now.

By now a whole contingent of police and television press had appeared from behind the bamboo grove. Her father's gunshot had brought them out, guns loaded and pointed toward him. To Lia's horror, he aimed his shotgun directly toward the police. One of the senior officers stepped forward with a bullhorn.

Then, with the loud squawk of the bullhorn, he called out. "Tomas, you do not want to do this. Put the gun down. You know we have to take this land. We've discussed this many times before. We have some other land already prepared for your family."

33

Tomas, choking with anger, shouted, "We ain't moving. This is our land. Nothing you can do or say will ever change my mind."

From the other end of the road, a loud roar began to grow. Lia strained to look in that direction without being seen and saw a line of trucks and heavy equipment moving toward the farm.

"Tomas," the stern officer demanded again, as he advanced with his assault rifle raised. "It's time. We've shut off your water. We can give you one hour, but you have to vacate the property this morning, or we will have to come in there and forcefully remove you and your family. I know you don't want that. It will be so much better if you decide to leave peacefully."

At that moment, a Jeep from the equipment convoy broke away from the line of vehicles and headed rapidly toward the police. It pulled up abruptly, with a spray of gravel, next to the officer, and a blond woman got out. Lia thought she might be an American by her Houston Astros T-shirt. Lia strained to make out the logo on the Jeep she'd stepped out of—AmVista Oil. Yes, she was definitely American.

The woman walked over to the officer, and they conferred for a moment.

The officer held up the bullhorn again. "Tomas, these people are now the legal owners of your land. They have been very patient but cannot wait any longer. We have to come in *now*. They are not willing to wait an hour. They need to start work on the land right away."

Lia had to get out of this tree. If her father didn't stop waving that shotgun around, he was going to get himself hurt. After stroking Cala on the shoulder and whispering to her to stay hidden, Lia crawled to the edge of the platform. She was just about to stand up to climb down the tree when she heard the sound of a shotgun being fired. She peered down on the scene below. The officer had collapsed on the ground, blood collecting on the left arm of his shirt. The woman from AmVista dove behind the Jeep.

But it was too late for Tomas. The police let loose with a volley of gunfire, and her father twisted in a heap to the ground. There was no question in Lia's mind that he was dead.

Lia collapsed back onto the deck, sheltering Cala as best she could as the police swarmed forward. Carrying flickering torches, they set fire to the palm thatch of the house, the outbuildings, and the barn. Cala started to cry out, but Lia silenced her with her hand and body. There was nothing they could do for the family against the ravaging army of police. She watched petrified, her heart pounding, as the barn turned into a hellish, blazing inferno and collapsed in a fiery implosion. Lia didn't see how any of her family could have survived that, even in the underground shelter.

The woman from the Jeep picked herself up from the ground. Lia followed her movements, watching her walk to the edge of the property, where she turned to face down the road. She waved a hand, and the heavy equipment began to lumber forward.

The police dragged her father's body toward the road to a waiting police van. They hoisted his body into the back and closed the doors. The injured officer had already been taken away.

Lia, still holding Cala tightly, watched as the police roamed the property making sure that every structure was fully demolished. It was all Lia could do not to cry out. But soon the police retreated and left, as the heavy equipment drove onto their land and began bulldozing and crushing the plastic greenhouse that was protecting the Baobab grafts and seedlings. The old tree itself was spared, as it was far too large to be taken down by even the heaviest equipment, so stood alone as smaller trees were knocked to the ground—the solitary real tree in the forest of oil rigs soon to be constructed all around it. Lia watched in horror as her work was destroyed before her eyes.

When the coast was clear, Lia held Cala in her arms and carefully descended the tree. She rushed to the remains of the barn but the embers were still too hot for her to search for a cellar door. She had to get Cala to safety as quickly as possible.

Her phone was gone; her laptop was gone; her research was destroyed; and she had no money. And now she had a six-year-old child she was responsible for.

☆☆☆

Ed Perez was campaigning in Kansas City when he was accosted by the pushing and shouting press corps. "Have you heard about the massacre of the Brazilian family by AmVista?" a reporter shouted out, as Ed stepped up to the bank of microphones.

Ed sneered. "Oh, I believe you press guys have got it all wrong, once again. The moment there is even the most minor event that involves a major American corporation you liberal media guys blow it all out of proportion and spread blame everywhere, like using a flamethrower to light a candle."

"Ah, come on Ed," the *NBC* reporter scoffed. "We have tape from the farm. Would you like to see exactly the extent of the damage? They pulled the bodies of a mother and five children from the cellar of a burned out barn, after killing the father who was trying to defend his family and property."

How Ed hated the press. A necessary evil, Martin had explained to him countless times before, but one Ed could happily live without. "Well, it is my understanding from reliable sources that these were unlawful resisters. They had been legally evicted from their property by the Brazilian government. They had been given every opportunity to leave peacefully, and I understand it was the father who instigated the event by firing on, and injuring, a police officer doing his duty."

From the cluster of reporters, a *New York Times* reporter shouted out. "But to wipe out a family and steal their land so one of our companies could drill for oil. Is that what you stand for, Mr. Perez?"

Ed waved the concern away like a pesky fly. "Brazil is a sovereign nation with its own rules and laws. It is not for me to comment on the actions of another country at this time. Now, I'd like to talk about my revolutionary new tax plan. You have all my handouts. Are there any questions on how this will benefit the American people?"

☆☆☆

Lia was frantic as she reached the river and headed toward the ferry dock. She clutched Cala closely to her, scanning the scene for a friendly face. Her friend Gilberto worked at the dock; if it was his shift, he'd let her cross the river for free, and might even lend her a few reais to help her get to Belém where her aunt lived. There she might be able to regroup, conceive a plan of action, and find a safe haven for Cala.

She was terrified the police would come looking for her and Cala once they realized they were missing. She was certain that someone would inform them she was visiting from the States and was still unaccounted for. And surely someone would know there was still another young child missing There was no way they wanted any witnesses remaining, she thought; they would not hesitant to eliminate them. Growing up, she'd realized people had a way of just disappearing in this region when they got to be an inconvenience for the authorities. It would be just a matter of time before they would come looking for her. And the ferry would be one of the first places they would search if they hadn't staked it out already.

Lia was at the edge of exhaustion carrying Cala. It was clear the child was in a state of shock; she was pale and nearly comatose. And it was all Lia could do to keep moving forward. But she called upon her reserves of inner strength and pushed forward. It was their only chance.

As they neared the dock, Lia could see the ferry was just pulling out. *Damn!* It would be another thirty to forty-five minutes before it returned and that much time again before it would leave this side of the river. But this would also give her an opportunity to recoup her strength, she thought with some relief. She searched the area and found a hiding place near the dock in a thicket of high grasses where she could observe the dock without being seen.

Lia settled in to wait and get as comfortable as she could, making a bed from the bent grass for Cala to rest, but Cala would not let go of her. Lia moved as gently as she could, finally managing to get in a comfortable position. This was the first quiet moment she'd had since they had fled the farm—the first opportunity Lia had to examine their situation and think about their circumstances.

Her first concern was for Cala; her second was how to get back to New York. As much as she would like to take Cala with her, Cala had no passport. There was no way Cala could leave the country at this time. By a stroke of luck—though it had irritated her at the time—Lia had left one of her bags at her aunt's when she visited her, right before she traveled on to the farm. In that bag was her passport, which meant she would be able to leave as soon as she could call Cran and arrange for him to book her a flight and wire her some cash. But first they would have to get to Aunt Elita's.

As she watched the dock from the thicket, Lia saw a Jeep race down the road and pull up at the dock. Two burly, uniformed policemen got out, searched the side of the road briefly, and finding nothing of interest, went over to confer with the attendant and Gilberto, who *was* working as she had hoped. After a long couple of minutes, the policemen seemed satisfied and drove away, and Lia allowed herself a sigh of relief. Still, she sat almost motionless, Cala still clinging to her, until the ferry returned, unloading its five passengers. When the stragglers had cleared, a few more passengers got on and sat down to await the ferry's departure. Lia could see Gilberto on the dock securing a line. It was time to act.

Gently Lia disengaged the now-sleeping Cala from her arms, leaving her for a moment in the protection of the thicket. Nervously, Lia crept along the river bank to near the dock. She called out to Gilberto as quietly as she could, hoping her voice would carry enough that she wouldn't have to shout louder and risk drawing attention to herself. He turned toward her but could not see her as she kept herself concealed below the dock.

"Over here. It's Lia," she called out again, waving to him from her hiding place.

Gilberto finished securing the line and came over to her, searching her out by her voice. "Lia? Why are you hiding under the dock? Come on up. Do you need to get across?"

"Have you not heard?"

"What?"

"The police—they—killed my father, took the farm, and I believe the rest of my family is dead too—except for Cala. She's with me."

He put a hand to his mouth. "Oh, my God, Lia. How can I help?"

I need to get to my aunt's in Belém." She reached out and urgently took hold of Gilberto's arm. "Please. Can you help us?" Lia looked around quickly in every direction. "I saw the police come and go. I'm sure they're looking for us."

"Yes they are." Gilberto thought for a moment. "I have an idea. Where's Cala?"

"Just over there."

"Go get her and come back."

Lia rushed to the grasses and retrieved Cala. She was still heavy with sleep, —but she put her arms around Lia's neck and fell back asleep as Lia carried her back to where Gilberto was waiting. He was on his cell phone, speaking softly. When she came up onto the dock, he put the phone away.

"I've arranged for my brother to pick you up at the dock across the river. He has a truck and will take you to your aunt's."

"Oh Gilberto, how can I ever thank you enough?" She wanted to throw her arms around him and give a hug, but Cala was still clinging closely to her, so all she could manage was a quick kiss on his cheek.

Gilberto grabbed Lia's arm and led her along the dock. "Quickly. The ferry will be leaving soon. We need to get you on board and out of here."

The ferry was small. It held no more than ten people plus the captain. Gilberto helped them into the boat, securing them a spot at the bow. They would be less visible there, he assured her. Lia hunkered down with Cala and tried to be as invisible as possible. Gilberto went back to the dock and spoke briefly to the ferry captain. When Gilberto turned to Lia and gave her a thumbs up, she relaxed for the first time that day. They would soon be on their way to her aunt's, and she could sort things out and get back to New York. Lia closed her eyes for a brief moment. She was suddenly very tired.

Then she heard it. She looked over the edge of the ferry and caught her breath—watching with mounting dread as the police Jeep tore down the road toward the dock.

It pulled to an immediate stop, and the same two policemen scrambled out, and charged down the dock toward the ferry. Gilberto pointed toward Lia, and the police jumped on the ferry and quickly pulled Lia and Cala to the dock without any struggle. She was too exhausted to resist. They forced them toward the Jeep, and one of the officers said to Gilberto as they passed, "Thanks for the tip, guy. You can collect your reward at the station."

Lia's stomach churned with the realization of Gilberto's betrayal, and she shot him a furious look as they passed. Gilberto shrugged, mouthed "Sorry," and began releasing the line to the ferry as it prepared to cross the river. Cala began to cry once they were in the Jeep.

Deborah Salcido was on the satellite phone to Houston, standing at the new drilling site where the heavy earth moving equipment was working furiously to destroy all the forest around one giant tree.

"Do you have any idea what the press is doing to us here?" Terrance's furious voice came through clear as a bell, despite the long distance. "They are skinning us alive and raking us over the coals—both at the same time, if that is possible. The Senate has called hearings. And the Brazilian government is denying all responsibility. What the fuck happened down there? I thought you were on top of this."

Deborah squirmed, but she was careful to control her voice so Terrance wouldn't know she was vulnerable. "Everything was in order. The paperwork was impeccable. The police proceeded exactly according to plan, but the old man just lost it and shot first, wounding one of the officers. Then the police went berserk and shot him dead and burned down the house and barn. They had no idea the wife and children were in the barn. It was all a tragic mistake."

Terrance sighed deeply. "I expected better of you, Deborah."

Deborah ignored his pique. "But there's some good news," she continued. "The eldest and youngest daughters survived. The police are searching for them now. They ran away after the fire."

Terrance did not take the news in the spirit that Deborah had hoped. "I'm not particularly concerned about them," he shot back. "What about the drilling? Has it started yet? You know what it costs us a day to have all that equipment out there in that Godforsaken place?"

Deborah was resolute, keeping her voice strong and loud over the noise of the machines. "You'll need to talk to Ben about the progress with the drilling. That's more his department than mine."

"Yes, but I put you in charge out there. Goddamn it, Deborah, do I have to do everything myself?"

"Sir, before you dismiss the two daughters, you should probably know that the eldest is a graduate student at Columbia. If the press learns about that, it will open up a whole new can of worms for us."

There was silence in Houston. Finally Terrance spoke. "Then, see what you can do to help them," he said a little more quietly. "Maybe we can salvage something out of this mess after all. The press loves a heartfelt success story. Might help mitigate the mess you've made down there."

Deborah felt her face flush—she was *not* about to take all the blame in this debacle. "I think the cause of this disaster might be viewed by the press as being anchored in Houston, so don't fucking pile it all on me, Terrance."

Again there was a long pause from Houston. "Just take care of things down there." Then the line went dead.

Cala would not stop crying even as Lia tried to soothe her, stroking her hair softly and whispering that everything was going to be all right, even as Lia knew it might not be. The Jeep jerked along the pitted road at a terrifying speed. The police would not answer any of her questions, so Lia was left to fear and imagine the worst. She was certain they would be taken to an out of the way swamp and disposed of—no questions asked or answered.

So it came as something of a surprise when the Jeep came to a screeching halt at their farm. Without anything more than a stern "Get out," the police deposited them by the side of the road and sped off. The giant Baobab tree towered across the field. But Lia's greenhouse was gone. The land had been cleared of all other trees, and crews were already at work setting up the first drilling sites and creating roads through the fields and forest stumps.

Lia was so distracted she didn't see the woman striding toward them from across the field.

"Looks like you could use a hand," the woman offered in English, surprising Lia, as her attention had been on Cala. The woman looked familiar, but then Lia had been expecting a firing squad—not someone offering to help, so she didn't recognize the woman immediately. "Here, let me hold her for a while. You look tired." The woman held out her arms and offered to hold Cala, and Lia, thoroughly exhausted, allowed her to.

"Do you have any water?" Lia asked.

The woman offered Lia a plastic water bottle, and Lia took it gratefully. Exhausted, she slumped to sit at the base of a tree, leaning back against it and closing her eyes after drinking deeply from the bottle.

Lia finally opened her eyes. The woman was holding out a bottle of water to Cala, but Cala was too tired, and too much in shock, to take more than a sip. Cala laid her head against the woman's shoulder and sucked her thumb. The woman held Cala closely to her and nestled the child's head by her neck.

"Who are you?" Lia demanded as her own shock wore off a little. "Do you know why the police dropped us here?"

"Sorry—I'm Deborah Salcido," the woman answered, lowering Cala back down to Lia. "I had the officers bring you here. I was very worried for your safety."

"And why would you do that? Who are you?"

"I'm with AmVista. We own the land now and are developing it for oil production." Lia stood up so she could look the woman in the face. Now she knew why she recognized her—of course, it was the American woman in the Jeep with the Houston Astro T-shirt she'd seen earlier that morning.

The woman was still talking. She pointed behind Lia. "See that land over there? We're going to be building a pipeline to the river where we'll be able to transport the oil down to the port. It's going to bring a lot of money and new development to your community. Almost all of your neighbors are rejoicing at their good fortune."

"Rejoicing?" Lia asked, almost stupefied. "How could anyone be rejoicing at all of this...devastation?"

The woman smiled a patronizing smile that rubbed Lia the wrong way. "It's a poor economy here. This will stimulate the area and bring many needed jobs and much prosperity to many of your neighbors."

"That is utter and complete bullshit." Lia focused a glare fully on Deborah. "And how exactly has my family prospered, do you think?"

Deborah looked down briefly so Lia could not read her expression. "Yes, well…I am truly sorry about that. A most unfortunate incident. But believe me, AmVista had nothing to do with that. It was the police. And I have to say, your father did instigate the episode by firing first." Lia could only stare at the woman. She couldn't think of a response to her brazen audacity. "But I want to help. How can I help you right now?"

Lia struggled with what to do. There was no doubt they needed help, but could she trust this stranger? This woman who had been instrumental in the violent deaths of most of her family? If it was just herself she would reject the offer, but she was not alone.

Lia looked down at Cala and decided what must be done. "She's in shock. I need to find a place for her. She needs food and rest. And I'm not in such great shape myself. We need some place to stay. We need some clothes. I need to call home. I need to get Cala to our aunt's, and I need money and a ticket back to New York."

Deborah's demeanor changed instantly; she became all business. "Okay, I can help you with all of that. And just let me add that, as the eldest in the family now, you will receive the proceeds from the sale of the farm. We could never get your father to respond to our efforts to settle with him." Deborah looked relieved to be able to help now.

"I will only accept because of Cala. And what about my family? We need to arrange for the funerals."

"Yes. Everything is already being taken care of. And I just want you to know that you are not in any danger. This is all over. I want to help you however I can, now or any time in the future. You can always call on me."

Lia was not greatly reassured.

☆☆☆

Terrance had had no interest whatsoever in even considering the president-elect's offer to serve as secretary of energy. Why would he leave his cushy position at AmVista to face the frustrations and uncertainties of a divided and gridlocked Washington? He had kindly thanked Edward, but staunchly declined the offer.

He was now somewhat regretting that decision, however, as he remembered the struggle to contain the Brazilian fiasco. He wistfully thought about the upcoming inauguration and, for a brief moment, contemplated standing with the president on the podium under the brilliant sky of the cold Washington afternoon, flags snapping in the brisk breeze. But that decision was done and the opportunity gone. There was no going back now.

It had taken months of hard diplomatic work to mollify the Brazilian government's outrage over the Braga family deaths, even though, as AmVista repeatedly pointed out, it was the local police who had started the fire. And except for the father, who was shot after firing on the police, all the rest of the deaths were accidental. None of the police officers knew the family was hiding in the barn.

And then there had been the US press to deal with. Thankfully, their attention span was usually a week or two at most, until some new sensation had them clawing after the latest breaking news. Terrance relished the lack of attention right now, three and a half months after the horrible incident.

But the really good news for Terrance was that the drilling and pumping at the new Brazilian oil field was progressing even faster than anticipated, and the oil pipeline was filling up innumerable barges to head down to the nearest Brazilian seaport for transfer by supertanker to the vast reaches of the world—mostly India and China these days, with their unflagging appetite for ever more energy to feed their rapidly expanding economies.

Terrance was sitting in the AmVista boardroom, drumming his fingers on the table and staring absently at Deborah in the seat across from him. Around the rest of the table was the AmVista marketing group— enthusiastic, yet exhausting young go-getters. It was just before the inauguration, and AmVista was planning its new marketing campaign with the new administration in mind.

Deborah had only just narrowly survived the prospect of losing her job—but her influence was now greatly diminished. Terrance wanted her in this meeting though. She had direct experience with the operations in

Brazil—however unfortunate, and that knowledge could be an asset.

The young hotshot, David Fiedler, head of marketing, was in the process of unveiling his new marketing strategy. He annoyed Terrance no end, but he did know his stuff and Terrance forced himself to put up with him.

"Green—we gotta go green. All our polling numbers indicate that it's the new direction for us."

Terrance could not restrain himself. "Are you kidding me? Did you see the guy the people just elected as the new president? He's about as green as a stop sign. I can't believe your data is up-to-date."

David was not at all intimidated. "I kid you not. These numbers are hot off the press. Sixty-three percent of the participants polled highly favor an aggressive green image. Twenty percent are swing, and the rest just don't give a fuck."

"But gas prices are skyrocketing. Surely all they want now is for us to drill. Isn't that why Perez and I so cleverly manipulated the oil supply—so they would elect him as president?"

Deborah was stunned. She shot a quick glance toward Terrance. While she suspected as much, she had never been able to confirm what Terrance had just blurted out. Did he realize she had not been privy to that information? She decided to do some research on her own after the meeting.

David jumped back in, "You would think so, but the underlying numbers indicate that they don't think the shortage can be fixed. What they are really clamoring for now are vastly improved and expanded alternative energies."

"You gotta be fuckin' kidding me." Terrance threw his pen down on the conference table.

"So how can we take advantage of this?" Deborah asked, trying to bring the meeting back to a favorable direction.

David continued, "We go green. Hey, how do you like this as the new slogan—'AmVista for a cleaner, greener tomorrow!'"

There was stunned silence from Terrance, and then he said, "Who the fuck is gonna believe that?"

"Look, there are a lot of directions we can take this—for example—we can tout our development of wind farms, solar fields, ethanol blends, refinery cleanup, improved well maintenance, and on and on. Remember it's not what we do, but how we're perceived at what we do. I've got some great guys in my film unit who can do hot little sixty second docu-ads that will knock your socks off."

Deborah looked at Terrance. She could tell from his intense expression that he was thinking this through, despite his initial annoyance.

"I've got an idea," Deborah interjected. "You know, besides a new slogan, how about a new logo as well? When I was at the new oil fields in Brazil there was this huge tree—very iconic. It would make a great logo for AmVista. I can just see it leading into our TV ads, plastered on the sides of our trucks, and standing tall and proud and green on all the signs at our service stations. Here...take a look at this." She pulled up a picture of the tree from her phone and slid her cell across the table to Terrance. "It's simple, it's graphic, and it's green."

He studied it for a moment and then showed it to David. "What do you think?"

David nodded and smiled. "If you give me the okay, I think we have our new campaign. It will go a long way in overcoming the stigma of the Brazil incident."

"Work it up, and let's take a look," Terrance concluded, rising from the table.

A Bright New Day

The first day of the new president's term

President Perez's inauguration was going well, without a hitch, and Washington was celebrating the event with abandon. There were a dozen Inaugural Balls scheduled—about half attended by the new president and his radiant, centerfold wife. Diego, though invited to the inauguration, had refused; Brandon had been discreetly omitted from the invitation. If Brandon wasn't invited, Diego had told his father months ago, then he wouldn't attend either.

So instead, Diego had rented a room for the day at The Drake, where he sat now with his mother and Brandon to enjoy a big screen TV gossip fest.

Diego's mother, Milly, had been a very great beauty in her day. After all, Ed Perez was known for his appreciation of a fine lady. Not that she wasn't still beautiful—she was. But now she radiated a more mature beauty. She was thin and elegant—perhaps, he thought a little unkindly, with just a little too much makeup. Her one or two face enhancements had given her a rather pinched look. But still, she was stunning, Diego thought—a lady very much to be reckoned with.

She loved very elegant jewelry and wore her very expensive rings and necklaces with a subtle "fuck you" nonchalance—which she totally carried off.

Diego was thoroughly enjoying his "Fuck You Mr. President Day." Already, the viewing party had drunk a lot of champagne and nibbled on smoked salmon and caviar treats, while making snide comments about the trampette wife's hair and the absurdly dreadful cut of her awful dress that resembled nothing more than hideous Victorian drapes. They fell all over themselves with laughter and had a thoroughly delicious time

47

mocking the Republican elite, parading around with the newly unleashed lobbyists lurking in the shadows, anxious to get back into action after eight years of what they considered Democratic oppression.

"So boys, have you settled comfortably into the family chateau yet?" Milly asked during a commercial break.

"We're still unpacking, Millicent," Brandon answered.

"Millicent! Oh no, no, no. Milly—please. Never Millicent. Millicent is, no doubt, some wretched savant from a horrid French children's book filled with annoying escapades and nasty stuffed animals."

Diego continued, "It's nice not to have the expense of the apartment for a couple of years—once we sublet it, of course. Dad was very gracious not to ask us for any rent."

Milly huffed out a snort of laughter. "Well, that doesn't sound like him at all. It's probably just because he hasn't thought of it yet. But just you wait..."

"Oh Mother, he's not that bad."

"What about Carmella?" Milly asked, instead of responding to the defense of her ex-husband.

"She'll visit during semester breaks when she doesn't go to the Michigan house. Says she misses you."

"How sweet."

Milly turned her attention back to the television. "Too bad we don't have any hot male strippers," she casually commented as she watched a hunky guy showering in a soap commercial. "Your father would *so* approve." They all burst out laughing. "That's the nice thing about having a gay son and son-in-law. We wouldn't have to hire both sexes to entertain ourselves. Just one stud would do the trick." That set them off again.

Then Milly leaned in closer and whispered. "Those new Secret Service agents outside the suite look pretty hot. Maybe we could invite them in and enlist them to do a couple of strip numbers for us."

Diego shook his head. "Mother, no wonder Dad divorced you. I think I would, too. You are too outrageous for Chicago—much less Washington."

"My, my, I do believe I have a bashful gay son. Who would have thought? You've become quite the prude lately, laddy."

"But only on the surface and during working hours. Remember, I'm a member of the respectable Gardner, Chappell, and Banks now. You wouldn't want your law firm represented by a flaming reprobate, would you?"

"Oh, I can only hope...," Milly replied, taking another sip of champagne. "And say, whatever happened to subverting the system from within? I've not heard a single subversive remark from you since you joined that stellar firm. Have you forsaken all your radical principles? Have the Repubs completely brainwashed your impressionable, childlike faculties?"

Diego shifted uncomfortably in his chair. "Mother, I just started. I need to insinuate myself into their good graces before I start the revolution. They are talking about establishing an environmental division, and with my experience I would be well placed to be a part of that."

"Well, don't take too long. I am looking for you to counterbalance the atrocious policies of your misguided father."

"Well, *I'm* scouting for just the right cause. I need an issue that will galvanize the public's imagination. Something really big."

"I hope you find what you're looking for very soon, sweetie. Since you will not be giving me any grandchildren, I need something substantial to talk about at bridge."

Diego leaned back on the sofa and looked questioningly at his mother. "How in the world did Dad ever marry a radical like you?"

"Hormones, darling. Simply young male hormones. You know all about those, don't you dear?"

"Yes, he does," Brandon added with a wry smile.

☆☆☆

At the local university bar, peanut shells littered the floor. Two pinball machines were dinging and ringing in the background. The smell of stale beer and cigarettes filled Cran's nostrils. He nursed a Heineken. He'd gone to the bar to drink with his buddies and watch the inauguration on the TV above the bar with the sound muted. Much better that way, he thought. And besides, he just couldn't stay in the apartment with Lia any longer today. Ever since she got back from Brazil four weeks ago, after that terrible tragedy with her family, she had become a difficult person to be around. She was letting her thesis and grades slip miserably, and though they both shared the household chores, she had completely ignored her end of the housekeeping. He could certainly understand her anguish, but she was impossible to be around for long periods, and he occasionally needed to flee for his own sanity.

Before Cran stormed out of the apartment in disgust this morning, he had done all the dishes in the kitchen sink, made the bed, cleaned the bathroom, and mopped the kitchen floor.

That wasn't even the most worrying part. Lia would often mysteriously leave the house in the wee hours of the morning, wrapped in her down coat, knit cap, and muffler, without any explanation. When pushed, she admitted that she was taking long walks along Central Park to think and clear her head. He tried explaining to her how dangerous it was for a solitary woman to be out that late alone, even around the university, but she just shrugged in response.

Cran's attention was only vaguely focused on the inauguration. Even with the sound off, it was annoying. He'd become so disillusioned with politics these past few years he could hardly bear to watch the news anymore. What had become of this country? Democracy was so obviously broken—if it even existed anymore.

But he was too weary to dwell on politics today. What he really thought about was Lia. He was gravely concerned for her well-being, but he had no idea how to help her. He was not looking forward to going back home later—she would almost certainly be worked up after the inauguration. He wondered as he sipped his beer if she would accept therapy.

☆☆☆

There were only two bright spots in her life these days, Lia reflected. One was her daily telephone call to Cala in Brazil. It was costing her a fortune, Cran pointed out, but Lia didn't care. Cala was all she had left of her immediate family, and besides, the money from the AmVista purchase of the farm allowed her this little luxury.

The other joy was her teaching. Though she had let her studies slide, she was totally engrossed in her teaching assignments. She loved working with "her kids" as she called her students. Only the other day one of her favorite students, Carmella Perez, had stopped by her office.

"Do you have a minute?" Carmella asked, poking her head inside the door.

"Sure, what can I do for you?"

Carmella edged her way inside the office. "It's a little embarrassing..."

"If it's about your grade on that last quiz, not to worry, it doesn't count against your average."

Carmella laughed. "No, it's not that. I ah..."

"It's okay, out with it."

"Well, you may or may not know, but my dad is going to be inaugurated on Wednesday—as president..."

"Oh, *that* Perez?" There was only the slightest edge of disapproval in her voice.

If Carmella noticed the slight, she didn't comment. Instead she nodded shyly. "Yes...and well, you see, I have to be assigned this Secret Service detail..."

"Oh my..."

"They have to go everywhere I go. They promise to be discreet and inconspicuous, but they will have to go along with us on all the field trips. Just thought you ought to know. I hope it's not a great inconvenience."

Lia leaned back in her chair. "Well, well, well...not encountered anything like that before. Can I have your autograph?"

Carmella blushed. "I think you've already got it at the top of all my test papers." They both laughed.

"Yes, I suppose I do." Lia was thoughtful for a moment, and Carmella turned to leave. Lia stopped her. "No, don't go yet. I would like to chat a bit more, if you have a moment."

"Sure." Carmella took a seat.

"Tell me, are you enjoying this course?"

"Oh yes, very much. I sort of took this course on a lark because my older brother suggested it, but now I'm really...I don't know...really loving it."

"Well, you are very good. Is it something you might be interested in as a career?"

"Might be."

"What year are you?"

"Junior."

Lia rummaged through some papers and pulled out a brochure. "I have an opening in a special advanced program I will be overseeing next year. It's at the graduate level, but I think you could handle it even as a senior. It takes sustainability management to the next level. It's cutting edge within the Earth Institute, and we are seeking career-oriented students like you to be in the program. Take a look at this prospectus and let me know if it's something you might be interested in." Lia handed her the brochure.

Carmella's face lit up. "Thank you, I'll certainly consider it."

Lia thought of Carmella now, as Lia stood on inauguration day, with a rolled-up newspaper in her hand, watching the TV as President Perez took his oath of office. She could not bear to sit. She paced the room swatting her other palm with the newspaper, only occasionally glancing at the TV screen. How could a man like this have such a sweet and endearing daughter, she pondered? She feared the new administration would radically divert the direction of the country to the right, undoing the many advances the previous administration had done for the environment. It would be incumbent upon her colleagues and herself to launch a fierce and consistent opposition. She wondered how Carmella could keep her footing in both worlds—her father's and that of the environmental community. How could she navigate her escape from her father's grasp if she was, indeed, intent upon a career in the environmental sciences?

Lia continued pacing. She glanced at the TV just as a commercial came on. She was jolted. It was an AmVista commercial—and there was her tree! She could hardly believe her senses. Since when had *her* tree become their new logo?

She felt she might become ill. The presidential inauguration was being sponsored by the rapists of her land and family.

Suddenly the inner turmoil around her family's tragedy coalesced into a flash of brilliant understanding. She knew what she had to do. The first thing tomorrow morning she would contact her bank and set up a trust of the AmVista money for Cala to be certain she was well provided for. Then she could move forward with developing a plan for well thought-out revenge.

☆☆☆

First Lady Elena Perez had a gift. She knew how to attract men without threatening other women. She had worked her routine since she was thirteen. She was also shrewd. She knew how much to give away to get what she wanted. But she kept most of herself to herself. What she eventually did give away was always carefully measured and calculated.

She did not know how good a thing she had stumbled upon when she first met Edward Perez. Perez? Wasn't that some kind of a South American name? But he had money and tons of it—Texas oil. She had managed to reinvent herself several times over as she transitioned from Selma drive-in waitress—to Dallas hostess—to Chicago fundraiser for impoverished children on the South Side. And, now, finally—her crowning achievement—First Lady of the United States.

She was certainly beautiful, even at thirty-eight. Her perfectly colored, blonde and lacquered hair and her expertly applied makeup only revealed her hard edges in certain lights and angles. She knew how to position her head to show off her neck to its best advantage, and her long legs distracted from her few unflattering features—her cleavage not being one of those. She knew exactly what profile to present to photographers, and she had managed to carry off her American Princess image to the vast majority of the voting population quite successfully.

"This is where Winston Churchill stayed when he visited Roosevelt before we entered the Second World War," the chief White House usher announced as he introduced Elena to the Queen's Bedroom. She was having her first detailed tour of the White House. The day of the inauguration was filled with too many other activities for her to familiarize herself with her new home until today.

"Was that the Roosevelt they named the Teddy Bear after?"

"No, ma'am, that was Theodore Roosevelt—number twenty-six," he explained politely. "The British prime minister was visiting Franklin Roosevelt—number thirty-two—at the time—commonly referred to as FDR."

"Oh it's lovely," she commented, examining the formal, rose-colored room with the Andrew Jackson bed. "It's so...queenly." Elena smiled and nodded. She executed a neat little Jackie Kennedy turn with a delicate wave of her hand. She had studied the black-and-white video of Jackie's tour of the White House. Of course, her tour would be in radiant color and high definition.

"Would you like to tour the kitchens now?" the chief usher asked.

Elena was startled. "Oh, will I have to cook? I didn't know..."

"No, ma'am, this is just a courtesy tour." He gave her another polite, inoffensive smile. "I would like to introduce you to the executive chef and his staff of five. They will be consulting with you on a daily basis about the family menus and, of course, all state and official functions when there may be up to twenty additional chefs. Your personal staff will be advising you on your duties and responsibilities and what's expected of you as first lady." He nodded toward the door, motioning that they were to leave the room. "I feel certain you must have many ambitious plans to personalize the office to your own special preferences and interests. And you can always call upon my help if you have any further questions or concerns. That is what I'm here for."

"Oh, that's okay then. You had me going there for a moment. I haven't even cooked a bean in...well, I can't even begin to tell you how long ago that was." She giggled, but realized she might be revealing her rural Alabama roots just a little too openly, and she recovered her poise. "I shall be happy to inspect the kitchens now, if that is convenient," she added graciously, allowing him to lead the way.

☆☆☆

"Gentlemen, please get back to me with your reports as soon as possible. I want to act swiftly, but I need all of your advice and expertise before I make a final decision."

President Perez leaned forward from his chair between the two couches in the Oval Office. The vice president, the secretaries of energy, defense, homeland security and the director of the CIA flanked him, sitting on the sofas. He stood up, indicating the meeting was over.

"How does it feel?" Malcolm Danzer, the Vice President, asked Ed as they were preparing to leave the room.

"How does what feel?"

"The Oval Office."

Ed turned to Malcolm and smiled. "Pretty damn nice, let me tell you. But don't get ahead of yourself and think it will be yours any time soon. Not for at least another eight years."

Malcolm laughed. "And don't *you* get ahead of *yourself* either, old buddy. It might be only four years. You know Washington."

Ed laughed in response and put his arm around the vice-president as he escorted him toward the door. Malcolm was just exiting as Ed spotted Elena peeking in from the secretary's office.

"Oopsie," she squeaked, withdrawing when she saw that Ed was busy. As soon as he was sure all the men had left, he went to fetch her, leading her back into the Oval Office.

"Well, this is it," he gestured around the office once they were alone.

"This is all yours?"

"All mine. Well, mine and the American people's."

"I see," she said, as she kicked off her shoes and shuffled over the carpet with the presidential seal in her stockinged feet. "This is nice. This rug is *so* soft."

"I'm glad you like it."

"But it's s-o-o-o *hot* in here. I don't know how you can stand it. Do any of those windows open?" She removed the jacket of her cashmere suit and draped it over a wingback chair. "What's that over there?" she asked, pointing to a door.

"That's my bathroom, honey."

She glided over, peeked through the door, and turned back to Ed.

"But it doesn't have a bathtub," she observed as she undid the top two buttons of her peach silk blouse.

"Don't need one of those down here. We have a quite luxurious tub in our private quarters. You must have seen that." He settled onto the presidential sofa, putting his feet up as he slid off his shoes.

"And where does this door go?" she asked as she ambled over to the doors that exited from the Oval Office to the outside portico.

"That goes outdoors, sweetie."

"Oh, that's nice. So you can go out for some fresh air and a little stroll whenever you want."

"I guess so."

"That must be very refreshing."

Ed patted the sofa cushion next to where he was stretched out. "Wouldn't you like to take a load off?"

She raced over to the sofa, spread her arms out wide and collapsed backwards onto the pillows next to Ed.

"This is very well upholstered, don't you think?" she purred, picking at the piping.

"I think it's just splendid." Ed reached over and pulled Elena toward him.

He groaned when there was a knock at the door. A moment later the door opened. Ed strained to see who it was, but couldn't see over the back of the sofa.

"Mr. President? Sir? Are you in here?"

Ed realized it was his secretary, and he couldn't escape.

Ed pushed Elena into the seat cushions as he raised himself to peek over the back of the sofa? "Yes?"

"Sir, the prime minister of Uzbekistan is on the telephone for you. There's a developing situation."

Strategic Reserves

Day 18 of the new president's term

Life hadn't always been like this for Deborah Salcido. Fifteen years ago, she had lived a most ordinary life—a husband, a daughter, and a house in the Houston suburbs. But then Melissa, her three-year-old daughter, had gotten sick, with a rare bout of whooping cough, and died. The experience was so devastating that she and her husband split soon after. But she eventually rallied and threw herself into work—first with her alarm company, and now with AmVista.

For a long time, this new life had worked. Being totally absorbed by her work helped her keep the pain and emptiness at bay. She'd worked diligently to create her hard exterior, the mask that allowed her to be ruthless in her work.

But something had happened to her in Brazil. When she held that little girl, Cala, and she nestled her head in Deborah's neck, the mask shattered, and she had not been the same person since.

Now, Deborah was adrift—not least because of Terrance's humiliating treatment of her since she returned from Brazil. He had shoved all the blame for the fiasco on her and shouldered none of the blame for himself. He had marginalized her, and she suspected he was secretly searching for her replacement.

She had fought too long and hard to let a man like that get the better of her. She needed some leverage to put him in his place and secure her position—and his slip of the tongue at the marketing meeting would do quite nicely. Terrance and Ed Perez, through AmVista, had manipulated the energy markets—and she was going to find out how. That revelation could be a dynamite card for her to play if Terrance did, indeed, threaten her with dismissal. Now she just needed to secure the concrete evidence.

But where to begin?

She was still the chief security officer, so she had full access to the entire AmVista complex. However, she was certain Terrance would have been exceptionally careful in hiding his dealings, and there would be very little evidence in the obvious places—the computer system, his office, or the AmVista banking records. She suspected that he probably went outside AmVista and used a subsidiary, or even an overseas source that would be difficult to trace—especially since Ed Perez had been involved as well.

She decided to begin with the Cayman Island contacts. All of the corporation's overseas subsidiary funds went through the Cayman accounts.

She had to deal frequently with Sir Neville Hargrove at the Cayman Security Bank on matters relating to security codes for some of their more complex financial transactions. She knew Margaret McPherson, his secretary, quite well—they were on a friendly, chatty basis and often shared intimate stories while she waited to be connected to Sir Neville on several occasions. She decided to start by giving her a call.

"Hello Margaret, it's Deborah Salcido at AmVista."

"You don't say," Margaret said in her soft Scottish brogue. "I was just making a cup of tea and thinking about your charming self. What a coincidence. And what are you up to these days, up there in that steamy, muggy Houston?"

"Well, it's February, so it's not too bad right now."

"I'm afraid Sir Neville is not in today, dearie. Got a touch of the phlegm, you know."

"Well, Margaret, it's not him I'm calling to speak to. It's you."

"Really, why that's a nice surprise. Why ever would you do that?"

"Can't I have a nice little chat with an old friend without any other motive?"

Margaret chortled. "I guess, but it never happens. Somebody always wants something. After all, we're not a charitable organization, you know."

Deborah laughed. "That certainly is true." She paused, then inched her way forward. "Margaret, I do need just a little favor..."

"What's that, dear?"

"I'm doing a little research project for Terrance Geiger. He's asked me to check up on the security of a special account that was set up probably eight or ten months ago. It is not connected directly to the AmVista accounts, and he wants to see if there have been any inquiries about it from any outside sources.

"Do you have the account name and number?" Margaret asked, once again all business.

"Yes, I have it here somewhere. Just a minute...oh where is that paper?" She rustled some papers into the phone. I know I have it...one sec..."

"It must be the Brightway account. It's the only one outside of AmVista that Mr. Geiger ever set up."

Deborah smiled. "Oh yes, the Brightway account. That's it. What can you tell me about it?"

Margaret clicked her tongue, her tone switching instantly to that of a school mistress. "Now, Deborah, you know I cannot divulge any further information about that. I mean you are checking on security, and what kind of security would that be if I just blurted it all out—even to you?"

Deborah thought quickly. "Excellent, exactly the response I would expect from a professional like yourself—ever the discreet one. Don't take it personally, but it's my job to try and compromise even you. Well done."

"Well, I should hope so. After all, that is what we pride ourselves in—security and confidentiality." She gathered herself together with a certain amount of justified indignation and continued in a new vein. "Now then, have I told you before about my Dora's very worrying high blood pressure...?"

☆☆☆

Brandon Dalius taught architecture at the University of Illinois-Chicago. He had given up the competitive world of cut-throat professional architecture in favor of the more subdued but mundane ivory towers of academia. Diego often chided Brandon for being such a wimp and several times tried to secure commissions for him to renovate a sprightly pizza palace, or to restore some sorry, semi-opulent but decaying apartment building. But Brandon's lofty dreams of soaring skyscrapers and multilevel mansions precluded working on such tawdry projects, and he preferred to fantasize about hobnobbing with the likes of Sullivan and Lloyd Wright from the comfort of his snug little faculty office.

Brandon was just a few years older than Diego. His famously flaxen hair was just beginning to recede, and while he was still considered handsome, his looks were beginning to soften, the first fingers of pudge clamping themselves around his middle. He still retained all the sharpness of mind he had in his youth and a quick biting humor, but he would never publically allow that physical change was creeping up upon him.

Late in the first month of Ed Perez's presidential term, Brandon was sitting at a cozy, corner window table grading sophomore structural engineering papers at one of the many university-adjacent coffee shops. He was working through his second soy latte when one of his architectural history students, Merlot McAllister, pulled out a chair, plopped down her books and macchiato, and slumped opposite him with fevered determination and terrible posture. Her all-black ensemble of eye shadow, lipstick, and nail polish, along with the silver nose ring, lent her a sinister, haunted look. She leaned forward, reaching for the sugar, nearly knocking over Brandon's tall coffee glass. He straightened up, jolted from the haze of semi-literate student scribblings, and stared stupefied at Merlot pouring a pyramid of sugar into her tiny cup.

"Miss McAllister, can't you see that I am engaged?"

"Don't worry about it," she said, dusting off the loose-spilled sugar with her elbow.

"No, I'm not apologizing, I'm complaining." She looked at him and scowled. "Now, if you will excuse me, I've got work to do," Brandon added, retreating behind his papers.

"Okay, okay, I won't be a minute. Just want to ask a quick question."

"All right, what?"

"You know that guy I'm always seeing you with, what's his name?

Diego Ferris?"

"No, Perez..."

"Yeah, that's the one."

"What about him?"

"Do you happen to know if he's seeing anyone? He's awfully cute."

"I know you only joined my class this semester, Miss McAllister, but he just happens to be my boyfriend—as almost anyone in the entire university could have told you. You really should do your homework before bothering me."

"But I got a B+ on my last quiz. I thought that was pretty good."

"That's *not* what I meant, you silly girl."

Brandon rose from his chair, gathering up his papers.

"I must go. Unfortunately, I'm certain to see you in class again very soon." He stuffed his papers into his briefcase, threw his scarf around his neck with an indignant flourish, and swept out of the coffee shop.

☆

Merlot watched him disappear down the street through the coffee shop window. Then she pulled out her phone. "Agent McAllister here...it's done. You should be able to track him now...oh yeah, I jizzeled him all up real good. He was totally distracted. Never saw me plant the tracker on his briefcase. You can tell the president I'm all over it now." She closed her phone and scowled. Yeah, like she would really be interested in dating some fag guy.

☆☆☆

Brightway. Brightway. What the fuck was Brightway? Deborah was pleased she had gotten something from Margaret—not much, but something. But she was not any closer to understanding what Brightway was all about. She couldn't be sure it was even what she was looking for.

She started with the obvious: an online search. There were some religious groups, some insurance stuff, and investment opportunities all under the Brightway search. Maybe the investment group was a front for Terrance's activities, she thought hopefully, but when she dug a little deeper, it was obvious this was not what she was looking for either.

The late hour left her free to search in privacy. It was after midnight; Deborah had the offices almost to herself. There were a few night staff, but they mostly answered to her. They had no reason to suspect that she was snooping around the building. She often did this as part of her security responsibilities.

The accounting department yielded no results either. She'd thoroughly rummaged through the files and in the databases looking for something about Brightway, but there was nothing there. She couldn't think of where to search next.

Then she had one more thought. She drifted down to the basement where the paper files were archived, hoping to stumble across something there. In a box at the back of a tall shelf, she found a folder on Terrance. She pulled it out and flicked through it. It was filled with travel documents. A quick perusal didn't signal anything out of the ordinary until she came across some documents for a trip to Cuba. That gave her some pause. The company was disallowed by federal law to do any business in Cuba. What was Terrance doing there? She peered at documents in the dim light. Terrance had taken a trip with someone who the documents didn't name at just about the time Ed Perez was becoming a serious contender for the Republican nomination for president.

Interesting, she thought—but still not enough to uncover what Brightway was all about.

Listening for any passersby who might interrupt, she hurried to the copier to make copies of the documents. Freshly made copies in hand, she put the originals back carefully and hurried back to her office.

As she passed by Terrance's office, she had a hunch. She doubted she'd find anything of importance there, but she should check out his office all the same. She swiped her pass key and pushed the door open quietly. The room was dark, but she only turned on his desk lamp to avoid drawing too much attention.

Quietly and quickly, she surveyed the desktop and searched through all his drawers, but there was nothing at all suspicious or revealing. She leaned forward, resting both hands on the desk, and bowed her head in resignation. She had exhausted all her options. Now she was at a complete dead end.

She was just about to turn off the lamp and leave the office when she noticed a silver-framed photograph at the edge of the desk. It was a photo of three men—Terrance, Ed Perez, and another figure she recognized but whose name she could not recall. She picked up the photo and sat at the desk, examining the picture more closely. The photo was taken in a café. The three men were standing at a bar drinking. They were casually dressed in golf shirts. Had they been golfing? She struggled to recall the name of the third man—military type, strong face, dark complexion, but with outrageously bleached, curly, blond hair. The face was distinctive but the name still escaped her. If she could just figure out who that third man was she felt certain she could solve this whole mystery.

She studied the surroundings of the bar, seeking a clue as to where they might be located. It was clearly an open-air bar—either at a beach or at an outdoor patio. There was hibiscus and bougainvillea; some palm trees, and what looked like shuttered windows—suggestive of the tropics.

Then she noticed a reflection in the mirror behind the bar. All she could make out was "yawt" in the top line and "egn" below it, the other letters of the words just out of shot.

Of course, the image was reversed in the mirror so she took a piece of paper and wrote the letters out in the correct order—"tway" and "nge." She hurriedly scribbled out "brigh" before the first word. That made sense, but the second word still eluded her. She pulled out her phone and took a photo of the picture. After making sure the frame was placed back exactly where she had found it, she turned out the light, and left Terrance's office. She felt very close now to the solution—after just a little more investigation.

☆☆☆

Lia stared down at Cran as he slept—his hair tousled, his breathing deep and regular. He could have been twelve, dreaming of climbing trees or discovering new treasure caves.

She wrestled with her feelings for him. She knew in her heart that it was over, as he certainly must have known as well, but still he held on. He was far too sweet and innocent—too much the dreamer—the romantic. She knew she would have to be the one to make the move and fracture their relationship. But not today. She had her teaching obligations.

In a few minutes, she would have to leave to attend a class field trip. Quietly, Lia pulled on some clothes and left the apartment before Cran could wake.

Lia had arranged a tour of housing developments in New Jersey that had been built on filled-in, native, freshwater wetlands that were now slowly reverting back to their natural state, endangering many suburban homes. Even the original populations of frogs and salamanders were returning. She'd told her students it was a wonderful opportunity to examine the regenerative force of nature that was constantly struggling to reestablish an ecological balance despite the abuse by humans.

Since the management program was small, with only a few students, it was decided that Lia would drive the group out to New Jersey in an SUV. But because of Carmella's special circumstances she would need to go on her own, accompanied by her Secret Service detail.

It was still dark when they'd gathered at the Institute. After a quick discussion between Lia and the Secret Service detail, it was agreed that the Secret Service car would lead the way as they would have a better view of the traffic and could more easily spot any potential threats or dangers.

It was a cold late February day, but there was no snow in the forecast. The sky was dark with low clouds. There was a bitter, biting wind scourging down the Hudson River Valley. Lia had her down coat tightly zipped up with the collar around her face, her head covered in a knit cap, and a wool muffler wound tightly around her head with only her eyes peeping out.

The rest of the students going on the outing were huddled inside the SUV with the engine running and the heat cranked up full blast. Carmella was in the car with the agents ready to leave when Lia gave the signal. Lia checked her list once more. Only one student was still missing, but Lia had steadfastly insisted they would leave on time, and all her students knew she meant what she said. She checked her watch. She had given the tardy student an extra five minutes, and that time was up. She signaled to Carmella's driver and hopped into the driver's seat of the SUV. The agents led the way, and before long they were crossing the George Washington Bridge. They headed west on I-95 switching over to I-80, passing Hackensack, headed toward Paterson.

By now the SUV had warmed up, and Lia's students were chatting softly as a morning talk show rattled on the radio.

"Did you guys read the reports I gave you yesterday?" All the students went silent except for one. Lia shook her head. "You guys..."

The agent's car was just ahead of them keeping a steady pace in the right lane. Cars, trucks and buses sped past them on the left. They were approaching an overpass just ahead.

As Lia watched in horror, a Creamrich Dairy truck started to skid on what Lia guessed was a patch of black ice on the overpass above. As the driver started to skid he overcorrected, struggling to get the vehicle back into his own lane. He began to spinout just as a Hackensack trash truck behind him hit the same patch of ice. This truck clipped the dairy truck's right rear, and the dairy truck slammed into the overpass guard rail, which collapsed in seconds. The truck catapulted down toward the highway below, landing nose first on the hood of the agent's car. The back of the dairy truck fell sideways across the rest of the car, which immediately burst into flames as the gas tank of the dairy truck burst, spilling fuel over the agent's car.

Lia was traveling about twenty yards behind Carmella's car when the dairy truck landed. The struck car stopped abruptly, spinning to the right.

Lia was headed toward an apparent collision with the agent's car, but with adrenalin surging through her system she managed to swerve to the side of the road, stopping just short of crashing into the overpass wall. She threw open her door and dashed toward the burning car.

Through the window, she could see that both agents had been crushed, and were certainly dead. But she could also see that Carmella had miraculously survived. She was wedged on the floor of the back seat.

Dave, one of her male graduate students jumped out of the car and raced to Lia's side. The fire was spreading across the car, strongest at the front and the left side of the car. The right back door was still free of fire. It must have sprung open when the dairy truck collapsed the car.

"I think we can get her out," Dave shouted.

"Let's do it," Lia answered.

Lia and the student crawled over to the car, staying low to the ground to avoid the searing heat of the flames above. Dave lay down on his back on the pavement, kicking the door with both feet to force the car door open even further. They were able to reach Carmella, drag her free of the car, and remove her to the side of the road.

When they'd pulled her to safety, Lia stared down at her bloodied student. Carmella was unconscious. There was no way to evaluate the extent of her injuries, but she was still alive and breathing.

Lia struggled out of her down coat and covered Carmella with it. She knelt down beside her and grabbed her hand.

"Carmella, can you hear me?" she whispered. "Squeeze my hand if you can hear me."

☆☆☆

Deborah was stopped in her car, waiting for the stupid light to change. She had been going over and over the puzzle in her mind since last night, trying to solve the riddle of "nge." She was going back to AmVista this evening—her staff was used to her working nights occasionally and taking the days off. She felt freer to poke around and investigate undisturbed when most of the workers were gone for the evening.

It was raining slightly, and the steady rhythm of the wipers was almost putting her to sleep at the long wait at the light. Her head nodded. A horn blast behind her alerted her to the fact that the light had changed to green. She turned her head slightly to make a left turn, and as she focused outside the car, she noticed a neon sign on a building to her left. The way her car was positioned, the frame of the front window blocked out part of the word and she saw just the end—"nge." She shifted her head and read the entire word "lounge"—Sundance Lounge and Bar.

That was it! The bar in the photo must have been the Brightway Lounge. As soon as she got to her office, she would do a search on the Brightway Lounge in Havana. Her guess was this was an old bar left over from the Batista days when there were many *Americanos*—thus the name of the bar in English.

She drove a little faster, propelled by the excitement of her hunch. In the quiet of her office, she was able to confirm that the Brightway Lounge was still a working bar in Havana today. That was one mystery solved. But could that be all there was to the Brightway name? She thought not. It had to mean something beyond just the name of the bar itself. Otherwise, why would there be a secret Cayman account under that name? Maybe the three men in the picture had created some kind of document or organization, using the name of the bar to christen their agreement. She might be reaching with her assumption, but she felt certain she was on the right track.

She had printed out a copy of the photo on Terrance's desk from her phone, and had it before her on her desk studying it. Why was it so difficult for her to identify the third man in the picture? She certainly recognized the face, but she could not put it into a workable context. She finally pushed the photo aside and decided to look once again at the travel documents she had copied from the archives.

Nothing new there. She was just about to set the papers aside when she noticed there was a second page to the itinerary that Terrance used for the trip that she had not studied when she made the copies. She turned to the second page anxiously. From Havana, it showed, Terrance had taken another plane to Caracas, Venezuela. Then the insight flashed. The third man in the picture was none other than the Venezuelan dictator, Benevito Casados. Imagine that—here was the CEO of the largest oil company in the US, the future president of the United States, and the dictator of Venezuela—one of the largest oil producing countries in South America—all together in the same place at the same time. Now that was a meeting to contemplate! She was definitely on track to solve the Brightway mystery. But she still didn't know exactly what Brightway *was*.

☆☆☆

"If you'll forgive me, Mr. President, this seems very personal," Donald offered.

"Of course it is. What the fuck do you think? What the hell good is it being president of the United States if I can't abuse the office a little now and then?" Ed let out a loud laugh.

President Perez was just finishing up a meeting with the director of the FBI, Donald Rappaport, in the Oval Office. "Yes, but in my opinion, it's not the best use of our resources."

"What's it costing? One agent, and a couple of lap dogs checking surveillance computers a couple of times a day? How big a deal is that?"

"Well, it's a big deal to the taxpayers, sir."

"Humor me."

Ed couldn't wait for this meeting to be over. Donald, a holdover from the previous administration, was as dry and flavorless as an eighty-year-old hooker.

"Why are you doing this anyway? This Brandon Dalius has no record. He appears to be no threat in any way."

"He's a fag who's fucking my son. I want to find out if he's cheating on Diego, and if I catch him so much as winking at some other guy, I want to let Diego know so he can dump him faster than a naked Eskimo pissing in the Arctic."

The door to the Oval Office opened, and Ed's secretary announced. "Sir, it's your wife on the phone."

"Isn't she upstairs?"

"Sorry, no, it's Milly, your *other* wife. Says it's very urgent. It concerns Carmella."

"Okay, okay." He rose and went to his desk. "What?" he bellowed into the phone. He listened in utter silence, his face ashen.

☆☆☆

Something about the interaction of Diego's left shoe and sock caused his sock to twist around his foot when he walked. He had just come back to work from lunch and had to take his shoe off to twist the

68

sock back around, once again, so the heel of the sock was back on *his* heel instead of twisted around to the top of his foot. It annoyed him greatly, but he had never been able to figure out why this happened, and why it didn't happen with any of his other shoes. One of the great mysteries of life. He was just retying his shoe when his desk phone rang. He picked it up. "Diego Perez..."

"What the fuck are you doing?" a male voice boomed.

"Who's this? Chester, is that you? I didn't recognize your voice at first."

Chester ignored the question. "When are you gonna quit farting around and do some real work up there in Lawyerland? How's Brandon, by the way? Give him my best."

"I will." Diego laughed to himself. Chester was such a blatant character. "What are you blowing up about? Huh?"

"You miss me? We sure miss you. It's not been the same here since you sold out to the enemy. We need you back at GreenPAC."

Diego sighed. "I haven't sold out, Chester. I'm just organizing a new strategy."

"Yeah, that's what you said nine months ago. So where's the beef? Haven't seen you at any rallies, at any parties—you haven't even come by for a condescending visit to the office to sprinkle us with your fairy dust of wisdom. And your *father*—president? Come on, don't tell me you haven't got some kind of clout somewhere from that." Chester loved ragging on Diego—had done since the time they were roommates at Princeton.

"Hey, I'm trying to do this on my own—without relying on Daddy's reactionary cachet. It takes time to build some trust around here, but I'm in line to be a part of their new environmental division. That should really put me in a position to do some good work. And I'm just waiting for the right blockbuster project. Something that will galvanize the general public and inspire them to action."

"Yeah, yeah, yeah. I've heard all that before. Get off your ass, kid. You are wasting your time and talent."

"You called me to tell me this?" Diego's cell buzzed and scooted across his desk. He picked it up to see who was calling. It was his mother.

69

"Chester, love ya to pieces, but my mom's calling. And when the dragon roars the prince must answer. Call you later. Bye." He answered his other phone. "Mom, what's up? What gala event do you have me scheduled for this weekend?"

"Diego, I'm on my way to New York. It's your sister. She's been in a terrible accident. Can you come out?"

Diego's mouth went dry. "Where?"

"Columbia Medical Center."

"I'll be there as soon as I can."

☆☆☆

Deborah was not fully prepared to face Terrance just yet—she had almost solved the Brightway mystery; she felt it in her bones—but he had summoned her to his office. He hadn't indicated what the meeting was about, but if it was to sack her, she wanted to be able to confront him about Brightway with all the evidence she had. Though it was not complete, it could still be damaging.

Before she headed to his office, she gathered together the papers she had, made copies of everything, and sent the copies by mail to her secret post office box in case he had her office searched. When she was prepared, she walked up the corridor to his office.

"Have a seat," Terrance said, without looking at her as she entered. He was seated in his desk chair, his back turned toward Deborah, returning a file folder to a lower desk drawer.

Deborah stole a quick glance at the silver framed photograph on Terrance's desk as she sat down in a comfortable arm chair across from Terrance. The photo appeared so innocent in the daylight.

"Now then," he smiled, as he turned back to face her. "So, what have you been up to these past few days?"

She couldn't read his tone or intention. He was being dangerously ambiguous. She decided to play the innocent card. "Oh, you know— regular routine. My office has been upgrading some software for the surveillance server. Hired a few new guards. Not very exciting stuff."

"Uh huh..." Terrance picked up a remote, turned on a TV, and started a DVD. "Let's watch a little television together, shall we?"

Deborah thought he was being unsettlingly cheery. She turned to the monitor. The DVD showed a security feed, and it clearly showed Deborah entering Terrance's office and going to his desk. Deborah froze, her mind racing.

Terrance leaned back in his chair with a smug smile, hands behind his head. "Very informative, don't you think? Bet you didn't know I have my own personal security system. I've always believed in having a watcher watching the watchers." He abruptly leaned forward again, his tone changing completely. "Now, tell me exactly what you were up to in my office. And don't tell me you were simply checking up on my security systems. It is clear from the video that it was much more than that."

She quickly calculated what lie she could fabricate but immediately decided against going that route. "I'm going to answer your question by asking you a question of my own. Exactly how do you explain Brightway?" She phrased her question like she knew the answer. Perhaps she could just bluff her way through this.

Terrance's face registered genuine surprise. He was not expecting this.

"How...?" He hesitated. "You..."

She was astonished. Why didn't he just deny knowing anything about Brightway? She realized she'd caught him off-guard.

"How in the world did you find out about the hidden oil reserves?" he asked.

Oil reserves. Of course. It all fell into place now. AmVista, in conjunction with Venezuela, was diverting oil to some secret location to create a shortage and drive up the price. And with Ed Perez involved, it was certainly a political strategy as well. The pieces were falling neatly into place. She realized: Brightway was a scam to manipulate the presidential election in favor of Perez. Drive up the price of oil and elect a president most likely to drill, drill, drill. And as a nice side effect, deregulate the oil industry as much as possible.

"I have my ways," Deborah finally answered his question. "After all, you didn't hire me for my stunning good looks."

Even Terrance had to smile at that. "Well, I'm sorry you had to stumble across our little secret. And exactly what do you intend to do

71

with this information, might I ask?"

Well, here it was then—the devil's bargain. Deborah was now at the point where she had to make a decision. Would she take the devil's coin and continue as part of a corrupt system, or was she ready to strike out on her own and blow the whole scandal wide open? In either case, she needed to determine the completion of the narrative.

She smiled, avoiding answering him directly for the moment, intent on getting as much information from him as she could. "I have to admit, it was an ingenious plan. Was it your idea to involve Casados?"

"It was," Terrance nodded, smug in his accomplishment.

"Did he supply the storage facilities?"

"Well, not directly. Salt caves in Mexico."

"How soon do you plan to release these reserves, and how will you do it without destabilizing the market and causing the price of oil to crash?"

Terrance studied her. "You've learned quite a lot around here, haven't you? Not bad for a filly."

She was intensely insulted by his condescension, but would not allow herself to show it. "I would really like to know how the master works. There's always more to learn."

Terrance shifted in his chair. He appeared to be enjoying this little conversation. "The oil will start being released very soon. China and India are eager buyers who don't mind paying a premium to keep us from releasing it into the US market. And they know how to keep their involvement a secret. After all, we need to keep the price up in the US to stimulate the demand for more drilling here. Pretty neat, huh?"

Deborah nodded, pretending to acknowledge the work of the master—feigning to be too overwhelmed for words.

He studied her again for a long few tantalizing moments before finally speaking again. "I think you are being wasted in security. With your smarts you should be assisting me on weightier projects. Does that interest you?"

From thinking she was going to be fired, to being offered a promotion. Now that was an interesting development.

Now she was even more confident and cheeky. "But what about my little breach of etiquette?" She pointed to the DVD still playing on screen.

"Yes...well, let's just say I admire your ingenuity. It shows you are willing to take risks. I'm sure I can put your subversive skills to better use for us in the future. And let's talk next week about your future. I have to go to Washington tonight. We'll meet when I get back."

"Will that include a pay increase?"

"Of course, I have always been one to reward appropriately applied misdeeds."

"I look forward to it. Thank you."

He indicated with a wave of his hand that the meeting was over. Deborah rose and left quietly, rushing back to her office where she closed and locked her door. She swept her room for any new surveillance camera or bug, and finding neither, she removed a pen from inside her jacket pocket. She took off the top of the pen, to remove a small SD card, which she then inserted into her computer, and immediately began downloading the audio file she had just recorded during her conversation with Terrance. She had all the evidence she needed to make her next move.

☆☆☆

The hospital heart monitor continued its steady and reassuring beep. Milly sat by Carmella's bedside, almost unable to keep her composure, as she surveyed the damage done to her beautiful daughter. Milly could see that Carmella was badly bruised and scraped on her face, arms, and torso. She had suffered a broken leg and foot. She was still undergoing tests for internal injuries, which if discovered could complicate the situation. However, for now she was considered stable. Lia sat opposite on the other side of the bed. Carmella was sleeping at the moment.

Milly had only just arrived this morning. Her entire focus had been on Carmella. She'd held herself together remarkably well, being the friendly gorgon that she was, and only now was she able to turn her attention to Lia.

"How can we ever thank you...?" Milly was for once at a loss for words. Her strong "competent mother" mask began to crumble, and she burst into tears.

"Please think nothing of it. Anyone would have helped her. She's going to be just fine, you'll see," Lia responded softly.

"Did you suffer any injuries, dear?

"A few burns but nothing significant." She held up her bandaged arm to Milly.

"You're her teacher, isn't that right?"

"More like a group leader. It's an exploratory seminar. We all share in the discoveries together. Carmella is very bright and seems intensely interested in environmental issues."

"Like her brother," Milly added.

Lia hesitated. "But not like her father," she finally blurted out.

Milly smiled her wry smile. "You got that right. Thank heavens my children take after me and not their father. Still, if there's anything I can do for you..."

"I appreciate that, thank you, but can't think of anything just now."

The hospital room door opened, and Diego peered in.

"Diego," Milly exclaimed, opening her arms to her son.

Diego came forward and asked in a whisper, "How's she doing?" straining to see Carmella, but locked in his mother's emotional embrace.

Carmella opened her eyes at the commotion.

Diego finally broke free of Milly and leaned over to Carmella, "Hey Pudge, how ya doin'? Just think, you get to pee in a pan—what fun."

Carmella took a deep breath but couldn't quite answer. She held out her hand to Diego. "Don't make me laugh," she whispered. "I hurt all over."

Diego nodded, "I'll bet you do, honey. But you'll have a great story for the grandkids though."

She squeezed his hand.

Milly spoke up, "Diego, this is Lia, she's the one who pulled Carmella from the burning car. Saved her life."

Diego nodded and smiled. "Guess we owe you a lot. Dad will probably give you the Medal of Honor or something—or at least a lifetime subscription to the *White House Gazette*."

Carmella swatted at Diego but missed. "Don't make me laugh. You promised."

He grimaced. "Oops. Sorry." Diego looked around the room, but no one seemed to have anything to add, so he chimed in. "There are enough Secret Service agents out in the corridor to start a soccer team. Are we all adjusting to having them peering over our shoulders twenty-four seven?"

Milly spoke up, "Actually, I am a persona non grata with the current administration and am not required to have them around me to take out the trash. More's the pity."

"Mom…," Carmella wailed, unable to keep from laughing again.

☆☆☆

Deborah picked up the phone but put it down again. She got up from her kitchen table and paced. She went to the kitchen window and looked out to the backyard where her daughter's swing set still sat, unused. She had pleaded with her ex to take it down, but he never got around to doing it before he split for good. She could have taken it down herself, but as it was one of her last links with the child, she hadn't been able to.

She thought once again of Cala and how soft the girl's cheek felt against her neck. She clinched her teeth and strode back to the table and picked up the phone. This time she dialed the number she had found online. She was ready to commit professional suicide.

"GreenPAC," a male voice answered on the phone.

"This is Deborah Salcido, Director of Corporate Security, from AmVista Petroleum. I have some very important information that I think will greatly interest your organization."

"What is its nature?" the receptionist asked.

"It's about a scandal that will blow the top off the energy market and greatly embarrass the president of the United States."

There was a brief pause, and then the receptionist answered as coolly as he could, "I'm putting you through to Chester Joyce. He's our CEO. I'm sure he'll want to hear what you have to say."

The Honeymoon is Almost Over

Day 40 of the new president's term

Diego was sprawled out on his bed in his New York City hotel room in a phone conversation with Brandon when he heard the click of an incoming call. He quickly glanced to see who it was.

"Are you ready yet, babe?" Brandon breathed heavily into the phone. "I'm almost there."

"Ah, Brandon...Brandon."

"Is that you coming?"

"No. Honey...Honey, I've got to take this call."

"What! You're kidding me? I'm just...just...ah-h-h-h-h...never mind."

"Brandon, it's really important. It's Chester." He had a feeling the call could be urgent. As much as Brandon might like him to, Diego couldn't put off answering the call from Chester.

"Well, that's the last time I'm going to wait for you."

"I'm really sorry, babe. I'll talk to you later. Love ya." He switched to the other line. "Chester?"

"You busy?" Chester asked.

"Well I was. Brandon is not too pleased with me just now, though." Chester got it. "You mean...?"

"Yeah."

"Need to finish?"

Diego didn't answer the question. "Chester, just what the fuck is it you want?" He sat up on the edge of the bed and rearranged himself, zipping up his fly.

"Okay, listen, this is it. I got you your great blockbuster project. Where are you? Can I come over now?"

"I'm in New York City."

"The city? Damn. This is really important. When you back?"

"Don't know. Maybe tomorrow. Carmella was in a car accident—I needed to come out here."

"Oh God, I'm sorry. Is she gonna be okay?"

Diego walked over to the window and looked out to check the weather—another gloomy, East Coast winter day. "Yeah, think so. Doctors are running a gaggle of tests, and they'll let us know this afternoon. If she's good, I'll catch the next flight home. Mom is here. She can hold Carmella's hand as well as I can. What's the big news? Can't you tell me now?"

"You got Secret Service guys all over you, don't you?"

"Yeah, a few." He turned toward the hotel room door, knowing the agents were right outside.

"And I'll bet anything your phone is tapped."

"Probably."

"Then it had better wait till you get back. You and Brandon still at your dad's place?"

"Yep."

"Call me when you get in, and we'll meet someplace secure."

"You gonna give me a hint?"

"Possible impeachment... How does that sound?"

"Oh boy... See you tomorrow—for sure." Diego smiled broadly and began to pack.

☆☆☆

"You can't go where I'm going," Lia spoke softly to Cran.

He was packing his last box. He paused before taping the box closed. He shook his head. "If you could just help me understand," he said, turning to face her. "Maybe there's something I could do to help you..."

"No..."

"It's what happened to your family, isn't it?"

"Yes, partially." She still felt raw and looked away, not wanting Cran to see the depth of her wound.

78

"Why 'partially'? What else is there?"

"It's what I have to do now." There was no way she could reveal her true intentions to Cran. She didn't want him to be implicated in any way. It was for his protection, but she couldn't tell him that.

"Can't you tell me?"

"No... Please Cran, let it be. We've been over it a million times. I just need to be alone."

He turned back to the box, marked its contents with a felt pen, and began taking his belongings to the car.

When he had finished, he hugged her good-bye, and left. She watched from the apartment window as he got into his car and drove away. It seemed certain that this would be the last time she would ever see him.

☆☆☆

Merlot yawned, covering it up with her hand. She was sitting in the back of Brandon's makeup class on architectural history. She was *so* bored. She didn't give a fuck about the lancet arch. When was she going to be reassigned? This was the most pointless assignment she had ever had.

This Brandon guy was a complete zero. There was nothing distinctive or dangerous about him at all. He was about as rambunctious as a marshmallow. If the higher ups were investigating Brandon as some kind of a security threat, they were way off track. This guy was oatmeal. And this ridiculous Goth makeup she had to wear as her "cover" was a joke. Did students still look like this anymore? Not in her class they didn't. She stood out like a giraffe at a gerbil convention.

She played with her pencil. She drew circles and swirls on her homework. Seven, six, five, four...she counted down the seconds on the wall clock till the class would be over. Three, two, one... She waited. Brandon didn't dismiss the class. *What the fuck?*

Oh no, she realized too late. It was a Saturday makeup class; it went on till the professor decided to end it. *SOMEBODY JUST KILL ME! PLEASE!*

She pulled out her phone and texted her chief:

Plez reassign me! This Brandon guy a snore. Suggest you get aggressive & send "specialized" agent—more in line with Brandon's unique tastes.

☆☆☆

Diego and Chester were both trolling the aisles of the Jewel supermarket near the GreenPAC headquarters with their grocery carts, casually picking up random items as they obliquely chatted, pretending not to know each other. It seemed a good place to meet, where they would be safe from prying Secret Service eyes or recording devices.

"How's Carmella?" Chester whispered to Diego. He prodded at a melon to see if it was ripe.

"Mending. The tests were clear."

"Terrific." Chester moved his attention to feeling up an avocado.

Diego was a little impatient. "So what's the deal here, Captain Marvel? Why are we meeting like this?"

Chester looked and him and surreptitiously pulled a DVD out of his briefcase. "Here, take a look at the document, audio, and video files on this when you get home. They will knock your socks off." He slipped the disk to Diego, the action covered by the bag of carrots he'd picked up.

"Where did you get this?" Diego asked, casually glancing at the disk Chester handed him before tucking it under his coat.

"Are you ready? From the head of security at AmVista in Houston."

"You're kidding me, right?"

"Don't you believe it," Chester added, swerving his cart to avoid colliding with a display of stacked canned tomatoes.

"You do realize AmVista is one of my firm's top three clients," Diego said finally.

Chester looked at him with mild shock then turned away quickly in case anyone might see. "That could be a problem."

"Yea-ah..."

"But you're the guy who wanted the big issue. So here it is. This would put you squarely in the spotlight and could launch your political career. Take a look at this stuff, and when you've considered it, get back to me. But if you're not going to move on it, we will. And it needs to be acted on pronto. But I really think we should do this together as a team—with you as the spokesperson and GreenPAC as the sponsoring organization."

Diego glanced quickly at his watch. "Hey, I gotta go. I told the Secret Service guys I would be just a minute and told them to wait in the car. Oh shit, they're coming in now looking for me. Can't seem to escape them for longer than ten minutes. I'll call you soon as I look this over." He tucked the disk beneath his coat and headed for the checkout.

Lia pulled the invitation out of the thick buff-colored envelope once again. The presidential seal embossed in formal federal blue and gold radiated like a small sun at the top. Lia ran her finger over the seal.

Carmella had personally delivered it to her in her office after class. Carmella's recovery was swift, which Lia had been glad to see, but still ongoing. She wore a cast and hobbled about on crutches, but she was mending well.

Carmella had explained that her father wanted to personally thank Lia for saving her life. The invitation was for an evening of music at the White House honoring a number of jazz musicians. Carmella gleefully explained her father would send a plane to fetch them and bring them back.

The invitation had lit a spark of anticipation in Lia. This was an opportunity she'd never dreamed of. All her previous plans for revenge evaporated as she began to formulate a new plan of action. Cala was never far from her mind, and the loss of her family continued to fester in her soul. Now her overriding passion was to act upon her desire for revenge.

And with this invitation she'd been granted unfettered access to get close to the heart of the dark, corrupt system that had fostered her family's obliteration. She abandoned all her former thoughts and plans and began to craft a new scheme.

Brandon had two hours before his next class, but the professor he shared his office with was holding office hours at the moment, so he needed somewhere else to go.

Just the right time to go to the library, Brandon decided, to find a quiet corner and work on his paper. He was scheduled for publication in the June issue of *Architect*. Though he'd completed the article, he wanted to edit it once again.

Having found a table to his liking in a quiet, secluded corner of the periodical section, he settled in. He took out his laptop and his water bottle and started to study the document for any changes. He was briefly distracted by an exquisitely handsome young man he had not seen around the campus before—a new student? A transfer? He turned back to his article, but he couldn't shake the image of the student. He discreetly looked up again to see where he might have gone. To his surprise, the man had taken a study table just across from him and was staring at Brandon quite openly.

The man had deep dark eyes and long jet hair. He had a stubble beard—was he Middle Eastern? Spanish? Italian? In any case, Brandon had to look away. The man's stare was too direct, too sexual. Brandon's stomach seized up with the unmistakable symptoms of desire. And that was not all that stirred.

It was quite clear that any more work on his article was impossible just now. Even though Brandon did not look up, he could still feel the man's penetrating gaze. Brandon had not been unfaithful to Diego since they had entered a committed relationship. There had been a few slipups when they first met, but that ended once they had decided to become a monogamous couple, and for the past two years, he had been steadfast since they moved in together. *But hey, gay men are gay men*, he heard himself rationalizing. He laughed to himself and amended his thought to *but hey, men are men*.

He had no choice. He needed to get out of there. He closed his laptop, stuffed it in his briefcase, and headed toward the stairs that led to the ground floor. He didn't want to risk being captured in an elevator with this man. It would be too dangerous. He was not sure if he could contain himself. He walked briskly along the row of stacks and turned

82

the corner to head toward the stairwell. The sexy hunk was already there waiting for him, leaning against the wall, blocking his way.

"What's the hurry?" the man asked.

"I'm sorry, I've got a class," Brandon evaded.

"No you don't. You've got an hour and a half. Plenty of time for what we want to do."

"I think you misunderstand...," Brandon tried to be firm and professor-ly.

"I'm Momo," the man said, extending his hand and lightly brushing Brandon's cheek.

This is where Brandon could have fled—should have fled. He was right at the top of the stairs, but he didn't. Instead he said, "I'm Brandon."

Momo nodded. He took Brandon by the arm and led him along the hallway toward the men's room. It was at the end of dead-end corridor and little used, except by the university gay underground for quickies.

"I don't think...," Diego's lovely smile flashed before him. Brandon tried one more time to extricate himself from this situation, but the fact that this hot man desired him kicked off his middle-aged hormones, and he just couldn't resist any longer.

"That's right...don't think...just feel." Momo led Brandon into a stall and closed and locked the door behind them.

☆☆☆

Brandon was devastated. How could he have let this happen? He pulled his car into the garage and leaned his head on the steering wheel. What was he going to tell Diego? They had promised each other to be open and honest and not keep any secrets. He knew he would have to face up to his obligation and tell Diego what he had done with Momo this afternoon. But he dreaded hurting Diego, and he hoped that Diego could forgive him. He took a deep breath, got out of the car, and headed to the kitchen entrance.

"Hello? Diego?" Brandon called out. The only response was Chiquita racing down from the upstairs, charging through the entrance hall, slipping on the polished wood floor, and jumping into Brandon's arms. "Not now, sweetie," he said sadly, putting Chiquita back on the floor.

Brandon went to his office, dropped off his briefcase, and then he went to their bedroom. No Diego. He called out again louder, but still no answer. Where could he be? He should be back from work by now. Maybe he had to work late. Brandon finally went to the living room and turned on the lights. There by the telephone was a note from Diego.

Had to go to DC - The Dad commands. Some kind of event this evening to honor the woman who saved Carmella's life. Will be good to see Pudge again. She seems to be healing well. Tried calling your cell, but no answer all afternoon—then your mailbox full. Probably out screwing some hottie—Ha Ha. I'll be back by mid-morning or early afternoon. Want to spend some time with Carmella. Miss you.
xoxoxo
D

Brandon was both relieved and upset. He wanted his confession to be over and to be forgiven. He thought of calling Diego on his cell but didn't want to discuss this over the phone. It needed to be done in person. It was only fair. Now he would have to wait until Diego returned.

He doubted he would sleep very well that night. But now that he was alone, and the pressure was off, his thoughts returned for just a brief moment to his very hot, and very satisfying, encounter with Momo in the bathroom this afternoon. It made him feel guilty all over again.

☆☆☆

Diego was about to board his plane to Washington, flanked by his Secret Service handlers. His phone rang—the call was from Chester. He stepped aside. He still demanded his privacy.

"Chester, I'm on my way to DC. Not the best time, right now. Can we chat later?" Diego glanced over to make sure he was not being overheard by the agents.

"We're on a tight deadline. Have you read the materials I gave you?"

"I have. Absolutely unbelievable stuff. But is it reliable?"

"Like gold. You can meet the source yourself if you like. I can set it up for any time that works for both of you."

Diego hesitated, watching a plane outside the window take off into the inky night sky. "It's very tempting, Chester, but I'm concerned that AmVista is my firm's client. It would be totally unethical for me to reveal this information as an employee. I'm sure you can understand that."

"I do. But it's your choice, good buddy. Are you gonna be a *part* of the system, or are you ready to *fight* the system? You can't do both."

Diego began to pace the floor. "I know. I know. I'm still mulling it over."

"Well, we don't have a lot of time. We want *you* to be our spokesperson. As the son of the president, it would carry major weight if you would stand with us. And remember, you are always welcome to come back to work at GreenPAC if you need to escape the clutches of the G, C & B legal lair."

Over a tinny speaker, the gate attendant announced the urgent plea for final boarding.

"Gotta go. We'll talk soon. Promise."

☆☆☆

The White House evening had not yet commenced. The guests were gathering and enjoying cocktails until the president and first lady arrived. Diego was pleased to see Carmella looking so well. The bruises and scrapes had almost disappeared, and though she was hobbling along on crutches, she seemed to have regained her spirits and greeted Diego with great enthusiasm.

"Hi, big bro." She limped along, her face lighting up at seeing him.

"Hey Pudge, you're lookin' great. When can you get back to your fencing?"

"Not for a while yet, sadly." Carmella turned to Lia who was just behind her. "You remember Lia, don't you? From the hospital."

"Of course." Diego took her hand and smiled.

"Pleasure," Lia replied. She did not warm to him immediately. She thought he looked like a rumpled, wooly dog, panting with too much eagerness—blowsy and sad—like a Christmas ornament discarded by

85

mistake when the tree was thrown out.

"We're so grateful for all you've done for Carmella. And she speaks so highly of your class as well. She just loves it," Diego said.

"I'm glad. She tells me you were instrumental in directing her to the Institute," Lia added.

"Well, big brothers do have their influence, you know. And it is my field as well."

"I didn't know. What field is that?"

"Activism. I'm a bit of a thorn in Dad's side. They barely let me in the door here, and they watch my every move like I'm about to spray green graffiti throughout the White House."

Lia laughed. She liked Diego much better now. "Can I help?" she joked. "Perhaps I could create a diversion by running naked through the halls. Maybe we could create a Rainbow House instead of a White House."

"Sounds good to me. The gay community would love that."

A presidential aide came up and leaned in toward Diego. "Sir, the president would like a word with you—privately."

"Excuse me. The Pater summons." Diego nodded to Lia. "Perhaps we can continue our subversive conversation later over drinks. I believe they serve a killer martini at the bar."

Lia nodded in reply. She'd like that.

☆

Diego was surprised, as he was ushered into the president's private office in the living quarters, to find an extremely handsome Mediterranean-looking young man already waiting on the sofa. Diego sat in a chair opposite and nervously tapped his right foot because he was so instantly attracted to the guy. He hoped the stranger hadn't noticed.

He nodded politely once to the man, keeping his gaze averted, though he could not resist a furtive look or two when he thought the guy wasn't looking.

"Diego…!" The president burst into the room, his hand extended for a handshake. This president did not do hugs. "Glad you could make it at such short notice. I know your sister appreciates that you could be here."

"Dad." Diego took his father's hand. "You wanted to see me privately?" He questioningly nodded toward the young man.

"Yes." Ed wasn't looking Diego in the eye, which unsettled him, instead pacing the room a couple of times before speaking. "Delicate matter. But important." He turned to the stranger. "Have you two met?"

The other man shook his head, and Diego answered, "No. But why is he here?"

"Well, let's just say it's about a domestic matter that concerns you and Brandon."

Diego's stomach knotted. Any time his father mentioned Brandon, it usually indicated trouble ahead.

"What?" Diego pounced, irritated by his father's interference in his private life.

"This is Mohammad Hamam. He's one of our FBI agents on special assignment. He was chosen for his very unique talents, and he has a little story you might find enlightening."

Diego did not like the sound of this—at all. "Dad, will you please get to the point? This is totally pissing me off."

"Tell him," Ed directed the agent, smiling widely.

Mohammad smiled and leaned back. "Sweet—very sweet. This is when I really love my work." He patted the cushion on the sofa next to him, inviting Diego to join him. Diego came over and sat down with trepidation.

"Okay spill it, what's the deal?"

"Guess where I was this afternoon?"

"I don't know—Saskatchewan."

Momo chuckled to himself. "Fucking your buddy in the men's room at the UIC library."

Diego turned gray and quickly looked up at his father. "What is this?"

"I was assigned to seduce your—what's his name? Brandon?"

"Just wanted you to see what your partner is really like," Ed smirked. "Isn't it time you dumped the jerk?"

Diego stood, angry, flustered, and confused, and faced his father.

87

"What I do or do not do with Brandon is between us and has absolutely nothing to do with you. I don't care if you *are* the fucking president of the United States—you shame yourself and are a disgrace to the office and a total...total..." Diego struggled to find a name harsh enough. "Rapscallion" was what he finally blurted out.

"Rapscallion?" the president guffawed. "Really? I'm a Rapscallion? God help me. You've cut me to the quick," he continued, laughing. Mohammad's eyes clinched in laughter. Diego could see the ridiculousness of his taunt, and he laughed, too—but his laughter was more to relieve the tension of his anger and sense of betrayal than from any great mirth.

Oh Brandon, he thought, *how are we ever going to get through this mess?* Annoyed, confused, and hurt, Diego fled the room without another word to his father.

Diego escaped the White House with just a quick good-bye to Carmella. Carmella urged him to stay so they could have an intimate breakfast together tomorrow morning, but Diego insisted on taking the red-eye back to Chicago that night. His mind was reeling, and he was in too great a turmoil to be sociable for the rest of the evening.

The East Room of the White House was filling up with guests for the intimate evening of light supper and jazz—one of the president's preferred musical styles. The program was ready to start, just awaiting the arrival of the president.

As this was the first public White House function since the inauguration, the DC social set was eager to measure the new president's entertainment style against the previous occupants. Texans tended to favor a looser, more populist approach. But this Texan had spent a considerable amount of time in Chicago as well, so the gossips refrained from rampant speculation for the time being. But each wanted to be the first to report on the degree of sophistication of the new White House.

"Ladies and gentlemen, the president of the United States and the first lady," the usher announced from the grand entrance. The orchestra broke into "Hail to the Chief."

Lia looked around for Diego, but he was not to be found. "Have you seen your brother?" she asked Carmella.

Carmella nodded sadly. "He was called to my father's office. They must have had some sort of a spat, as he rushed away with just a quick good-bye. Took a flight back to Chicago."

"Pity. I was looking forward to continuing our conversation," Lia said, unable to keep the sincere disappointment from her voice.

☆

After they were done greeting the most prominent dignitaries, the president and Elena came over to Carmella and Lia. Ed put his hand on his daughter's shoulder and leaned in to kiss her cheek. The White House photographer took several photos of the group—the camera flashes dazzled, Elena smiling through it, and tightening her grip on the president.

"So this must be the famous Lia Braga," the president said, offering his hand and examining Lia up and down—with a new sparkle in his eye. "And very charming, indeed." The president extricated himself from Elena, who stepped back with a pained expression.

"How very grateful I am at your rapid intervention on my dearest daughter's behalf." The president held on to Lia's hand a little too long. "If there is ever *anything* our family can do for you, please do not hesitate to ask," he added. "I do have just a little influence around here, you know." He laughed at his little joke.

Lia joined in the laughter, perhaps just a little too eagerly. Elena held tightly to her forced smile. "Why, Mr. President, how very generous of you to offer," Lia added.

Carmella put her hand on her father's arm. "Dad, did you and Diego have a fight? He rushed away so quickly back to Chicago. We were going to have breakfast together tomorrow. I really wanted some alone time with him."

"Let's not talk about that right now," Ed responded without looking at his daughter, keeping his eyes intently focused on Lia.

Lia was acutely aware of the effect this was having on Elena.

Elena pulled on Ed's arm, but to no avail. With a quick glance

89

around, she found a distraction. She leaned in and whispered in the president's ear, "Honey, we need to chat with some of the other guests now. The secretary of state is looking awfully blue."

"Duty calls," the president announced and then turned to Lia just before he left and quietly spoke to her. "It's been a great pleasure, Miss Braga." He leaned in and whispered to her, "I'm going to be in New York in a few days. Would you have a private lunch with me?"

"That would be delightful," Lia said, smiling.

"Someone will be in touch with the details." He turned away, hosting Elena on his arm. She threw a murderous glance back at Lia as they departed.

"Mr. Secretary"—Ed strode toward State—"my wife tells me you are looking awfully blue this evening. Is it China or Iran?"

☆☆☆

Diego tried snoozing on the plane, his flushed forehead resting against the cool plastic of the airplane window. The jittery buzz of the fuselage cut into his efforts to sleep, so he turned to the other side of his seat, curled into a ball, and hugged himself—seeking warmth and to withdraw from the world—a wounded animal seeking refuge.

It was still dark when the plane landed. It was far too early to call Chester for a very important talk, even though he was filled with a new resolve, so he climbed into the Secret Service agent's car and headed home. Would Brandon still be asleep? How would he start the conversation? Would they be able to heal this wound? He didn't know. He wasn't even sure how he felt at this moment—numb, he decided, as he wrapped his arms around himself.

The agent's car pulled up in front of the Perez family home just as dawn was breaking. Diego wondered if Brandon would be up yet. As an early riser, he might even be out on his run already. Diego dismissed the agents and headed for the house, dreading the inevitable confrontation with Brandon.

It was strange being back in the house where he'd grown up—so many associations with the past. It had been difficult to adjust to his life with Brandon in a place where he expected to see one of his parents every time he entered a room. Now he wondered if they had made the right decision to live here, even though the rent was free.

His throat was dry and his hand shook slightly as he unlocked the door and entered the front hall. He stopped and listened. The house was quiet—though not completely. Diego heard muted activity in the kitchen.

"Brandon, you up?" he called out. Chiquita raced to greet him. "Hey, baby." Diego reached down to let the dog lick his hand.

"Diego?" Brandon called from the back of the house.

Chiquita jumped at his heels as Diego headed for the kitchen. The scene, when he entered, was so achingly normal—Brandon making a smoothie like he usually did before his run.

"I didn't think you'd be back till later this morning. Did you get any sleep?" Brandon inquired, not looking at Diego directly.

"Not much." Diego placed his bag on the floor by the kitchen table and sat down. "Got any coffee?

"Not yet. Want me to make some now?"

"Please."

Brandon busied himself with making coffee. They hid behind small domestic chitchat for the moment, neither looking the other in the eye.

Finally, Brandon brought Diego his mug of coffee and sat down at the table opposite him. There was a pause, and then Brandon took a deep breath. "We gotta talk."

"Yeah." Diego finally looked up and recognized how sad Brandon looked. It broke his heart to see his friend and lover looking that vulnerable.

"I did something terrible," Brandon admitted, casting his eyes down.

"I know."

Brandon gazed at him in surprise. "How?"

"You were set up."

"What? How? I don't understand."

"My father orchestrated this little seductive episode to disgrace you with the hope that I would be so angry I would dump you." Brandon looked stunned. Diego continued, "I know all about the guy at the library."

"I'm so sorry. Don't know what came over me."

Diego smiled. "I do. I met the guy. He was hot. Not sure I could have resisted him myself." Diego proceeded to explain all that happened in his father's office.

"That bastard." Brandon bowed his head. "I am so sorry. I really have no excuse. Can you accept that? Will you forgive me?"

"I've gone around and around about this. I know we chose monogamy, and I want you to know I have never cheated on you. And it's not that I haven't been temped—many times, believe me." Diego tapered off into silence. He sat with his hands folded, not looking at Brandon. "But I have something I want to tell you as well." He looked up at Brandon.

Brandon winced.

"I've made a decision..."

"You want us to separate?" Brandon's words were strangled.

Diego shook his head. "No. Not at all. That's not what I was going to say." Brandon looked relieved.

Diego continued, "I can't judge you. I'm not at all sure what I would have done under those circumstances." Diego smiled. "He *was* very hot, wasn't he?"

Brandon nodded and smiled sheepishly. "I'm afraid so. And he came on to me so strong." He looked directly at Diego. "Then you forgive me?"

"Yeah, I do."

"I'm so glad. I've been suffering all night. I felt so guilty."

Diego reached out and took Brandon's hand. "I know. But what I'm going to say will change our lives."

"Tell me." Brandon was so relieved that Diego had forgiven him, Diego could say anything now, and it wouldn't matter.

"I'm going to resign my position at the law firm."

Brandon just stared at him dumbfounded. "Really? Why? I thought everything was going well there. Aren't they about to invite you to join their new environmental division?"

"Well, yes, but things have changed." Diego explained about

Chester's offer to have him lead the exposure of AmVista's suppression of the oil supply, and his father's involvement leading up to the election.

"Wow. That is some story."

"Yeah, I know. But AmVista is one of our firm's top clients, and if I do this I will have to resign from G, C and B. And if I join GreenPAC again it means a big cut in my salary and a lot of very controversial exposure for me. I need you to be okay with this before I commit. It's going to be a big deal and may be rough going for us for a while. I need you to be on board."

At first, Brandon looked undecided but then said, "Of course. Go for it. I know it's what you really want."

"Then I'll call Chester this morning and resign from the firm this afternoon."

Brandon reached across the table and took Diego's hands. "Perhaps we should think about leaving this house as well. Don't see how we can stay on here under the circumstances. We still haven't sublet our apartment. We could easily move back. What do you think?"

Diego smiled in agreement and nodded. He'd have to craft a scathing email to his father later, explaining why neither he nor Brandon could continue living there after what he'd done to Brandon. Ed could get some other schmuck to look after the house. And, oh yeah, by the way, he'd write, Diego was not about to dump Brandon, as mature adults can work things out—so the president could just go fuck himself with a really super-big, black dildo.

☆☆☆

Diego's plane was late arriving in Houston. He checked his watch for the tenth time that hour. He hoped that Deborah would still be at the Taco Bell where they'd arranged to meet. He knew she was still working at AmVista and would probably have limited time to meet with him. He rushed from the arrival gate as quickly as he could. The airport was a bit of a maze, and he had some difficulty locating the restaurant. But there she was, a copy of *Middlemarch* on the table, as they had arranged—his means of identifying her.

"Ms. Salcido, thank you so much for waiting. I'm so sorry, but my plane was delayed. We had to fly around storms over St. Louis."

"Yes, I've been watching the arrival monitors. Please sit." She indicated the chair opposite. "But I cannot down one more Crunchy Taco. Perhaps you would like this last one."

"I am rather hungry, thanks." He eagerly devoured the last taco.

"You can call me Deborah, by the way."

"And I'm Diego. Pleasure," he answered with his mouth full and salsa dripping.

Deborah seemed anxious. "I haven't got a lot of time. Do you mind if we get right down to it?"

"Not at all—my return flight is in just under an hour."

"What exactly is it you want to know?"

"The material you sent us is dynamite." He wiped his mouth with a napkin. "But the force of our revelations to the press is going to depend upon the power of our evidence. What you gave us is great, but it would mean so much more if you could be a co-presenter of the evidence. The fact that you collected it, and that you are the chief security officer at AmVista is very significant. Having you as the face of the disclosure would give it added power."

Deborah looked resigned. "Of course, it means the end of my employment if I do that."

"I understand. Same for me. My law firm represents AmVista, and because I'm working with GreenPAC to reveal this information, I've had to terminate my employment with my firm."

Deborah toyed with her empty soda cup. "But it's not just about employment. These Texas oil folks have a mean streak when it comes to betrayal. I could easily find myself floating face down in a bayou if I'm not careful."

"I see. Well, Chicago is not without its violent precedents also. But I do understand. It will have to be your decision. But it'll make such a huge difference if you do join us."

"I'll think about it."

Diego leaned in toward Deborah, "Tell me, why are you doing this, anyway? I don't see the incentive."

"It's personal. But if we get good and drunk together some time, I might just tell you."

Diego laughed. "I look forward to it."

Deborah suddenly got up to leave. "I really must go. It was great to meet you. I'll let you know my decision in the next couple of days."

"As quickly as possible, please. Time is of the essence here."

Deborah rose to go.

Diego added, "By the way, you know my father is the president, don't you? There's a lot of turmoil in this whole business for me as well."

Deborah smiled. "Kill the king, long live the king. Is that it? Neat."

Diego shook his head ever so slightly. "No. That is certainly not my motivation."

Deborah considered the answer for a moment, nodded, and left. Diego sat for another moment to finish the taco and then rushed to the gate to catch his plane home.

Unseen by either of them, a man at a table not far from where Diego and Deborah sat, put away a small camera and a telescopic sound recording device. He rose, gathered up his newspaper, and left, keeping a safe distance behind as he followed Deborah.

Now the Honeymoon is Over

Day 67 of the president's term

"I hope you like lobster," the president said to Lia as she stared out of the floor to ceiling windows overlooking Central Park from New York's West Side.

"I do." She sipped at her champagne. "This is a very comfortable apartment. Is it yours?"

"A friend's. I have a house in Chicago and a summer home on the lake in Michigan. You must come for a visit to the lake. It's very nice."

"What will your wife think about that?" Lia smiled.

"We don't always keep the same schedules. There are ways."

Lia looked at Ed over the edge of her glass—narrowing her dark brown eyes a little to make them richly seductive. It was clear from his hungry expression her strategy was working. "How is it you are in New York today?" She diverted the questioning to a less suggestive topic for the moment. She did not want to rush the seduction. It was in her interest to hook the old geezer well before she reeled him in.

"I had a speech at the UN this morning. Perhaps you heard it?"

"Sorry, not much time for the news these days. Too busy trying to save the environment."

He smiled. "So you're the one putting all those radical ideas into my daughter's head."

"Afraid so. But I shouldn't worry. I'm sure you'll be able to persuade her against such fancies with the force of your intelligent and well thought out, scientifically supported arguments."

Ed paused. He looked troubled, but recovered quickly. "More champagne?" He passed around the luncheon table, bringing the bottle to fill her glass.

"Don't you usually have people to serve the food and wine?" Lia asked, with a knowing smile.

The subtle dig landed. "I do, but I wanted to give you my most personal attention. I don't often have the pleasure of serving someone directly—my life is all so managed and remote."

"I'm sure your wife must appreciate your personal attentions to her."

☆

Ed smiled and stared at the woman in front of him with admiration. This little filly liked to play games. He was up for that. "So tell me, do you have a boyfriend?"

"We separated recently."

"I'm sorry."

"Oh, I'm sure you're quite indifferent—relieved even."

"That's harsh."

"And that must be refreshing as well. I bet everyone sucks up to you all the time. Does anyone ever deliver you the uncomfortable truth?"

"I have many plain-speaking advisors."

"Really? Are you one of those presidents who actively seeks advisors with opposing views, or do you only seek advisors who parrot your views?"

"Now you're becoming impertinent." He was getting uncomfortable with her frankness and was regretting his invitation to her.

She laughed. "Ooooh, bit of a thin skin, I see."

"That will do. Let's have lunch." He abruptly pulled out her chair, demanding she sit. She complied. He went to his place, whipped his napkin into his lap, and served the lobster and salad without further conversation.

She looked up at him and smiled. "Don't be hurt. I'm just a bit of a tease is all."

He looked at her. He was right on the verge of abandoning any thought of wooing her, but he was also excited by her feistiness. He did enjoy a good spar from time to time. He'd bet she would be a tiger in bed. And that excited him even more.

"I'm sorry if I've upset you. Can we start again?" She reached over and placed her hand on top of his.

"Don't see why not." He took her hand in his. The way she looked at him was so soft and gentle and pleading. Her dark eyes and caramel skin captivated him. Her tender red mouth was so inviting. He was becoming sexually aroused. His Latin blood began to surge. He could barely contain himself.

Lia leaned closer. "I'll tell you what, Edward, would you mind terribly if we skipped dessert? I think we must make love immediately, don't you?"

Ed had never had a woman be that direct with him before. Well, at least not one he wasn't paying for.

Lia rose from her chair, took both of Edward's hands, and raising him from his chair asked, "Bedroom?"

"Over there."

She led him directly to the bed, tossing back the covers on her side of the bed as he undressed. "I'm very glad the Secret Service agents don't have to attend," she added, as she slipped naked under the covers and threw back the sheets on his side of the bed to invite him in. He readily complied.

He looked at her one last time before he climbed in beside her. "God, you are gorgeous."

Lia hummed to herself as she cleaned up in the bathroom after their encounter. She carefully picked Ed's used condom from the waste can, then rummaged through her shoulder bag for a plastic bag to put it in. She concealed it carefully in a zippered pocket. They had a very efficient DNA lab at the Institute, and the director owed her several favors.

"Lia?" Ed called, after knocking on the bathroom door.

"Ed?" she mocked slightly in response.

"I need to go now. You can stay as long as you like. Just shut and lock the door from the inside as you leave."

Lia opened the bathroom door quickly, surprising Ed who was leaning against it.

"Oh," he exclaimed, startled.

She took his arm. "I'm ready. We can go out together." She reached up and gave him a very deep and sexy kiss, totally disarming him.

"Ah...I was going to say we have to leave separately. I'm sure you understand." He looked like he was still reeling from the kiss.

"Oh, Ed, I can't believe a man like you is concerned about being seen with the woman who saved his daughter and who had his picture taken with her at the White House reception."

"Well...I guess it's all right then."

She whispered in his ear. "I just want to spend every second I can with you."

He smiled and looked at her appreciatively. Lia smiled in return but for different reasons.

Preceded by the Secret Service agents, they exited the back of the building where the president's limo was discreetly stationed. Just before Ed climbed into the back seat of the car, he leaned forward and kissed Lia once again. "There's a car out front ready to take you wherever you want to go." He got into the limo and drove off under police escort.

After the car had completely disappeared, Lia looked across the street as David, her photographer friend, stepped out from behind a large dumpster. He gave her a thumbs-up and smiled.

☆☆☆

Deborah knew she was being followed. You can't trap a trapper. She was not sure how much Terrance knew, or suspected, about what she was up to, but she knew she was—or soon could be—in great danger. She had seen the man at the airport surveilling her and knew now was the time to make some preparations of her own.

She believed Terrance underestimated her—the fallacy of male superiority. She could work that to her advantage. She would play clueless with him, and her presumed innocence would be her shield—for the time being. He would not be looking to her as a real threat just yet—he was too certain he had seduced her with his proposed promotion for that—at least until she made her big announcement through GreenPAC.

But she had her own little bag of tricks and a plan to use them. She wanted to know every nefarious action Terrance was plotting, and if she failed to thwart him, or if she became bayou fish food, she would have a complete record of his actions, one she could arrange to be made public whether she was still around or not.

She had already successfully bugged his office, his mobile phone, and his car—now all she needed to do was get inside his home and complete the total surveillance of Terrance's world.

She had long ago fashioned an escape route, knowing one day she might have to lose her tail. She could see the familiar rusted out old Chrysler just down the street as she drove out of her driveway. And sure enough, as she headed away, the car followed.

She drove to Dillard's department store, parked, and went inside. Once there, she glanced into the cosmetic counter mirror. The man had followed her. She headed toward ladies dresses, and when she arrived, she glimpsed him browsing the sale rack as she selected a series of outfits. With her arms loaded with dresses, she approached the man tailing her.

"Excuse me, I hope you don't mind," she said sweetly. "I really need a man's opinion on this. Which do you think is a better color for me?" She held up a blue dress. "This one?" Then she switched to a green dress. "Or this one? I just can't seem to make up my mind. You know how we ladies are. I like the green one myself, but my husband thinks blue is a better color on me. What do you think?"

She was amused by how totally flustered he was by having her approach him. He was supposed to be undercover, after all. "I ah...well, I..." He tried backing away from her.

"Oh, now don't be shy. It's just going to take a minute." He looked around for an escape. "Here, I'll tell you what. Why don't I try these two on and you can tell me which you like best. I won't be any time at all." She handed him a whole arm full of dresses. "Here, hold these, I'll be right back." She dashed off with the two dresses to the fitting rooms, suppressing a laugh at how paralyzed with confusion he looked.

Once inside the fitting room, Deborah discarded the two dresses, pulled a raincoat out of her bag, a pair of sunglasses, and a scarf, and put them on hastily. Disguise on, she dashed out a second dressing room entrance and disappeared out of the store, leaving the poor tail languishing with an armload of dresses as he waited for her to return. The poor man was obviously not one of Terrance's more qualified employees, Deborah thought, and it was certain his employ would now be cut abruptly short. Deborah would not have to concern herself with him anymore.

Clear of the tail, Deborah went straight to her car and drove to Terrance's house. Today was the perfect day to implement her plan. She'd done her research. Tuesdays at eleven the pool guy cleaned the swimming pool. Terrance's house was surrounded by a high fence with a key-padded locked gate. She did not have the gate code, so she needed the pool guy to open the gate so she could follow him in. She got to Terrance's house at ten forty-five.

Almost right on time, just after eleven, Pepe's Pool Service truck pulled up to the gate. She waited as he punched in the code and drove up the drive. As soon as he was clear of the gates, Deborah charged up the drive after the truck, and just made it through the gate before it closed. Pepe appeared visibly startled by the surprise visitor.

Deborah got out of her car and dashed over to Pepe. "Is my brother in? I just have to speak with him. He's got my divorce papers, and I needed to take them to the court—an hour ago."

"He work," Pepe answered in broken English.

"Oh yeah, of course he is. What about his wife, Kathy? Is she around?"

"She work too, I think, maybe." She kind of felt sorry for the pool guy. Poor Pepe was not sure quite what to do with this lady. He had never seen her before. "I can call him if you want?" He started to take out his cell phone.

"Oh, that's all right. I've got a key. I know right where he keeps the papers on his desk. Don't you worry about a thing." She rushed back to her car, took out a large shoulder bag, and headed for the front door. She waved and smiled.

Pepe looked at her in confusion for a few more moments before he began to unload the pool cleaning equipment from his truck.

She'd told more than one little white lie to Pepe. Deborah did *not* have a key. That's where being an expert at picking locks came in useful. She'd been worried the alarm system might pose a problem, but when she checked, to her good fortune, she'd discovered the alarm service Terrance used was owned by her family. She had been able to extract the code before she came over.

Once inside, and after the alarm was turned off, she began her work as quickly as possible. She had been to several parties at Terrance's house, so she knew the layout and exactly where she needed to work.

First, she went to Terrance's library where he had his desk. She began by scanning the room for bugs—it was not impossible that someone else was observing his actions—but the room was clean.

She then worked her way through the house concealing various audio and video receptors. She would use the house's internal electrical wiring system to transmit the information from the receptors, bundle it at a staging device, and then transmit it to her company's satellite. She found the house's electrical switch box in the garage, dismantled it quickly, and installed her staging and transmission equipment behind the panel, and she was done.

☆☆☆

Diego's new work environment at GreenPAC definitely took some getting used to. His cubicle at G, C & B seemed like an amphitheater compared to this old metal desk crammed into a corner of an office filled with at least ten other assorted desks, a copy machine, and a multitude of file cabinets—*life at a nonprofit*, he thought wryly. He didn't even have his own desk phone but had to share one with the desk next to his. Fortunately that person was frequently out of the office, so Diego could hoard the phone mostly to himself.

On the brighter side, it was so nice not to have to wear a suit and tie and to be able to show up at work in jeans and a sweatshirt. That he did enjoy.

Chester was at his door—Chester was the only one to have his own office—and he motioned for Diego to come over.

"How you settling in?" Chester asked, as Diego took a chair

opposite.

"Well...," Diego hedged, with some uncertainty.

"That bad, huh?" They both laughed.

"So, how was your trip to Houston? Is she going to be onboard with us or not?"

"I believe so. Just waiting to hear her final answer. She has some reservations. Feels there may be some safety issues."

"Yeah, can imagine. But we need to set the press conference date and time. Time is of the essence here."

Diego nodded. "I expect to hear from her today or tomorrow. If not, I'll call her again. If I were you I would go ahead and schedule the conference. We can proceed without her if need be."

"Okay," Chester checked his desk calendar. "How about the 28th of April? The president is going to be in China. It will be doubly embarrassing for him to have this story break while he's there. The Chinese are all about saving face. And he's going to have to really scramble to get back home to address this issue. It should throw him completely off his game."

"Excellent. I'll follow up with Deborah, and let you know if she's onboard." Diego rose to go.

"Diego?"

Diego turned back to Chester.

"Are you okay with this? It is your father, after all. Will this destroy your family relationship?"

Diego pondered that for a moment. He remembered the smug look on his father's face as he gloated over the revelation of Brandon's indiscretion. "He deserves everything coming to him. The only one I'm afraid might be hurt by this is Carmella. But I really think she'll understand."

☆☆☆

Elena never knew Ed had so many socks. She only knew now because she was rummaging through his dresser drawers. She didn't know exactly what she was looking for, but she was desperate to find something. The evening he had come back from New York after the UN speech, he reeked of sex. She knew that smell—had smelled it on him far too many times before. But now she was the first lady and she was not going to put up with this outrage any longer. He would see. She would assert herself and demand... What? Demand what? She had no idea.

She was so frustrated she took all his socks out of the drawer and tied each one in a tight knot and threw them all about the bedroom. That would teach him real good.

She then rang up the kitchen and ordered a peanut butter and salami sandwich even though lunch was hours away. It was only ten-thirty on a Thursday morning.

She would show him, she would. Let her put on ten pounds, then he would be sorry. She would become all blowsy and let her hair go its natural color. She would wear housedresses, and mules, and smoke in public. She would become a national disgrace, and he would never be re-elected. Oh yes, that would serve him just right.

On her way out of the dressing room, however, she passed a mirror—she glanced. She looked damn good. She tucked in her tummy just a skosh. A curl fell over her forehead at just the wrong angle. She shook her head, and it jiggled back into its perfect place. *Damn girl— you am hot!*

Then she remembered, all of a sudden, that incredibly cute intern in the West Wing who had given her the eye several times. She thought she might just wander down that way and say hi to the chief of staff. She would pass right by the intern's desk on the way.

☆☆☆

Though they hadn't thought it before, it was proving to be fortunate that Diego and Brandon had not been able to sublet their furnished apartment. When they moved back, there was very little they had to do to settle back in again. No hoard of boxes to unpack, just a few suitcases with their clothes, and a few boxes of files, personal documents, and effects.

Still, though neither would say it, their much smaller apartment felt a little bit cramped now compared to the spaciousness of the large Perez family home.

And although forgiven, Brandon still felt a certain twinge of guilt and awkwardness around Diego. They had not had sex since Brandon's indiscretion. Brandon was unsure how to breech the barrier between them.

Diego, for his part, was also preoccupied with the upcoming press conference. Even though he didn't want to admit it, the disclosure of the AmVista scandal *would* hurt his father. And although he had been hurt by his father's actions, he still worried about how his actions might affect Carmella.

Brandon and Diego had been awkwardly dancing around each other the last couple of days. Diego felt they both wanted to reach out and start the healing process, but neither quite knew how to break through to the other.

"Oh crap," Diego exclaimed.

"What?"

"Paper cut."

"Let me see." Brandon came over to where Diego was putting folders back in his file drawer.

Brandon took Diego's finger in his hand. "Poor baby," he crooned. He gave a sly smile and put the injured finger in his mouth and began sucking. "Papa make it better."

Diego closed his eyes. "You'd better watch out. This could lead to something..."

"Would you like that?"

"M-m-m."

Brandon took Diego in his arms, walking Diego backwards toward the bedroom.

Chiquita looked at the two men and thought that it was playtime. She charged around the living room searching for her ball. Finding it, she scooted over as her humans disappeared into the bedroom. Chiquita dropped the ball and barked for immediate attention. The bedroom door stayed closed, leaving Chiquita outside to ponder the mystery of how anyone could refuse a bouncing ball.

☆☆☆

The mountain range of bubbles mounding over Elena was beginning to collapse, and the bath water was turning tepid. She had fallen asleep with a lit cigarette dangling from her limp hand on the edge of the tub. The cigarette fell onto the bath mat and began to smolder.

Ed was alerted to the scene as he caught a whiff of smoke from the adjacent room. He peeked into the bathroom and rushed forward as he saw the smoldering embers start to spread. Disgusted, he squashed the butt out with the toe of his shoe. He turned on the shower's cold water, and Elena jumped awake, flinging suds over the edge of the tub.

"What the fuck?" Ed boomed. "You should be ready by now. Goddamn it, Elena, the banquet is in half an hour. Madame Ying Tao is expecting you in her chambers in fifteen minutes. Get your butt out of that tub and get dressed."

"Well, I *am* the first lady. She can just wait." Elena leisurely slipped on her robe and took her time gliding over to her private quarters.

Goddammit, that woman wasn't about to make him late. The president was already dressed and ready to meet with the Chinese head of state. If need be, he would leave Elena to make her own way to the banquet hall. He was not about to be inconvenienced by her shenanigans.

There was a knock at the suite door, followed the urgent entry of Madison Burk, the president's scrawny, puckered press secretary.

"Mr. President, you have to see this now."

"What is it, Mads?"

"This was just sent to us from the White House press office. I think it will speak for itself." Madison turned his tablet to the president to show a paused video.

"Can't this wait? Got a goddamn state banquet in fifteen minutes."

"The banquet can be delayed. You've got to look at this right now." Madison pressed play and Ed followed the activity, turning slightly grey as it played out.

"Who's the woman?" he asked.

"Deborah Salcido, head of security at AmVista."

"And that's Diego?" He suddenly recognized his son.

"Afraid so."

"Goddamn it to hell!" he shouted.

Elena replied from the other room. "Did you call me, dear?"

"No!" he bellowed, and started pacing the room. "How did they get hold of this crazy shit?"

"From the Salcido woman. Don't know why she would sabotage her own company, but now she's gonna be toast."

"And what about me? Do you realize what this is going to do to ME? Linking me with the CEO of AmVista and that commie goon who runs Venezuela in an oil price manipulation scheme. Jesus Harold fuckin' Christ!" He pulled a cigar out of his jacket and lit it as he paced and thought.

"Well, you know there's nothing to worry about if it's not true," Madison tried to comfort.

"Oh, come on, Mads, of course it's true."

Madison cleared his throat. "Oh, sir..."

Ed couldn't look at this goon any longer. "Get me Martin."

"Yes, sir."

As Madison dialed the president's chief of staff, another knock came at the door. Cradling the cell phone between his ear and shoulder, Madison opened the door.

The American ambassador to China stepped inside.

"Mr. President, the Chinese president is waiting. He's becoming agitated."

"Tell him to go fuck himself."

The ambassador blanched. "Sir, I can't do that."

"Then tell him to go fuck you."

Without another word, the ambassador withdrew.

"Sir, I have Martin on the phone for you."

The president grabbed the phone from his hands.

"Have you...? What can be done...?" Ed listened for a minute. "I'm coming back tonight. This goddamn mess has got to be contained. Muster all our resources, and we'll hold our own press conference tomorrow when I get back... I don't care about any of that. We'll do what we have to do."

Madison spoke up. "Sir, you can't go back tomorrow. You have a full schedule with the Chinese president for the next four days—it would cause an international uproar if you were to stand him up."

Ed reeled on him. "I don't give a good goddamn. We'll tell him we have a national emergency." Ed threw the phone across the room, striking a fifteenth century Ming Dynasty vase, which shattered as it hit the floor.

Elena appeared at the dressing room door. "I am ready, my dear," she declared, all smiles and radiance.

The president turned to look at her. She was dressed in a gold lamé gown with bands of ruby sequins running in bands around the bodice. She looked as garish as a Kung Fu porno movie poster.

"No," was all Ed could muster in response. "Go change."

"I don't see why. This is so chicly oriental."

"Go!"

She turned with a pout, and retreated back into her dressing room, slamming the door behind her.

☆

The Chinese president—already a permanently angry-looking man—glowered as Ed finally came forth with Elena on his arm in a plain, dark-green dress this time. They were accompanied by the Chinese president's wife.

Servers stood ready at the kitchen entrance, and they signaled to the chefs that the US president had finally arrived.

The guests took their seats next to the American ambassador to China as the Chinese president remained standing and paused, glass raised, to propose a toast. Ed's translator hovered at his shoulder. The Chinese president forced a smile and rhapsodized about the friendship of their two countries, and how trade created peace and mutual understanding. He talked about cultural exchanges, and trade agreements, and the harmony of the heavens. Elena squirmed—Ed knew the lush was itching to sip her champagne. He didn't take in a word of the Chinese president's speech—thoughts of the GreenPAC news conference were racing through his mind.

The American ambassador coughed and Ed realized it was his turn to toast. He stood up. He looked out over the guests filling the great hall. The bright lights, focused on the guest table, dazzled. The room felt stifling. There was a buzzing in his head. He felt faint, and leaned forward to support himself to keep from falling. The ambassador rose and crossed to Ed.

"Sir, are you okay?" he asked.

"I...ah...don't feel right."

The ambassador looked around frantically and tried to give Ed support.

Ed pulled at his shirt collar, and then collapsed, falling across Elena, who threw her champagne in the air and let out a shriek.

☆☆☆

"Watcha gonna do now?" Diego asked Deborah, as they drank beers in Chester's office, trying to relax after the explosive news conference earlier that morning. They had ignited a fire storm in the media and had been besieged for hours by the press. Only now were they free to kick back.

"Oh boy..." She held up her cell phone. "Thirty-seven calls from Terrance. Fourteen from my attorney. And eight from my father. How about I disappear somewhere in the south Pacific?"

"Now that sounds like the perfect solution. Can we join you?" Chester asked.

"Only if you are masters at grass hut construction."

The three laughed and took swigs of their beers—their laughter tinged with anxiety.

Diego became serious and leaned toward Deborah. "How can we ever thank you? Without you..." He shook his head. "Do you feel safe going back to Texas?"

Deborah's cell phone rang. She glanced at it. "Terrance again." She waved the phone in the air and muted the call.

"Think he might be a little pissed?" Diego joked.

"Umm. Good possibility. Well, one thing I am sure of—I won't be going back to AmVista."

"Want to stay in Chicago? I'm sure we could find a position for you here, if that would interest you," Chester offered.

"Nah, don't think so. Not really my scene. Helped you guys for a personal reason. But it's not something I want to do regularly."

Diego turned to her. "That reminds me. You said if we ever got drunk enough you would tell me what motivated you to do this—wreck your career and expose yourself to danger." He paused. "Had enough beers yet to tell us?"

"Yeah…" Deborah took another sip of her beer before she continued. "Do you remember that incident several months back when there was the big ruckus in Brazil because the Braga family got burned to death in a barn?"

"Sure do. AmVista was involved, wasn't it?" Chester replied.

Deborah nodded. "Only two family members survived—two sisters. It was a terrible incident, and even though AmVista was technically blameless, I was so devastated by the event that it turned me completely against my own company."

"You were there?" Diego asked.

"It was I who found them. They were pretty shook up—hungry, thirsty, in shock. The little one, Cala, just touched my heart, and I had to do something. I helped them cope. The little one went to her aunt's nearby, and the older one, Lia, lived in New York—some kind of a college instructor. I helped her get back to the US"

Deborah's phone rang—again. It was Terrance—again. "Hey, listen, I'm no saint here. I've done plenty of pretty nasty stuff in my day. Not looking for any Mother Teresa tributes, if you know what I mean. But that one incident—well, it did something to me. I had to respond in some meaningful way."

"So what now?"

"Probably go back to the family business—alarm and security service. Pretty dull after all of this. But hey, it's family, and it's a living. Maybe something else will come along some day. Who knows?"

"Well, you take good care of yourself. I don't imagine all those calls from AmVista were congratulations."

"I've taken a few precautions. Wasn't born in a turnip patch, you know."

111

"Well, if there's ever anything we can do—just contact us." Chester offered his hand to Deborah.

"You'll be my backup."

Diego was glad to walk Deborah to the street to catch a taxi to the airport—partly because he wanted to keep up the conversation and partly because he was worried about her.

"It's been great working with you," he told her as they neared a cab. "Thank you so much for your help."

"I should say it's my pleasure, but not so sure it was, if you know what I mean."

Diego nodded. He held the taxi door for her as she slid into the back seat. "Bye. Be safe."

As he watched the taxi speeding off, things started to click in Diego's mind. The woman Deborah had befriended in Brazil—he thought he knew her. If correct, that Lia Braga was the same Lia who had saved his sister and was her teacher. *Small world*, he thought.

☆☆☆

President Ed was resting comfortably in an armchair, snoozing under the influence of a sedative on Air Force One. Elena was snuggled up on a sofa in a corner of the small room, flipping through the *Congressional Quarterly*—but as it had no pictures, she got bored quickly.

The president's doctor had done a thorough examination and determined that the president had not suffered a heart attack or a stroke. It was most likely a case of stress and exhaustion, brought about by the overseas trip, the shock of the scandalous news conference, and Elena's sequined lamé dress. But the whole fainting incident at the banquet accomplished exactly what the president had desired: it got them out of "goddamned China"—the president's words. Given that it was a legitimate medical emergency, no American warships had to be dispatched to ply the Taiwan Strait to support the president's honor.

The doctor had expressly forbidden the president to have any communications with his staff in DC until he got back to Washington. He needed complete rest, which meant that Elena was instructed to keep watch and make sure that Ed didn't cheat. She was thoroughly bored with the task. Given that the president was drugged and soundly asleep, she figured it would be okay for her to take a little cat nap. She stretched out on the sofa and nodded off.

In the rear of the plane, the press corps, traveling with the president, bombarded poor Madison with endless rounds of questions about both the GreenPAC press conference and the president's collapse at the banquet. But Madison had almost no additional information or answers. He just had to wing it.

Ed opened his eyes groggily. It took a moment for him to realize where he was and what had happened. He looked about the room and saw Elena stretched out on the sofa asleep.

He would have to move quietly so as not to wake her—he was in no mood to deal with anything she might have to say to him just now. He carefully slipped the blanket off his legs and stood up. He was a bit wobbly but steadied himself using the back of the arm chair before carefully slipping out of the room and going directly to his private office.

He sat at his desk, resting his head for a moment on its cooling surface and then righted himself. He took a small slip of paper out of his wallet, picked up his secure phone, and dialed.

"Guess who?" a voice on the line said playfully.

"Ed?" Lia responded. She was thrown by hearing his voice. She'd never thought he would be free to call her without a half dozen aids listening in to his every word.

"How ya doin', honey?"

"Where are you?" Lia asked as she settled back in her chair. She put the book she'd been reading on her lap.

"I don't know, over the Pacific, or the North Pole, or some goddamned place like that. Air Force One."

"I thought you were in China till the end of the week."

"Supposed to be but ditched it."

"Can you just do that?"

"Well, I did."

"I suppose you know about the press conference?" she asked, faintly smiling.

"Can't we talk about something else? I miss you. I want to see you."

"Oh Ed, you are so sweet." It was a good thing he couldn't see the grimace she was making. "But wasn't that Diego at the GreenPAC press conference? I'm sure it was him." She couldn't help digging the knife in a little deeper.

"This is not why I called you, to talk about that stuff. I need some lovin'." Lia shuddered, imagining his embrace. "When can I see you?"

"Just say when and where. You're the one with the hectic and restricted lifestyle."

"Okay, remember we talked about you visiting the house in Michigan?"

"Yeah."

"I'm going to send Elena off to stay with her mother for a while, and I'm going up to the Michigan house for a rest—had a little incident at the Chinese banquet..."

"Are you all right?"

"Will be. Just need some rest and quiet. I want you to be with me. Will you do that?"

Lia paused. She was not sure what she wanted her next step to be. She wanted to think about it more before she made a decision. "Let me know when and where and how I am to get there, and I will let you know if I can make it. I do have some teaching obligations, you know. Can't be gone for too long."

"I'll get back to you when I know the dates. Really want to see you. Can't stop thinking about you, sweetheart."

"Yeah, me too you." She leaned her head back, silently imploring the heavens for this conversation to end.

"Gotta go. Will get back to you soon. Can't wait to see you." He hung up.

Lia leaned back in her chair. She contemplated where she was with

114

her plan. She couldn't believe the good news of the GreenPAC revelations about the president's involvement with the oil scam. She knew this would play out as a major scandal, and it fit perfectly with her plans to destroy him. She had the DNA evidence from the condom, and she had pictures of her and the president kissing in front of the president's limo. But she wanted more—something more damning and conclusive. A trip to the Michigan White House could be just the opportunity to gather more evidence for when she went public of her affair with the president. It would only be a matter of time before she hammered the final nail in his coffin. How perfect that he and AmVista were in the crosshairs of a public scandal. Soon her family would finally be free to rest in peace.

☆☆☆

Diego hurriedly answered his office phone. He was busy.

"Lunch," Milly commanded Diego. "La Cazuela at one. My treat."

"Mom, we are really very busy. I usually eat lunch at my desk. I can't just up and go out to lunch whenever I want.

"Of course you can. It's only a non-profit, for heaven's sake. They have to work around your schedule. They hardly pay you anything. Think of it as a perk."

"I'll see what I can do."

"Do that."

"What's this about? You never invite me to lunch unless it's about—something."

"A little celebration."

"Oh really? What about?"

"You'll see—at one."

Milly was already seated at a garden table with a commanding view of the restaurant and everyone coming and going. She waved to Diego when he arrived.

"You are ten minutes late," she said in her most withering mock-stern voice as Diego sat opposite her.

"Well, I see you have comforted yourself with a pitcher of margaritas in my absence. I'm sure that has blunted the edge of your disappointment."

"Don't you be snide with me, young man. Some of this is for you as well."

"So grateful, but I *am* working, and I've decided I shouldn't drink at lunch anymore."

"Pity." Milly topped up her glass.

"But I'm sure you won't let any of it go to waste." His eyes danced with wickedness.

"How observant of you."

"So what's this all about?" Diego asked after they had ordered and been served.

"Well, your father called me."

"Ah, ho, ho," Diego snorted out a laugh. "That must have been a royal treat."

"Well yes, as always." She smiled her little conspiratorial smile. "He is furious with you just now and can't bring himself to talk to you directly."

"I'll bet."

"He has asked me to talk to you for him."

"Oh boy, here it comes."

"I said I would. But, of course, I didn't say what I would talk to you *about*."

Diego held out his hand to her, palm up. "You may smack it if you please," he joked.

Milly tapped it lightly. "I'm sure there is no need to repeat to you what he said to me. I'm certain you can surmise that on your own. However, I do want to add a word or two of my own."

"All right."

"I'm sorry you are not drinking. I would like to propose a little toast."

"Really?" Diego held up his water glass. "Go for it."

Milly tipped her margarita glass against it. "To my darling boy. I am so proud of you. Here's to the fall of the Washington Caligula."

"Well, nothing's happened yet."

"Oh, but it will. Congress is just itching to hold investigations." Milly leaned in toward Diego conspiratorially. "Can you just imagine, your father consorting with the likes of Casados and that oily Terrance Geiger? Pun intended, of course."

"Of course. Thank you..."

Milly tapped the side of her nose. "Now then, just a word of caution. I know your father. I know his cronies. You just be careful and watch out for yourself. You hear me?"

"Yes ma'am." He paused and considered her for a moment. "And this is what you call a celebration. This is why you bid me here?"

"Oh no, that was purely incidental. The grand news is that I am being courted again." She smiled and began applying fresh lipstick.

"And who might the lucky fellow be?"

"Dexter Matthews."

"*The* Dexter Matthews? That TV personality and star of stage, screen, and international media? The Dexter Matthews of *Confidential Confessions*?"

"The very one and the very same."

Diego laughed. "Well, aren't you the saucy one."

"Just thought you should know in case you heard any malicious rumors."

"I'm at a loss for words."

Milly put the lipstick back in her purse and checked her hair in her compact mirror. "Also a little bird told me a charming story involving a university professor and a restroom... Anything to that little yarn?"

"Mother, I do not discuss those kinds of things. You know that."

"Well, being a woman of some considerable experience in these matters, if you ever want to chat about it, feel free. You will find me completely nonjudgmental and somewhat experienced in the intricacies of infidelity, after multitudinous episodes with your father."

"I appreciate that. But all I want to say is that the whole incident was a setup, engineered by you-know-who."

"Shocking." She emptied the margarita pitcher and thought about ordering another, but then thought better of it.

"But Brandon and I have worked it out. And you will be relieved to know that all is back to normal between us."

"So pleased. Do give him my regards." Milly set her purse in her lap. She motioned for the check. She was ready to go. "So tell me, are you free this Saturday evening? There's this charming little event at the Hudson Gallery..."

"Wouldn't you rather take Mr. TV Personality instead?

"I would, but he will be unavailable as he will be attending his wife's birthday party."

"Oh really?" Diego smiled slyly.

☆☆☆

Deborah had flown back to Dallas rather than Houston. At the airport, she rented a car and drove to the offices of her family's Houston offices. She needed to collect some vital information there. She was certain they would be looking out for her at Bush International and at her house. No need to make oneself too conspicuous. She had given a lot of thought to what she would do next. Now it was time to implement her plan as quickly and expeditiously as possible.

First she needed to get into her house to make the final arrangements. She waited till dark and then drove to her block and parked across the street and down several houses to avoid anyone who might be staking out her house. She then walked around to the street behind her house and snuck through her neighbors' backyard to hers. She waited and watched. As far as she could see, no one was observing her house from the back. She scurried across the lawn to a basement window that she had purposefully left unlocked. She crawled in and quietly ascended the basement stairs. She softly opened the door into the kitchen. She listened, and hearing nothing, entered the kitchen. The house was still. She was safe.

☆☆☆

Diego threw his bag on the floor by his desk. Coffee. He needed a hit of coffee. He went to the break room and rummaged in the sink for his mug from yesterday. It seemed that no one in GreenPAC had been assigned to do the dishes. Chester looked in.

"Was hoping I'd find you. Have you seen the news from Houston?" Diego shook his head. "Better come."

Chester led Diego to his office. "Take a look." He pointed to his computer monitor. Diego went over and sat in Chester's chair to read.

The photograph was of a suburban house totally destroyed by fire. The attending article read: *Tragedy struck in the upscale neighborhood of Tanglewood last night. The home of Deborah Salcido, Head of Security at Houston's AmVista Petroleum, was engulfed in flames after what was described by neighbors as a "horrific explosion." The house was completely destroyed, but luckily fire fighters were able to prevent the fire from spreading to adjacent homes.*

Local fire authorities have no reason to suspect that arson was the cause. The explosion appears to be the consequence of a gas leak, which may have originated in the basement where the gas had built up, causing the enormous explosion.

It was only recently reported by the HPD that a body was discovered in the remnants of the house. It was burned beyond recognition but is believed to be that of the home's owner, Deborah Salcido.

"Oh my God," Diego exclaimed.

Ms. Salcido was recently in the news as the result of startling revelations by her and the environmental activist group GreenPAC in Chicago. They asserted that President Edward Perez, AmVista President Terrance Geiger, and Venezuelan President Benevito Casados conspired to sequester vast amounts of oil in salt caves in Mexico. Their intention was to manipulate the oil market to drive up oil prices, benefiting the Perez Presidential campaign that had based the campaign on energy independence through unlimited drilling. The incident has become known as the Brightway Scandal and is being investigated by Congress and the Department of Justice.

Diego looked up at Chester. "I feel just terrible. Do you think it was an accident as they claim?"

"Here... Move over. You gotta see this." Diego scooted to an adjoining chair as Chester moved in to the keyboard. He brought up an email. It was from Deborah.

"I haven't had time to study this fully yet, but this email contains dozens of document, video, and audio files. She says they will prove beyond a shadow of a doubt that Terrance Geiger and AmVista were making plans to eliminate her."

"She must have sent this just before she died. She told us she suspected they might come after her." Diego took a deep breath. "We need to download these and get them into safekeeping. We also need to contact an attorney."

"That's your department. I'll let you take care of that. And I hate to say this, but we may need bodyguards as well."

"Well, I have my Secret Service guys already."

"And you trust them now, after all of this?"

"My father would never..." Diego looked at Chester.

"Your father, perhaps...but what about Geiger?"

☆☆☆

The president's most intimate cadre surrounded him in the Oval Office. They were still in severe damage control after the GreenPAC news conference, even at the expense of doing the country's business.

"Deny—just deny the fuck out of it," Madison suggested.

"Are you kidding?" the president exclaimed. "There are photos. There are travel receipts. There is the physical evidence of the goddamned oil in the Mexican caves. This is not like pissing in the swimming pool. You can't just swim to the other end and say, 'I don't know what you're talking about'."

"Justice is setting up an independent investigation with Congress. There are going to be hearings and shit on this for weeks—if not months," Martin added, already thinking of moving on as Ed's chief of staff. He had to think beyond just this administration. The stench from this mess could last for years, if not decades. This might make Nixon's indiscretions look like refusing to share crayons in kindergarten.

"And what about your son?" Carson McDaniel, Chief White House

Counsel, asked. "How could you let him be a part of this? You know how that looks to all the family values folks?"

"He's thirty-two, for chriz sake. It's not like I can just cut off his allowance, ya know."

"But there are other, more persuasive ways," Madison hinted.

Ed stared him down. "If what you're suggesting is what I think it is, then just back up. There will be no violence against my family by me or anybody else. Is that abundantly clear?" The group nodded.

"And then there is the press and the polls. Your numbers are tanking, and the media is characterizing you as just south of Vlad the Impaler. Madison needed Ed to understand just where he was. Ed's whole agenda as president was at stake. If he could not get through this mess, he would be next to useless in advancing the party's conservative priorities.

"Okay, we know where we are—now how do we get out in front of it?" Ed asked.

Madison drummed his fingers nervously on the table and then exclaimed, "What about a united family? You know, the kids, the ex-wife—the mother of your children—all cheeky and cuddly in front of the fireplace…"

"Christmas photos!" Martin suggested. "Always warms the heart."

"Yeah, like a fireside chat," Madison suggested.

"Too FDR," Ed observed. "You guys are trying to take down dragons with fly swatters. This is far too big and dangerous for mere photo ops. Let's get radical in our thinking here."

"What we need is a good war, California falling into the ocean, or a terrorist attack—something to unite the citizens. Deflect all attention from your little indiscretion. Get them united behind you as commander in chief during a time of crisis," Carson speculated.

Ed cringed. "I don't know…" He began pacing.

"Hey, and let's not forget that even the harshest scandal subsides with time. Maybe the best way to handle this is to just ride it out. Play humble and contrite. Grovel a little, and before long some other goon will catch the press' attention, and you can just move on." Martin seemed pleased with his solution.

"Yeah, you wish," Madison derided. "You're forgetting the Congressional investigations. They're not just going to melt away."

Ed thought aloud. "No, Carson might be right. What we need is an opportunity. Something to deflect attention from this whole mess. Something big and dangerous. Maybe we don't have the perfect opportunity right now. But something will come along. Just you wait and see."

☆☆☆

Carmella was just thrilled to be at the Michigan house with Lia. Classes were over. Finals were over. The summer stretched out before her—the last lazy summer before her senior year and graduation. She meant to spend her whole vacation time at the lake, reading, writing, and contemplating life after college. She was all mended now. No more crutches, but her fencing career was over. The breaks had made her leg and foot too fragile—they might not stand up to the rigors of a prolonged fencing competition, the doctors had said.

Carmella had been pleasantly surprised when her father called and asked if she would like to invite Lia to join them at the lake. After all, Lia had saved Carmella's life, he added—like Carmella needed convincing. He had suffered from stress and exhaustion after the China trip, he explained, so he was going to spend a week with them. Lia could only commit to a week or two, herself, as she still had many duties at the Institute.

Carmella and Lia were sunning themselves on a float about thirty yards off the end of the pier, the float rocking in the waves of a passing speed boat. A fly landed on Carmella's left hand but she didn't bother to brush it away. The sun felt so nice and warm—she just surrendered like a melting stick of butter.

They had arrived in Michigan just yesterday, and Carmella was still amazed that the two of them had been whisked up the lake from the Milwaukee airport in a Marine helicopter. She guessed there were a few nice things about having a father as president.

"I know it's terrible, but I can't tell you how glad I am that Elena is not here right now," Carmella spoke up.

"Really, and why is that?" Lia finally responded after rousing herself from near slumber.

"I know you don't know her, but she's...well...not exactly a Rhodes Scholar, if you get my meaning."

Lia looked thoughtful for a moment. "Now, now, Carmella, you shouldn't say harsh things about the disadvantaged. I'm sure she can't help it."

They both began to giggle.

"Oh, I can be *so* catty. I'm afraid I get that from Mother—and you know her," Carmella added. "Sorry."

Lia had almost fallen asleep again when the roar of an engine grabbed her attention. She pried her eyes open as the Marine helicopter that had brought them to the lake house yesterday once again skimmed across the face of the lake toward them.

"Oh, that must be Daddy." Carmella raised herself on her elbows to watch the helicopter land behind the house. She rose from the float, dove into the water, and swam back to the pier. Lia reluctantly followed. Grim as it was for her, she had a mission to accomplish, and it would require her full commitment to the task of damping down her revulsion at being intimate with Edward Perez, President of the United States of America.

Carmella ran to the back of the house to greet her father. Lia lagged behind.

"Hi, honey," Ed greeted, as Carmella threw herself into his arms.

When Lia caught up, attendants were busy removing luggage and boxes from the helicopter. Carmella ran up and handed Lia her phone "Here, take a picture of us. I want one for my desk."

When Lia had taken a couple, Carmella ran back to her.

"Here, let me take some of you two."

Ed stepped forward and shook his head. "Not now, sweetie. I've got to make a very important call. I'll meet you both at dinner." He turned to Lia. "So happy Carmella could persuade you to join us. Very nice having you here. I know it means a lot to her." He winked at Lia and then turned and went straight to his office in the house.

☆

Carmella was looking down at her plate quizzically.

"Is something wrong with the food?" Ed asked.

"Oh no. The food's great, but I just wondered, where did you get all of this?" She pointed to the plates and silverware all emblazoned with the presidential seal. "Isn't this a bit formal for use in a summer cottage?"

"My people brought it with us. It's part of the prescribed service," Ed responded.

"Your *people*?" Carmella let out a hoot of laughter. "Really, Daddy... Get a grip."

"It's a sign of respect for the office of the president. It's not personal, you understand."

"Do you have a presidential seal on your underwear, as well?" Lia giggled.

Ed made a point of changing the subject. There was no way he was going to discuss his underwear around his daughter. What was Lia thinking?

"Hope you like the vegetable lasagna, ladies. Had it made especially for you, Carmella—I know it's one of your favorites."

Carmella smiled and for a few minutes each person was lost in their own thoughts.

Carmella took a deep breath and Ed looked up at her.

"I'm sorry, Daddy, about that Brightway business. It wasn't very nice of Diego to treat you that way. Did he upset you greatly?"

"He and I are not speaking right now," Ed said sternly.

Carmella flashed her father a wicked grin. "But did you really do all that business with the oil? Seems kind of sneaky, if you ask me, and probably not very legal." Probably nobody else in the world could have asked the question like that and not lost their head. But she *was* Daddy's favorite.

Lia audibly suppressed a snicker.

"Well, no one asked you," Ed glared at Carmella.

"And I think you need to forgive Diego. After all, he was just doing what he believed was the right thing. Seems to me a lot of other people agreed with him as well."

"Where do you get all of this freshness from? If you ask me, you are way too much like your mother."

"Thank you. That is very sweet."

"It wasn't meant as a compliment."

"That's all right, I forgive you, anyway." Carmella smiled sweetly.

After dinner, Carmella turned to Lia, an eager and endearing look on her face. "It's such a lovely evening. Want to go for a walk along the shore?"

Lia put her hands together over her head and stretched. "I'm just a little tired. Why don't you go on? Certainly another time, though."

"Okay then, I'll say good night. I'm going to my room to read for a while when I get back. You guys enjoy yourselves." Carmella threw a shawl over her shoulders and gave a small wave before she left the house.

"Do you think she suspects anything?" Lia asked, as she rose and began collecting the supper dishes.

"Leave that. The staff will take care of those," Ed instructed. He paused to consider her question. "No, Carmella is still far too innocent and simple to suspect anything—as long as we're discreet." He stood by the dining room window and lit a cigar. He turned to her. "Come, it's much nicer outside." Ed strolled to a swing on the long porch overlooking the lake and Lia sat with him a moment later. They were silent for a moment before Lia spoke. "I must say, it was very clever of you to have Carmella invite me out here. The perfect cover. I wondered how you were going to manage our little get-together. And Elena is where?"

"At her mother's in Alabama. She's still pouting about her fashion faux pas in China. She's never quite forgiven me nixing her spangled dress at the banquet. Women continue to mystify me every day. Running the country is far easier."

Ed chuckled at his own joke, and Lia smiled. Ed reached over for Lia's hand, but she spotted Carmella coming up the walkway, and she snatched her hand away. "I think I'll take a long hot bath," she said, rising from the swing.

"I'll see you later?" Ed whispered.

"What about your handlers?" she asked. "It's hard to slip by them unseen."

"I can take care of that. You just be ready after ten. I'll come and get you."

☆

The walk had been so lovely Carmella wished Lia had joined her. "Hello you two." Carmella smiled as she came up on the porch. "I always forget how great the stars are out here after the glare of the city lights. You leaving?" Carmella asked Lia.

"Hot bath."

"Sounds yummy—me too." But she sat down next to her father and put her arm through his. With a small nod, Lia went inside.

"Daddy, how you holding up? I'm sorry if I was rude at dinner."

"It's okay. I understand. You young folk are all so idealistic at your age."

"But you were a naughty boy, weren't you?" Carmella teased. She loved teasing her father, and he usually took it in good grace.

But this time, Ed snapped. "Can we just drop it, please? It was enough at dinner."

Carmella gave him her sweetest smile. "But remember, it was you who always taught Diego to think for himself. See what happens?"

"Hum."

"Don't be sad. I'm just joking with ya."

"I know. Now what about you? All mended?" Ed asked.

"Hunky dory."

"Good."

They sat together for a spell without speaking. The last glow in the evening sky was finally disappearing, and the crickets were now louder than the waves lapping against the boat tied to the pier.

"Oh, Daddy..." Carmella sighed, thinking of everything and nothing. Finally she stirred and stood up. "Hot bath. Are you all right alone?"

"Never better. You've no idea how nice that is for me after the constant frenzy of the White House."

"Good night then, Daddy."

"Good night."

☆

Ed knocked softly on Lia's bedroom door.

"Yes?"

Ed looked in. "Come along, baby. Coast is clear. Quickly now."

He ushered Lia down the hall to his room, closing the door softly behind them.

"How did you get rid of the agents?" Lia asked, as they entered Ed's bedroom.

"Sent one to check the perimeter of the house, and the other to check on Carmella. Only had about a minute."

"But you've left yourself exposed."

"Only to you." Ed reached over and gave her a kiss. He picked her up and carried her to the bed, throwing her back onto the spread, and then throwing himself on top of her. He began showering her with passionate kisses. "You just drive me crazy, you minx." Ed pulled at her blouse with one hand and reached frantically into the nightstand drawer for a condom. He struggled with the wrapper. Lia started to laugh.

"What?" he asked defensively.

"I was just wondering if your condoms also had the presidential seal—like everything else around here."

That sent them both into a swell of laughter. Ed laughed so hard he slipped off the bed with a thump. There was a knock at the door.

"Is everything all right in there, sir? Do you need assistance?" an agent asked through the door.

"Ask him how he is at unfastening bra straps," Lia whispered. He pressed his fingers to Lia's lips as she started to laugh again, though he was struggling to suppress his own laughter, as well. He tried pulling himself together enough to answer. He went over to the door and leaned in.

"Everything's fine, Agent Samuels. Just laughing at a book I'm

127

reading and it fell on the floor."

"Very good, sir."

Lia took her opportunity as Ed was distracted with Samuels. She pulled out a safety pin hidden in her blouse, and unfastening it, quickly punctured the condom several times through the wrapper, tossing the safety pin under the bed as Ed turned his attention back to her.

"Now then, where were we?" He came over, pulled back the covers from the bed, and lifting her up, deposited her on the satin sheets.

She handed him the punctured condom. "You were just about to use this," she whispered.

PART II: A NEW SUNSET FOR AMERICA

Now the Honeymoon is *Really* Over

Day 226 of the president's term

Benevito Casados never met a terrorist he didn't like, at least a terrorist bent on destroying the *yanqui* imperialist empire. But *any* homegrown Venezuelan protestor was labeled a foreign subversive and summarily thrown into a hidden cell—rarely, if ever, to be seen again. It was interesting how one man's terrorist became another man's freedom fighter.

Benevito had a mane of newly peroxided blond, permed, and curly hair—some of it his own—some of it from the very best New York City House of Rugs. And it seemed he took sartorial advice from the Marx Brothers. The epaulets on his Freedonia style dress uniform jacket dangled more fringe than a Victorian sofa—with medals plastered across the front of his chest like a North Korean general. (That was, of course, when he wasn't purposely antagonizing somebody. He delighted in wearing clown shoes at the United Nations, dancing in a lady's satin nightgown at the president of Brazil's inauguration, and going in black face to a meeting of the Organization of African Nations. He rejoiced in offending any- and everyone.)

But this man was no joke. And he was also not stupid. He spoke fluent English and French as well as his native language, Spanish. He loved to rant and rave against US imperialism to his people, but he consistently watched BBC World News and CNN. He knew everything that was going on in the world—with added briefings from his all-encompassing intelligence agency.

He certainly enjoyed watching Ed Perez squirm over the revelations of the Brightway incident. Benevito had only participated with Ed and Terrance because he controlled the caves in Mexico, and he relished watching the price of oil climb after the successful completion of their

131

little scheme. At that time Ed was not president, so Benevito had no qualms about assisting in this project. And it had certainly come back now to bite Ed in the ass—having consorted with the Scourge of South America.

☆

This afternoon Benevito was entertaining the minister for foreign affairs of the Islamic Republic of Iran—Faraz Khorshid—at the Venezuelan honorable leader for life's seaside villa. They were seated by the pool, shaded by lush falls of bougainvillea as Benevito's two kids jumped and splashed in rowdy pool play.

"Kids..." Benevito said to Faraz, after observing them for a moment, "Not a care in the world. Life is just all play for them."

"The Prophet says the greatest gift a father can give to his son is to teach him good manners," Faraz calmly pointed out.

"I'm sure the Prophet was ever wise, but I don't think he knew my little rebels," Benevito pointed out. "Besides, I like a little bit of sass in a kid."

"Sass, I do not know this word," Faraz questioned. Both were speaking English to avoid the need for translators hovering over them; they could be more open and direct with no one else around.

"Sass...saucy...outspoken."

"Ah, yes. Now I understand."

"Not unlike me... You might be familiar with my reputation."

"Yes, I have heard. How you like to outrage the establishment..."

They both enjoyed a good laugh, but Benevito quickly plunged ahead.

"But I know you are not here only to jest at the foibles of our mutual adversaries."

"Of course not. First let me extend the very best wishes and heartfelt admiration to your government from mine. We have long followed your many exploits with much joy and would like to explore further our mutual interests and goals."

"In other words, you want something from us."

Faraz thought carefully before answering. "General Casados, in my culture we find that the winding, scenic road is ever so much more charming and engaging than the direct route. It provides a much more satisfying journey, with delightful scenery along the way, don't you agree?" He let the implications hang in the air.

"And in my culture, we dance in the streets for almost no reason at all," Benevito replied, smiling.

"I don't understand." Faraz was becoming a little frustrated with this meeting.

"Well, let's just say our ways and styles are different. Now, I would like to know exactly what it is you are looking for—your government, I mean, of course."

"Very well. As you know, Europe and America have become very nervous about our nuclear research. They have made many postures and threats. And because both of our countries find this kind of behavior unacceptable, it might be to our mutual advantage to form an alliance— for our *mutual* benefit, of course."

"And what exactly is it you want? You have plenty of oil—certainly that is not what you are looking for from us."

"That is so. But we understand you have been doing some uranium exploration. That certainly interests us as it is becoming increasingly difficult for us to find reliable sources of this valuable resource in the general market—sanctions, you understand."

"And you would like to purchase that from us?"

"I'm sure you will find that we would be very grateful and generous, with, of course, an ample finder's fee for your personal services."

"Certainly something worth considering. Anything else?"

Casados' house was located near an area of sand dunes, and when the wind was in a southerly direction, the house was plagued by flies. The Ambassador waved his hand in front of his face, annoyed by the pests. The sun was now directly in his eyes, and he had to squint to see Casados.

"Well, there is something a little more subversive we have in mind as well, Faraz continued."

"I like the sound of that. You have my complete attention."

Casados had a riding crop with horsehair at the far end and casually shooed the flies away from his face with little effort. And the sun was *not* in his eyes.

"We have conclusive intelligence that either Israel or the US—or both—are making plans to try to destroy our nuclear research facilities. It is foolish to think that they can succeed. But we were thinking it might be very useful to have sleeper cells of our agents in a friendly harbor in this hemisphere, which could be activated to retaliate quickly and decisively. We were hoping you might be willing to host these cells in your country."

Casados leaned forward. "And if this retaliation was perceived to be coming from Venezuela, how do think they would respond to us?"

"No, no, you misunderstand. The agents would not launch any activity from here. They would just be harbored here until they were needed. The actual attacks would take place in the heartland of the infidel, after the agents reach their destination, creating considerable havoc."

Just then four-year-old Carlito—his slightly too big swimsuit nearly falling off—came running around the edge of the pool, crying, having scraped his knee. He jumped up on Benevito's lap and buried his face in his father's shirt. Benevito applied a paper napkin to the scrape.

"Now, now, no need to cry. We can amputate just here." He mimed cutting Carlito's leg off just above the knee.

"No!" the boy shouted out, not quite sure if his father was serious or not.

"Then how about here?" Benevito asked again, this time cutting just below the knee.

Carlito started to giggle, understanding that his father was teasing him now. "No, not there either."

"Then here?" Benevito cut at the boy's ankle.

"*N-o-o-o.* Not anywhere." The boy was laughing now. His father reached over and blew a loud raspberry on the boy's neck, and Carlito squirmed off this father's lap and jumped back into the pool—suddenly all better.

Benevito leaned back in his chair, took out a case of cigars, and offered the Minister one. He refused. Benevito took his time lighting his cigar. He blew smoke up in the air, and continued in his silence. Finally he spoke. "And what exactly will you offer us in exchange?"

Faraz was taken somewhat off guard, but being the consummate diplomat that he was, he quickly recovered. "What is it you would like us to offer?"

"We are looking around for some nuclear capability."

"But we have no weapons, you understand."

"Yes, yes. You can save that camel shit for the Americans."

Faraz shifted uncomfortably in his chair.

"Coffee?" Hortencia, Benevito's wife, came out of the villa with a tray of coffee and Venezuelan sweet delicacies. "Time for a little break, don't you think? You gentlemen have been working so very hard remaking the world."

Benevito smiled at his wife and then at Faraz. "This is my wife, Hortencia, the Foreign Minister of Venezuela. I like to keep the reins of government in the family as much as possible. Much safer that way."

"Such a pleasure to meet you. I have heard a great deal about you and your fine country," Hortencia said and then leaned in closer toward Faraz. "After you two have finished your little meeting, we'll have a nice chat, shall we? Just the two of us. Have a couple of details to go over with you."

She placed the tray on the table between the two men and took a plate of cinnamon sugar cookies over to the kids at the other end of the pool. They quickly scrambled out of the water and sat next to their mother to enjoy her treats, their faces soon smeared with cinnamon and sugar.

The minister sipped on his coffee and turned again to Benevito. "And if you don't mind my asking, why exactly do you need nuclear capabilities? It would seem to me that you are well fortified—as our military intelligence quite reliably informs us."

Benevito rose from his chair. "Come, I would like to show you something."

Benevito led Faraz through a gate in the wall surrounding the pool. He led the minister through a lush garden filled with towering palm trees. "These must remind you of parts of your country, no?" Benevito asked.

Faraz nodded. "Very like. And very beautiful. A most enchanting garden. So much of our poetry is framed in garden imagery. A truly pacific place where many beautiful thoughts can blossom."

Benevito led the way through the rest of the garden and through another gate to the top of a hill overlooking the expanse of a vast military base. Faraz looked stunned. "Very impressive. This must keep the American satellites occupied and the Pentagon scrambling."

"We do what we can to promote world peace." Benevito smiled.

"But this does not explain your need for a nuclear capability."

"I am preparing a little surprise in the not-too-distant future and being a reliable nuclear threat would provide me with added protection."

Faraz carefully considered his response. "I am sure our government will give your concerns our immediate, fullest, and most comprehensive attention."

☆☆☆

Diego, Chester, and Wuf—Diego's buddy from G, C & B—sat sequestered in the GreenPAC conference room, getting ready to study the files from Deborah's email. The room seemed so small after the G, C & B conference room. Even with just the three of them it felt crowded.

"Isn't it a conflict of interest for you to be here with us, Mr. Moskowitz?" Chester asked, eyeing Wuf suspiciously. "Your firm does represent AmVista, after all."

"I'm not here officially," Wuf answered simply.

Diego smiled to reassure Chester. "I asked him to sit in to give us his perspective. Thought it would be good to have an outside opinion. Even though I'm an attorney, I'm a bit too close to this to be fully objective right now. Deborah's death has really upset me. I feel at least partially responsible."

Chester nodded but thought for a moment. "Excuse me for asking, but how do we know the information we share with you here won't go straight back to your firm and AmVista?" Chester turned his suspicious gaze back on Moskowitz.

"You don't. But I promise I won't betray any confidences here. I would be happy to sign a nondisclosure agreement if you like." He shrugged. "If you're still uncertain, I can certainly leave."

Diego patted Chester on the arm. "He's a good guy. I can vouch for him, and I think we need his perspective. We are not asking him to do anything for us—but just listen and advise."

"Very well," Chester said spreading his hands out in front of him in acquiesce. "If you're comfortable, I'll accept that.

"Now." He turned his attention back to the files on the table. "I've been going through these, and they are pretty amazing. I don't know how she did it, but Deborah amassed a damning amount of information against AmVista and especially Terrance Geiger. You know him, don't you, Diego?"

Diego rolled his eyes. "I certainly do. He worked closely with my dad, and we frequently crossed paths and occasionally swords. If you remember, we had an encounter with him last summer while we were picketing the Oil and Gas Conference."

Chester chuckled. "Oh yes, the $500 donation..."

"Right. By the way, did you ever send him the receipt he requested?"

"We certainly did." Chester laughed. "Now then, I've gone through all of Deborah's files, and I've picked out the most pertinent."

Wuf spoke up, "May I ask, what you intend to do with this evidence?"

"Good question," Diego responded. "We haven't discussed that yet, have we?" he said, turning to Chester.

"I ask because if there is criminal intent, and it can be proved, or even suspected, that Geiger actually committed a crime, you need to get the FBI involved. I wouldn't trust the local Houston police—too many good old boys down there watching each other's backs. But before you decide what you want to do, let's see what you've got."

Chester opened his laptop and played a number of recordings and videos showing Terrance in his office and at home, plotting and then planning Deborah's demise. Each video had a date and time stamp, and they followed the sequence of the scheme, each piece of recording more damning than the last. The final recording was just several days before the explosion at Deborah's house. In the final video recording at Geiger's house, it was evident that Terrance was passing a great deal of cash to a very suspect-looking individual with instructions to "complete the assignment in the next couple of days" clearly distinguishable on the audio. Diego shook his head in disbelief.

Everyone was silent after the last video finished.

"This should definitely go to the FBI." Wuf finally spoke up.

"Yeah," Chester and Diego answered at the same time.

Diego had a second thought. "And what about us? Should we go public with any of this?"

Wuf slowly shook his head. "I wouldn't. You've already rocked the boat enough with the Brightway disclosure—the waves you've created with that will have a life of their own for quite some time. I would just let the consequences of that play out—as they surely will. For now, I would turn these files over to the authorities, and let them handle this. It's definitely a criminal matter."

☆☆☆

Congress was now in full uproar, with House and Senate hearings delving into the Brightway scandal—the name shortened and now affectionately called Brightgate by the news media.

The president had so far refused to testify, citing separation of powers and executive privilege. And, of course, Benevito Casados could not be touched, as a much despised head of state of a renegade country. Nor could Congress subpoena any of the Mexican officials with knowledge of the oil storage caves. That left poor Terrance Geiger, the sole remaining Brightway participant, under the glare of Congressional investigation.

That approach wasn't exactly working for the House or Senate. To each and every question put forth to him by both Senators and Representatives, he had the same steadfast answer: "Under advice of counsel I refuse to answer, and I claim my privileges under the Fifth Amendment to the US Constitution against self-incrimination."

It was—a most unsatisfactory conclusion for the frustrated Congress.

But the investigating committees still had the physical evidence provided by Deborah Salcido. The fact that she was no longer living made things a bit trickier, however, as it was nearly impossible to verify their authenticity. That left Diego and Chester as the only witnesses who were knowledgeable of the scandal, given that they were the ones who revealed it and who were willing to testify.

Again, the thorny problem of the evidence always came back to the fact that Diego and Chester were not first-party participants and had only the evidence provided by Deborah Salcido—which could still not be verified because she was dead.

Thus the whole comic charade continued to revolve in vicious circles—much to the delight of Ed Perez—until finally the investigating committees had to conclude that there was nothing more they could do to pin the blame on anyone.

What they could do, they did. They managed to persuade the Mexican government to pump out all the oil and move it back into the open market, lowering the price of oil and gas for a short while, and the bevy of Senators and Representatives claimed a decisive victory for themselves and all the American people.

Ed knew it would be only a short time before the furor would die down and slide into the miasma of forgotten Washington and presidential scandals.

Ed was very relieved, pleased, and ready for another little discreet visit with Lia.

☆☆☆

Elena had resolved to watch Ed like a hawk—silently and at a distance. She had found out Carmella had invited that woman to the Michigan White House during the week Ed was supposedly there resting. Resting—ha! She suspected what kind of resting he had been doing out there. Resting on top of that tramp, no doubt. And all that time she, poor Elena, had had to spend an endless visit with her boring and ailing mother in the sweltering Alabama heat and humidity—with a half-dozen brothers and sisters constantly pestering her with questions about life in Washington and the White House and showing her off to their goonish neighbors.

Embarrassingly, two of her sisters tried to seduce her Secret Service agents. More embarrassingly, one of her brothers tried to pick a fight with one. Elena escaped back to Washington as soon as she possibly could and hid in the family quarters until the president returned from Michigan.

Now that Congress had officially dropped the Brightgate investigation, Ed was feeling frisky again, and she knew it would only be a matter of time before he sought out his new little playmate again. But Elena would be ready. She had made a close, though not intimate, friend with Thomas, the intern in the West Wing. He was most obliging and open to her flirtations, but neither would *ever* dare act on them. He was in charge of communicating the president's daily—minute by minute—and weekly schedule to all West Wing departments. While the president might fudge his whereabouts to Elena, she could always get the true account of his whereabouts from Thomas. She would be watching—and waiting.

☆☆☆

Right after the meeting with Wuf, Diego and Chester traveled to the Chicago branch of the FBI and presented their evidence and were assured that the matter would be looked into. Diego, being all too familiar with the vagaries of government agencies, cautioned Chester not to expect too much too soon.

After what had happened to Deborah, Diego urged Chester to consider security for the office and for himself. Chester, although he felt no need for personal security, did contract for a more sophisticated alarm system and an armed guard standing watch during office hours.

Milly, true to form, had inveigled Diego to escort her to one of her functions. It was a party at the sumptuous Evanston home of one of her bridge ladies—the charming, but somewhat overbearing Barbara Fincher, nee Daily of the Daily political dynasty. Mr. Fincher was Chairman of the Board for Arvko Aviation, and he was also the Illinois Democratic Party Chairman.

As they drove over to the event, Diego quizzed Milly about who this Barbara Fincher was.

"The lady is a bridge partner," Milly explained. "Highly connected and *very* influential in Democratic politics. However, I must warn you, she also has a wicked sense of rumor. One must tread very carefully around her. Never share a confidence for it will be broadcast citywide. And absolutely *no one* escapes her razor claws, as she is an equal opportunity offender. So do be forewarned."

"And you say she's your *friend*?"

"Absolutely. We lived down the block from one another as girls and were in the same class at Northwestern."

Diego turned to her and smiled. "Well, I can certainly see why you two are friends, as you have also accurately described yourself."

Millie lifted her head in a haughty self-righteous glare, but absolutely refused to either look at Diego or answer his inaccurate assertion.

"My dear, how charming to meet you. Your mother has told me about all of your many exploits." Barbara smiled and took Diego's hand as Diego and Milly arrived at the function.

"Pure hyperbole. You know mothers."

"Well, I do. But being a mother of three, I am often in the stratosphere over their many accomplishments myself."

"And all very well deserved, I am quite sure." Diego bowed slightly, taking her hand in both of his.

"Charming boy, Milly," Barbara said to her friend. She pulled Milly aside, just within earshot of Diego, and he had to stifle a laugh when he heard Barbara whisper too loudly, "He should meet my Cynthia. They would make such a darling couple, don't you think?"

Milly laughed. "That would be barking up the wrong tree, I'm afraid. However, if you had a son..."

"Oh, I see..." She nodded in understanding, savoring the latest gossip. "And you are okay with that? What about grandchildren?"

"My dear, for the moment I am spared the necessity of endless babysitting. However, I have a daughter who I am sure will supply the requisite progeny in due course."

Barbara's corporate executive husband, Horace, ex-Navy, and still sporting a military style buzz-cut, walked over to their group and extended his hand to Diego. "So this is the young Perez boy?"

"Sir," Diego acknowledged, shaking hands.

"Come. I have some people I want you to meet." Horace put his arm around Diego's shoulder and led him away. Diego cast a quick look at his mother. She nodded in assent and offered him her conspiratorial smile.

Horace led Diego to a garden room where there were several other moth-balled elderly gentlemen—self-satisfied power brokers, infatuated with their illusion of relevance.

"My friends, this is Diego Perez, our somewhat compromised president's son."

There was a gentle chuckle amongst the party.

"Pleasure to meet you, lad," one of the guests said, offering his hand.

Horace proceeded, "Diego here, as we all know, was instrumental in uncovering and making public the terrible Brightgate scandal. He is currently with GreenPAC, a champion environmental group that we have all subscribed to. He worked for a number of other environment groups before that and spent a time at G, C & B as an attorney. Quite an impressive resume, wouldn't you agree, gentlemen?"

The men nodded. One sizable, red-faced gentleman spoke up. "How does your father feel about your activities? Certainly he didn't expect his own son to expose him like that. Is that quite right?"

Diego put his hands together in prayer fashion and tapped his mouth as he considered how to answer. "Sir, my allegiance is to a greater cause than family loyalty. I sincerely believe my father's policies are ruinous to our nation and to the planet's environment. I will continue to follow my conscience when it comes to whom I serve."

"Admirable," Horace said. He turned to his colleagues with a questioning nod. They responded by answering his nod with theirs. "Son, we would like to sound you out on something. As you probably know, I am Chairman of the local Democratic Party. These other gentlemen are my colleagues." Diego silently waited. "We think you have a bright future and believe you would make a strong showing in an election in this state, say as a congressman or even as a senator in the state government—as a Democrat, of course. We would be very happy to sponsor you, if that is something that would interest you. What do you say?"

Diego thought for a moment. "Gentlemen, I would be very happy to consider your request, as I believe I could serve well in politics. However, I would need to discuss this matter first with my partner, Brandon."

"You have a business partner?"

"No, my domestic partner—my boyfriend, my lover."

There was a stunned silence.

"Oh...," Horace finally responded in a reedy voice. He looked furtively to the others. None of them could quite look Diego in the eye.

"Hmmm. That's what I was afraid of. Gentlemen, good evening." Diego nodded and turned to leave the room but stopped and turned back. "So happy to see your progressive, enlightened, Democratic principles in action. Let me know if, and when, you all grow some balls."

Horace stammered, "But it's all about electability, you understand."

"Oh yes, I certainly do understand—perfectly."

☆☆☆

"Sir, you need to take a look at this." The secretary of defense pushed a memo across the table to Ed at his morning national security briefing. He picked up the paper and studied it.

Ed stood up. "Is this saying what I think it's saying? Ships carrying Iranian missiles with warheads heading toward Venezuela?"

"I'm afraid so, sir."

"Nuclear or conventional?"

"Not sure at this point. But if they're from Iran they could be nuclear."

Ed strode over to the conference table and pounded. "Goddamn it, it's Cuba all over again."

"Except none have been delivered or set up yet, unlike Cuba in '62. We have a chance to make a preemptive strike if necessary."

"Why Venezuela?"

"Intelligence tells us Casados requested them. Trading for raw uranium."

"Yes, but why missiles? They are heavily fortified. He must be up to something else." Ed turned toward the window and stared out across the White House lawn.

"There does seem to be a lot of activity at his military bases. A lot of buildup—but we don't have indication why."

The secretary of state spoke up, a little hesitant to bring the subject up. "You know this Casados fellow, sir. Couldn't you have a word with him? Diplomacy should always be the first and best course, don't you agree?"

"What makes you think I know this brute?"

"But sir, the Bright..." State caught himself and stopped.

Ed glowered at him. "All supposition," Ed answered. He turned to Defense. "What are my options?"

The secretary smoothed his hair back. "Well, diplomacy, of course. Always the best start. But we are tracking the Iranian ships and know exactly where they are and could take them out at any point up to the time of delivery. And a blockade is also possible. But we would have to move our fleet soon."

"Where are the Iranian ships now?"

"Just off Cape Town."

Ed turned to State. "What would result if we took the ships out?"

State stood up and looked the president straight in the eye. "Well, Iran would probably shut the Strait of Hormuz to all shipping. That would crash the stock market, and the price of oil could surge to over $150 to $200 a barrel. In addition, there might be protests throughout the Middle East. Israel could feel threatened and attack Iran. Iran would retaliate against our troops anywhere they could reach us and no doubt rain missiles down on Israel."

"Ouch." Ed winced. He thought for a moment. "I'd better have a word with Casados then." He turned back to Defense. "But draw up a detailed list of military options, just in case."

"Well, Mr. President, you finally got your wish," Madison reminded Ed, smiling slightly.

"Yeah? And what's that?"

"The emergency diversion to unite the American people behind you."

"Did I really say that? Must have been out of my fuckin' mind," Ed sighed.

☆☆☆

Diego put his key in the lock of the apartment door. But he was surprised to find the door was already unlocked. Brandon home early? Wasn't it his late class today? He shouldn't be home until after seven, and it was now just five fifteen. Diego opened the door quietly and peered inside. The apartment was dark. There was no sound—except from the kitchen with the refrigerator kicking-in. But something was not right. It was too quiet. What was it? Then he realized—no Chiquita. She always came scrambling to greet the first one home. Diego quickly stepped back and closed the apartment door.

Diego had been insistent on minimal Secret Service protection, demanding the agents keep outside his residence and only observe from the street. The agents' work shift had just started, and he was being guarded this evening by Darcy and Danberry—the third team and the newest agents. He charged down the stairs to the street and went directly to the agents' car.

"Something's wrong," he shouted, knocking at the car window. Danberry rolled down the window.

"What's up?"

"The apartment was unlocked. Brandon's not there. And the dog is not responding. I think we've been broken into."

"Okay, let's take a look." The two agents got out of the car. "Stay here in the car while we check out the apartment."

"No, I want to come too," Diego said. Darcy was insistent. "It's not safe till we check the place out. You stay here in the locked car—we'll come and get you—not to worry." The agents headed toward the apartment but first walked around the entire perimeter of the building, poking in the bushes and looking for breaks in basement windows. Apparently finding nothing suspicious, they entered. Diego was too nervous—he couldn't just wait outside. He scrambled out of the car and followed the agents inside.

☆

The agents had proceeded up the stairs to the second floor. Danberry held back to act as watch in case curious neighbors intruded, as Darcy entered the apartment. Darcy was gone for a few moments but returned with his gun drawn.

He said, "You can go get him now. I'm ready. We gotta get this done."

☆

But Diego was already coming up the stairs.

"Thought we told you to stay in the car till we called you," Darcy scolded.

Diego ignored Darcy's comment and pushed through into the apartment. "What did you find?"

Darcy put out his hands to stop Diego. "I'm sorry, but your dog has been killed." Diego froze. "Someone's been here. And I found this." He held up a note in his latex-gloved hand. Diego, shocked and shaking, reached for it, but Darcy refused to give it to him. "Prints," the agent commented.

Diego stammered, "What does it say?"

"'Don't mess with Texas.'"

"What? What the fuck does that mean?"

"It's a Texas anti-littering campaign slogan. But, my guess is, it's trying to send another message," Danberry said. "We know about the FBI investigation in Houston. It's probably hitting a little too close to home for some folks down there."

Just then Brandon came in the apartment putting his briefcase on the floor and taking off his coat. "What's going on?" he asked, seeing the agents.

"What are you doing back so early?" Diego asked.

"Blackout on the campus. Classes cancelled." He strode over to

Diego. "So what is all this?"

"Somebody broke in," Diego answered. Taking Brandon in his arms, he whispered, "They killed Chiquita."

As he disengaged from Diego, Brandon was fired with anger. "What the fuck?" He tried to barge past the agents.

"Sir, I wouldn't go in there if I were you. Don't think you want to see that," Danberry advised. "Let us take care of the cleanup."

"I don't understand," Brandon said, suddenly quiet, his voice hollow.

Darcy took charge. "I think we'd better get you both to a secure location tonight. Don't think you should stay here."

"But our things...," Brandon protested.

"You can get only what you need for tonight," Darcy assured. He turned to Danberry. "You'd better call this in and see where they want us to take them."

"Done."

Diego watched the other agent leave through the front door, too frozen in shock to really register what was happening. Darcy grabbed hold of Diego's arm gently, prompting him back to the present.

"Go get what you need, but don't go into the kitchen," Darcy directed.

Brandon and Diego did as they were told; from the bedroom, bathroom, and office, they hurriedly collected what they needed for that night and the next morning.

"How long do you think we'll be gone?" Diego called to Darcy. There was no response. "Did you hear me?" Diego called again. *Was the guy deaf?* He left Brandon to pick up a couple of backpacks with their things, along with two jackets; it was nippy outside.

He didn't leave Brandon in the room for long. "Oh shit!" Diego exclaimed, running back to Brandon.

"What?"

"He's dead. Darcy's dead. We gotta get outta here."

Brandon turned in a circle, unsure which way to go. "Here," he shouted, and in the confusion handed his jacket to Diego, "you go out the back way, and then head for the car. I'll go out the front. At least one of us might make it."

Diego took the jacket, gave Brandon a quick kiss, and then headed through the back door, clambering down the wooden staircase that connected the apartments and served as a fire escape. As he was putting on the jacket, he realized it was Brandon's jacket, which was larger than his. The sleeves nearly covered his hands. He rushed down the stairs to the backyard.

He was just rounding the corner from the back of the apartment building when he saw Brandon getting into the agents' car. It was then he heard what sounded like a sharp crack. He hesitated a moment and was stunned to see the agents' car explode into a massive inferno so large and explosive it ignited the surrounding trees and knocked one tree into the street, striking a number of parked cars.

The explosion was so far reaching that it knocked Diego down and blasted out all the windows of the surrounding buildings. Diego went momentarily deaf, but he had the presence of mind to pick himself up and look around. He surveyed the damage. No one could have survived that blast. He suddenly realized he needed to flee. If *he* had been the target, there might be others coming after him.

He looked around and headed to the back of the property where there was a wall with a gate that led to a back alley. When he glanced back at the apartment building, he could see a man bounding down the back stairs—probably the man who killed Agent Darcy. There was no doubt that he was now after Diego.

Diego charged through the gate, heading down the alley as fast as he could, thinking only that he must find a place of safety. No time to mourn Brandon. Diego looked back as he reached the end of the alley and saw the man charge out of the gate and run down the alley after him, waving his arms and shouting something Diego couldn't hear. Diego didn't stop to find out what it was. Instead, he turned to his left toward the business district. He thought he might lose the guy in a crowd or at least be safe in a commercial district where it would be difficult for the man to attack him without initiating a police response. Diego reached the busy main street, but the man continued to run full speed after him, still calling out.

A crowd had gathered after the blast occurred and people were craning their necks, intently watching the police and fire activity at his apartment building. What if they thought Diego was responsible for the blast, and the man coming after him was a witness chasing him down?

Diego shot down another alleyway, looking for a place to hide. He spotted a large dumpster behind a restaurant. Next to that were three large, commercial recycling bins. The dumpster seemed too obvious a place to hide, so he opened the recycling bin with plastic bottles and wiggled his way to the bottom, covering himself with a thick layer of plastic bottles. He held his breath and waited.

His hearing had returned; even though he still had some buzzing in his ears, he could hear the man search the dumpster, muttering profanities. Diego then heard the man check the first recycling bin containing discarded glass and slamming the lid when he did not see Diego. The second bin contained paper and cardboard. Again the man cursed. Then he came to where Diego was hiding—kicking the bin hard in audible frustration. Because of Diego's weight in the bin, it tottered but did not fall. The man threw open the lid, but seeing nothing except plastic bottles stuffing the bin to the top, he smashed the lid down and continued on, muttering as he continued his search. Diego tried to control his breathing, which was difficult to do in the claustrophobic bin. He sensed, with an abstract logic, that he was in shock. He realized that Brandon was gone and that he himself was in grave danger, but he felt nothing. He had to form a plan and get away from there as quickly as possible. He had no idea how many other men might be out there looking for him.

After what felt like a safe enough amount of time, Diego hauled himself up and crawled out of the recycling bin. He looked around, but the man chasing him was nowhere in sight. He brushed himself off as best he could—he needed to look somewhat presentable when he went begging to use a phone. He had no money, and had left his cell phone behind in the apartment when he fled. He went back up the alley to the commercial district. He first went into an ice cream shop, but they were too busy with customers to pay him any mind, ignoring his request to use their phone.

He chanced the yarn shop next door.

"Please, I'm desperate. I've been robbed, and I need to use your phone to call the police," he pleaded with the kindly looking, elderly lady running the shop.

"Oh, you poor dear," she clucked. "I'll call them for you." She picked up the phone to call. Diego suddenly realized that it might not be the best idea to get the police involved just now. He panicked, and fled the shop, turning to see a look of bewilderment on the old woman's face as he left.

He saw a store across the street—Shazam, a comic book store. Without stopping to think, and barely aware of the traffic, he raced over and fled inside.

The clerk was a tall, lanky kid of about nineteen who sported a variety of action hero tattoos and piercings. He only glanced up briefly when Diego came in.

"Please, can I use your phone? Don't have any change."

The kid looked up. It was obvious to Diego by the way the kid looked at him that he was gay, and the two exchanged a momentary look of recognition and a smile.

"Sure, help yourself." The kid pointed to the phone on the counter. He went back to reading his graphic novel.

Diego called Milly. "Oh please be in, please be in," he chanted to himself as the phone rang.

"Hello?" she answered.

He'd never been so happy for her to pick up the phone.

"Mom?" He spoke softly, and tears filled his eyes.

"Diego? Where are you calling from? The caller ID says Shazam?"

"I need you to come pick me up, as quickly as possible—*please*." His voice was on the edge of breaking.

Milly hesitated just a moment. "Of course, just give me the address. I'll leave right now."

"I'm just a block and a half from my apartment on Clark—across from the ice cream shop we always go to. I'll be just inside Shazam. Pull up in front, and I'll run out when you get here."

☆

Milly pulled up in front of the shop. She tried peering into the shop window but she needn't have bothered. Diego dashed out, and jumped into the front seat, leaning down so that he couldn't be seen from the street.

"Take me to your place," he ordered hoarsely.

Though she didn't know exactly what was going on, Diego's panic had shaken Milly. She knew better than to ask Diego what was going on just yet—at least not until they were home, safe and alone. Her eyes darted around the street looking for hazards. On the way here, she'd been forced to take a detour; the street in front of Diego's apartment was closed off by the police, with a half dozen police cruisers blocking the way and two fire trucks dousing a vehicle fire.

Milly carefully pulled the car out into the traffic and drove back streets to get to home. She checked her rearview mirror again to see if they were being followed. Diego lay on the seat and placed his head in Milly's lap. She could see he was in shock. She stroked his head. "It's gonna be okay, baby."

Showdown

Day 324 of the president's term

"Did any of you get a report from Terrance Geiger describing his concerns that there was trouble brewing in Venezuela?" No one spoke up. Ed Perez was in the White House Situation Room with his political and military advisers.

"Damn. He spoke to me just after the election. But I never got the details. I sure would like to know what he'd discovered."

They had been monitoring the progress of the Iranian ships laden with the missiles.

Ed picked up the phone. "Get me Terrance Geiger at AmVista." There were a number of furtive looks around the room. Brightgate was still fresh in the memories of *everyone* in the room.

A smooth jazz CD was unwinding on the player as Terrance waited in his Mercedes under the I-610 freeway. He closed his eyes to listen, opening them again at the sound of a knock at the passenger side window. Terrance looked over to see the man he was waiting for. He motioned for the man to get inside the car.

"Mr. Geiger." The man nodded. Other than the fact that he was probably in his mid-forties, there was nothing exceptional about him. He was the type of man you would pass on the street or sit next to on the bus and could never describe later, Terrance noted—a distinct advantage in his line of work. The man zipped up his windbreaker in the cool of the air-conditioned car.

"So what happened?" Terrance asked sternly.

"Well, it weren't so easy, ya know. With them Secret Service guys, ya never know...they keep a sharp lookout for sure. And I only had a few minutes to rig the car when they went inside the apartment building. I know you said I shoulda got both the agents, but one a' them never came out." The man laughed. "But at least I got one a' them faggots."

"But the wrong goddamned one, you screwup. Now, I gotta get someone else to finish the job properly."

The man flailed his hands in agitation. "Hey, where's my money? You promised me my money. I done the job. Can't account for unforeseen circumstances, ya know. How was I to know the boyfriend would come out wearing Diego's jacket? I had to keep a good distance, ya know, to do the blow. Couldn't tell it wasn't the right one."

"Half. You get half. The half I've already paid you. You don't get a penny more."

The man leaned in, threateningly. "Fucker. If you think..."

Terrance's cell phone rang. He held his finger up to indicate 'one second.' It was from the dedicated office line. It was to be used only under the most important circumstances.

"Yes," Terrance barked.

"The President of the United States. Please hold," a sharp woman's voice crackled.

"Terrance, this is Ed."

"Mr. President, what a surprise." Terrance bounced with an air of jovial camaraderie. "I hardly expected to hear from you again, after...you know."

The hired goon wasn't going to put up with this bullshit. He leaned in again toward Terrance. "I want the rest of my money—now," he hissed loudly, grabbing hold of Terrance's arm.

"Are you with someone?" Ed asked.

Terrance pushed the man's hand away. "Just a minute," Terrance whispered to the man. Terrance returned to the phone. "Mr. President, what can I do for you today?"

"Do you remember calling me right after the election with some concerns you had about Venezuela?"

Terrance didn't get a chance to respond. The impatient hitman grabbed the phone out of Terrance's hand, reached across and opened the driver's door, and pushed Terrance out of the car. Terrance landed with a thud on the ground. The man slid across to the driver's seat, threw the phone on the passenger seat, closed the door, and drove the Mercedes off with a spray of gravel covering Terrance.

Terrance struggled to stand up. And just as he was recovering, someone from the freeway above tossed out a fast food drink cup filled with ice, striking Terrance on the face, the straw scratching his eye.

"Fuck, fuck, double, triple, quadruple fuck!" Terrance stormed off to find a pay phone, covering his injured eye with his hand.

As the man drove away, he heard shouting on the phone. He picked it up from the seat. "What?"

The president asked, "Who's this? Terrance...Terrance?"

The man opened the car window and tossed the phone onto the street.

Ed looked at the phone in disbelief. "Terrance? Terrance?" The line was dead. "The fucker hung up on me. Can you believe that?" he said, turning to his colleagues. Nobody answered his question.

"Sir, we need to know what to do here. Time is running out for us to act," the secretary of defense said impatiently.

"Yes, I know. Call Casados, and put it on speaker phone."

Benevito was in his Jacuzzi tub, smoking a cigar and reading *Mother Jones*. His private line rang. "Yes?"

"General Casados, this is Ed Perez."

"Mr. President, what a pleasant surprise. How fondly I remember our pleasant conversations in Havana. How very nice of you to call. And just think, here you are, president of your great vast country calling a poor little insignificant backwater like us. What an honor to hear from the grand yanqui US of A."

"Don't be a shit, Benevito. This is serious."

"Then how can I help you, Mr. President?" Casados nudged a rubber ducky with his toe to watch it scoot across the tub like a wayward battleship.

"What the fuck's going on with those goddamn Iranian missiles? You know we can't have them parked down there that close to DC. What game are you playing?"

Benevito laughed. "I think you call it hide and seek."

"That's not funny. We are not playing games here. There could well be consequences if you persist in this course."

"Oh, really? Tell me, Ed, what would you do if I told you we already have the missiles? You think we are stupid? Those missiles you are tracking on the ships are decoys—just to annoy your asses. Our Iranian buddies love a good joke too, you know. We received and set up, very cleverly, I might assure you, a full range of tactical missiles—with nuclear warheads—from our good friends in North Korea over a month ago. If you even think about attacking us, we will launch a barrage of hellfire you can't begin to imagine." He paused for effect. "Oh, and Ed, you have yourself a really lovely and pleasant day." He hung up.

☆

There was deathly silence in the Situation Room. Immediately after that bombshell, Ed's cell phone rang. It was used only for family business. No one else had that number. He glanced at the screen—*Milly*.

He didn't want any shit from her right now. He almost didn't answer, but he did, remembering the frantic call about Carmella's accident.

"Yes?" As she spoke, he began to pace the room. "Where is he? Is he hurt? Both agents? Brandon too? We need to get him sequestered as soon as possible. I'll have the Secret Service contact you immediately... What do you mean you don't trust them? They're the fucking Secret Service for Christ's sake... Don't you dare..." Ed threw the phone across the room. "Goddamn it to hell." He paced the room. "Secret Service agents dead and a bomb trying to take out my son," he shouted to the room.

"Sir, we need to address this Venezuelan situation right now," the secretary of defense insisted, standing up and trying to focus the president on the exigency of the crisis.

Ed stopped. "Yes, you're right. But what do we do now? They've already got the goddamned weapons. The situation has changed. Work on some new options and call me when you have something I can use. I've got a family crisis to deal with." He stormed out of the room, leaving a group of puzzled and upset military and White House officials.

☆☆☆

Milly thought the best thing to do was to get Diego out of Chicago as quickly as possible. She had talked to Ed that afternoon, and he was ranting on about sequestering Diego with more Secret Service agents. She was having none of that.

So, at ten o'clock on the same evening as the bombing, Diego was driving Milly up to Lake Geneva in Wisconsin, just north of Chicago, to his mother's lakeside house. If anyone was still looking for him, he'd more likely be safe there. They had told no one where they were going. The servants' quarters over the garage was where they'd hole up, Milly decided—they would be far less conspicuous there than in the main house.

"Are you sure you're okay to drive?" Milly asked.

"Yes." He was curt.

She looked over at him and put her hand on his arm. "Honey..."

He looked over at her. "Sorry."

They drove on in silence for some time, and then he said quite simply, "It wasn't meant for him; it was supposed to be me."

She couldn't answer that. She tried to find something more comforting to say but came up short. Instead she asked, "Have you talked to his parents yet?"

"No. What could I possibly say?"

"You want me to call?"

Diego shook his head. "No, I want to talk to Betty and Don myself—

but later."

"Whatever you think's best."

The rest of the journey passed mainly in silence. Milly didn't even turn the radio on. It was nearly midnight when they finally drove past the main lake house and over to the garage with the servant's quarters above.

Milly had Diego bring in her bags—better to keep him occupied, she figured. Diego's gym bag contained just a few of his old clothes from his mother's house since he had nothing of his own from the apartment.

"Can I fix you something to eat?" Milly asked, crossing to the fridge. "I'm starving." Finding the refrigerator was empty, she poked into the cupboards.

"I can't eat right now," Diego said quietly.

"Well, at least you'll be safe up here," Milly said, opening a can of tomato soup. "I don't think anybody would ever *dream* to look for you here."

She poured the soup into a pot and turned on the stove to heat it. A November storm had moved in, and it was starting to snow. Diego stood by the window watching the snow swirling across the lake and starting to pile up on the window sill.

Milly walked over, carrying a bowl of soup with a handful of crushed saltine crackers on top, and sat down on the sofa to watch the storm with Diego. He came over and lay on the sofa beside her. A few quiet moments passed before he reached over and grabbed at her blouse and skirt, his pain tumbling out raw and childlike.

"Mommy, Mommy," he sobbed helplessly. It was the first moment he had been able to let go and grieve for Brandon.

☆☆☆

Carmella had invited Lia over to her apartment for some spaghetti and a bottle of not too bad Chianti. She had so enjoyed the couple of weeks they had spent together at the lake, and she considered Lia her friend now, besides the fact that Lia had saved her life. Carmella tried to brighten her walkup apartment with some supermarket flowers, but they only made the apartment seem sadder.

Carmella was beginning to realize that she might have deeper feelings for Lia than she had been willing to admit to herself until now. Maybe the genes that made her brother gay were in her as well. She had fussed all afternoon while preparing dinner, thinking about what she might say to Lia. Should she or shouldn't she? She was conflicted and would just have to see in the moment if she had enough courage to reveal her feelings.

Carmella, in her eagerness to please Lia, had made Bosc pears poached in red wine for dessert. As Lia thoroughly enjoyed her pears, Carmella fumbled for words. "Ah, there's something I wanted to talk to you about..." she started, but her phone rang. It was her father.

"Daddy." She beamed, relieved that she didn't have to reveal herself to Lia just yet. "Guess who's here with me?"

Ed sounded hesitant, Carmella thought. "Is it Lia?" he asked.

"That's right, our darling Lia."

"My baby, I have something very important to tell you." As Carmella listened, her heart accelerated. "Oh my God." She turned to Lia. "Brandon, Diego's boyfriend, has been killed in a car bombing, and Diego is missing."

"Now listen," Ed continued, "I want you to come to Washington. I'm going to have extra Secret Service protection for you till you get here. I can't take any chances with your safety."

"But my classes..."

"Don't worry about them right now. You can make them up later. Right now your safety is the first priority."

"But it's my senior year, and I want to graduate with my class."

"We'll discuss that when you get here."

"But Diego—is he going to be okay?"

Ed sighed. "I believe he may be hiding out with your mother. I think he's safe for the time being. Listen, your agents will be instructed to take great care of you. See you when you get here."

"Okay."

"Let me have a quick word with Lia. Just want to say hi."

Carmella handed the phone to Lia. "He wants to speak to you."

"Mr. President." Lia feigned formality in front of Carmella.

Ed spoke softly into the phone, "Baby, I want to see you so bad, but I just can't get away right now. There's a major problem brewing with the chief prick in Venezuela, and I've got to stay on top of this situation with Diego. Sorry. But I'm sure you understand."

"Thank you, Mr. President. Very nice of you to take the time to say hello. Yes, I too remember the time at the lake with great pleasure."

"That a girl," Ed replied. "I promise I'll make every effort to see you as soon as I can."

He hung up and Lia handed the phone back to Carmella. "Now then, you wanted to tell me something?"

Lia liked Carmella, but Lia's passion to destroy the president overrode all other feelings. How could she possibly explain that to Carmella when it became time to act? Lia had decided to gradually wean Carmella from her friendship, and she decided tonight was to be the last time she would see Carmella outside of the classroom.

Carmella panicked. "I've got to pack. Daddy insists I stay with him for a while—he feels I might be in danger. We'll talk when I get back, okay?"

"Not a problem. I should go then. Thank you for a lovely dinner." She rose to go.

Carmella suddenly rushed over and grabbed Lia in a bear hug. "I'm going to miss you," she blurted out.

"My... Oh, okay." Lia disengaged from Carmella. "See you in class when you get back." Lia picked up her backpack, waved good-bye, and left.

Carmella stood in the empty apartment and began to cry—for everything.

160

The chief of the FBI's Houston office was doing his Monday morning review of open cases. He paused as one stood out at him. He studied it and then called the two agents working the case into his office.

"What's this?" He tossed the file to the lead agent.

"Oh, that... The Chicago office sent that on to us. Gave it a look but don't think it's anything of importance."

"Really? You consider conspiracy and a possible murder nothing of importance?"

"Ah, well, that's Chicago's take on it. Jim and I, well, we looked it over and don't think there's anything to it." The agent leaned in toward the chief and spoke softly. "It concerns a principal hotshot at AmVista...and well, you know..." He slid a cash-filled envelope across the desk to the chief who swiftly deposited it in a drawer.

"I see... Okay then, we'll just file it here, shall we?" He placed the file at the very bottom of a stack of inactive cases. "Let me know if you get any more pertinent information." He winked at the agent.

"You bet."

☆☆☆

It had snowed about six inches at the lake during the night. Diego was feeling a little more settled but still couldn't believe Brandon was gone. The first thing he wanted to do that morning after he awoke was to call Brandon—then he remembered.

Instead, he borrowed his mother's phone to call Chester.

"Ches, it's Diego," he said cautiously. He wasn't sure if Chester had heard the news about the bombing yet.

"Oh my God, where are you? Are you okay? It's all over the news."

"Can't tell you where I am, but I just wanted to let you know I'm fine and to urge you to look out for yourself. Whoever came after me could well be coming after you as well. Please, please, please be extra careful. I worry about you."

Chester paused a moment. "I have good protection now—don't worry about me. And, Diego, I saw on the news about Brandon. I know there's nothing I can adequately say—except that I am *so* very, very sorry, old buddy. He was such a great guy."

Diego looked out over the lake and shut his eyes. "Appreciate that. Gotta go now. But I *will* be in touch again soon—once I figure out what's next."

"Love ya."

"Yeah, me too."

☆

Milly stood behind Diego, studying him as he sat on the sofa and stared into the void. "We need to go to the market."

"I'll go," Diego offered. "I need to get out of here."

"Are you sure you're up to that?" Milly asked, concern lacing her voice.

Diego rose and paced impatiently, "Mother, we need groceries, and I need a break. I've been jerking around here like a dog on a short chain."

"I'll make a list," Milly said, picking up a pad and pen to become useful. "I could go with you."

"No. Alone. I need to be alone for a while—please."

☆

As he headed toward the car with his shopping list, his mind reeled with the image of the car exploding outside the apartment, and he was flooded with new grief and concern. He suddenly froze. There were tracks in the snow around the car. Then he saw a note sticking in the driver's side window. He looked around but couldn't see anyone, so he went over, pulled it out and read:

Please don't be alarmed. We are a group of like-minded people dedicated to the same causes as you. No one else knows you are up here but us. Let's meet and talk—10:30 a.m. at The Starving Artists Coffee Shop on Lakeside. It's very important. No need to look for us—we will find you.

The Franklin Society

Diego was greatly conflicted. He had to admit he was intrigued with the message and wanted to find out more, but he was also extremely cautious after the attempt on his life. He reread the note. It didn't *seem* like the sort of ploy a hitman would devise—far too arcane and sophisticated. His curiosity overcame his caution. He was taking a chance, he knew—but he decided to go to the café.

☆☆☆

General Casados stood at the head of a grand table in his war room. His marshals, commanders, and war ministry officials lined both sides of the table. The general was wearing jodhpurs and riding boots, his Freedonia military jacket, and waving his riding crop in the air like a policeman directing traffic at a busy Caracas intersection. His foreign minister, Hortencia, stood by his side and discreetly picked off a loose thread from the back of his sleeve.

"Well boys, are we ready to rock and roll?" Casados shouted, in an effort to rally his commanders.

A chorus of "*Vamanos*" rang out from the assembly.

"Excellent. Then we shall advance tomorrow morning at six hundred hours. All of you have your orders and know exactly what you are to do. Yie-yie-yie!" he shouted like a triumphant vaquero, pumping his fist and turning to give his foreign minister a kiss on the cheek.

☆☆☆

Terrance had a scratched cornea from the freeway incident—but he would live. His Mercedes, however, fared less well. It was discovered in a Louisiana swamp with the body of the hitman slumped over the wheel. It was surmised that he had fallen asleep and driven into the bayou without even gaining consciousness. A couple of cheap vodka bottles were on the seat beside him. His blood alcohol level was twice the legal limit. *How eminently delightful and justified*, Terrance thought to himself. *Well rid of the lout.*

Terrance had spent some major, non-tax deductible bucks arranging the hit on Diego and bribing the Houston FBI establishment to bury the investigation on Deborah's sudden death. And what did he have? Nothing. Diego had disappeared, and that Chester fellow was now more securely guarded than an ayatollah.

Time to take a breather and re-evaluate the situation. Of course, that Salcido woman had been disposed of. That was something. But too bad, too—Terrance had rather liked her chutzpa. *Oh well*, he thought. *They come; they go.*

And then there was that son-of-a-bitch Edward Perez, fucking President of the United States. And after all Terrance had done to help him get elected, Ed hadn't done one damn thing to support Terrance during the congressional hearings. Not even a thank-you note on presidential stationary when Terrance had refused to implicate Ed in the Brightgate business. And even the price of oil had plummeted over the whole mess. Terrance figured he was having a pretty lousy batting average.

The one place he *had* been fortunate was in discovering his home, office, and car had been bugged with Deborah's clever little listening and viewing devices. Once he made the discovery, he'd had everything swept, and all the surveillance equipment removed. Once again, he had to marvel at how clever that Salcido woman was. But he would not be so easily fooled again. It was time to disregard the mistakes and errors of the past and move forward.

☆☆☆

The sun was beginning to break through the clouds after last night's storm. The packed snow on the roads was already beginning to turn to slush in the sun's warmth. Diego sat with his latte, watching the light and shadows from the scuttling clouds play across the surface of the lake.

"Mr. Perez?"

Diego turned from sipping his coffee and looked up at a man in his early to mid-thirties. He had a kindly face, like the bud of a rose about to open—not quite revealing but pleasing to look at and filled with potential. He either needed a haircut or was growing his hair out. He was dark and strong looking, like he had just stepped forth from the north woods after a grand adventure in the wilderness.

"You can call me Diego." He smiled, offering his hand.

"I'm Dominic," said the man, taking Diego's hand.

"Italian?"

Dominic sat down opposite Diego, plunking down a cup of black coffee on the table. "Nope. American as jazz." He looked down at his hands.

Could he be shy, Diego wondered? "I got your note, as you can see."

"Thank you for coming." He looked up, directly at Diego, but seemed hesitant to speak. "Excuse me. I'm finding it difficult to know where to begin."

"You might start by telling me about this Franklin Society. That is how you signed the note. That has certainly sparked my curiosity. Never heard of you guys, but I have to say I am curious."

Dominic laughed. "Yes, that was a bit mysterious and pompous, wasn't it?"

"Well, I don't know about pompous, but I would sure like to know what you can tell me about it." Diego scooted his chair up close to the table. He didn't want to miss a word.

"Guess that's as good a place to start as any. As I said in my note, we are a like-minded group, dedicated to many of the same causes that you support. However, our interests go far beyond just environmental issues. For reasons I cannot explain just now, we are a secret society. Let's just say there are many prominent members of our group who, for various reasons, wish to remain anonymous for now—thus the secrecy. It's not because we are doing anything subversive."

"Too bad, I like a little rabble rousing subversion now and then. The establishment definitely needs shaking up."

Dominic chuckled and nodded. "Certainly agree with you there. But our secrecy is strategic rather than criminal."

"And yourself?" Diego asked. "What is your part in all of this?"

"Foot soldier—a mere pawn."

Diego was amused. "I doubt that."

Dominic smiled with a twinkle in his eye. "Well, at least that is what I am today."

"Continue, please," Diego urged.

"To be brief—we strongly believe in this country and in the Constitution. We have become very concerned in the past few years, as our country has been gradually weakened by the corrupting influence of money from Wall Street, as well as big national and international corporations."

A waiter came by with a coffee pot. "More coffee, gentlemen?"

"No thanks, Dominic said.

"A splash for me, please," Diego consented.

Dominic waited until the waiter left before speaking more softly. "We have transitioned from a true democracy to an oligarchy, or some might say, a technocracy. And these groups have succeeded in a large part because they have been able to polarize the country into the extremes of right and left. There is no center anymore. And they use this polarization to paralyze the government so they can amass vast fortunes for themselves by pillaging our financial institutions, both private and governmental."

Diego folded his arms and leaned in even closer.

"The way they do it is not illegal, but it *is* destructive. With a paralyzed government there are no effective regulations to stop them— and they can and do rob us blind." Dominic sat back in his chair to make his final point. "And we, the Franklin Society, mean to put a stop to that. We want to rebalance the electorate by removing the corruptive power of corporate money in elections and thus recreate a thriving center once again."

"Wow. That is quite some statement. And ambitious as well"

"But, unfortunately, all too true."

Diego had answers to some of his questions, but he was still puzzled. "And what does this have to do with me? I mean, I know I'm kind of out there with my environmental work and my gay rights rantings, but I don't see why you've contacted me." He suddenly realized. "And by the way, how the fuck did you find me up here? I've just come through a horrible experience. You know I'm in hiding, don't you?"

"Oh yes, we know everything. In fact, I bet we know a lot more about your situation than even you know." Dominic smiled slyly.

"Oh really? I would like to hear about that." Still, Diego the prospect of an answer made Diego nervous, and he began to crunch his empty paper coffee cup.

Dominic stopped and considered for a moment before proceeding. "Let's take our collective breaths and sum up. We basically have two issues here today. The first is to introduce you to us and to let you know how we would like you to work with us. The second is—you need to know exactly who is behind the bombing, the death of your partner, and the dangers that you continue to be under. Which do you want to hear about first?"

"I don't think it matters. Obviously, I want to hear both."

Dominic nodded. "There's someone I want you to meet. He can do a better job of presenting the big picture to you than I can."

"Where do we have to go?"

"Go?"

"To meet this guy."

"We don't have to go anywhere." Dominic pulled out his laptop. "We're going to meet him right here. The marvels of Wi-Fi. But we need to find a more secluded corner first." He looked around the room and spotted a table at the back of the cafe with no one nearby. "Let's go back there. Can I get you anything?"

"A regular coffee and a couple of chocolate biscotti would be great," he said. "I didn't have any breakfast this morning." Diego rose from the table, took his bag, and moved to the back. Dominic walked over to the coffee counter.

After Dominic returned, he opened his computer and logged on. "Now then, I want you to meet our director, Richard Buller." Dominic turned his laptop so that both could see the screen.

"Mr. Perez, it's such a great pleasure." The weathered face of an older man greeted from the computer.

"Good morning, sir." Diego nodded.

"I know you must have a dozen questions. But I would ask you to wait until I've had my say. I'm certain I will answer most of what you want to ask me. Is that all right with you?"

"It is."

"Very well then, let me start by saying we have been following your career and activism for some years now. We're very impressed with what you've been able to accomplish. I was especially taken with the courage you displayed in revealing your father's connection to the Brightway scandal."

"Thank you, but it was just something I had to do. There were ethical considerations."

"I appreciate that. And by taking that positon you have put yourself in danger. Let me address the incident at your apartment the other day and the death of your partner." Diego felt queasy. Richard could see that Diego was troubled. "Would you prefer not to hear this?"

"Oh, no—I need to know."

"Very well. You royally pissed off Terrance Geiger of AmVista—well, you and Deborah Salcido did—with your revelations of the Brightway incident. You already know what happened to her. Then Terrance set his sights on you. Now what you don't know is that the very people assigned to protect you—those two agents—Darcy and Danberry—had been bribed by Geiger to kill you."

Diego grew angry and wanted so much to flee, but he needed to hear the rest. "Go on."

"Before they started their shift, while you were still at GreenPAC that afternoon, the two agents went to your house, broke in, and killed your dog. They figured you would call them to come up to investigate as they would be on duty at that time. They had planned to kill you then and make it look like a robbery or some such. When Brandon came home unexpectedly early, it interrupted their plan. They even concocted a note to show you, implicating Terrance—figuring you would eagerly seek their closer protection, allowing them to more easily dispense with you.

"Now what the agents didn't know was that Geiger had also arranged to blow up their car. We didn't learn about this till after the event. You see, Terrance figured if the agents killed you, he could then eliminate the agents and not have to worry about them turning on him later. But as you know, things rarely work out as planned. We knew about the plan for the agents to kill you in the apartment, and we stationed one of our people in the apartment to protect you."

"What?"

"As you may remember, you discovered Agent Darcy sprawled out on the kitchen floor. You assumed he was dead, but our man had merely incapacitated him to protect you, as Darcy had intended to kill the both of you before you left the apartment. But the two of you panicked and quickly fled. And unfortunately, Brandon made it to the car before you. Whoever blew up the car saw Brandon get into the car wearing your green jacket, and thinking it was you, decided to execute the assassination right then."

"Oh, my God..." He briefly buried his face in his hands.

"And I suppose the other thing you should know is that the person who saved your life by thwarting Darcy is sitting right next to you." Richard grinned.

Diego shot a look at Dominic, who was smiling shyly. "You? Are you the one who chased me down the street?"

"I was calling out to you like crazy, but you either didn't hear me, or you ignored me. I was afraid you would be in more danger out there on the street. How in the world did you get away? I looked everywhere."

"I couldn't hear very well just then because of the blast, and I thought you were the killer coming after me. I fled. I hid in the plastic bottle recycling bin."

Dominic laughed. "Oh, that was good. I remember that I was a little suspicious when I kicked the bin, but when I looked inside all I could see were plastic bottles up to the top."

"So, I guess I owe you my life."

"I'm only sorry I couldn't save the both of you."

Diego addressed Richard. "If you knew about the plot to have the agents kill me, why didn't you know about the bomb?"

"I have to be honest and say we missed that. I'm sorry. Terrance used resources that we did not have access to."

Diego considered this. "Then how do I know you can really keep me safe now? Remember, I can't stay out here in the cold forever. I have to get back to my work and my life. And I must have Secret Service agents around me again."

Dominic answered. "Diego, there will always be risks. But I promise you I will personally do my very best to keep you safe."

"You will be my bodyguard?"

"Actually, I'll be in deeper background, but I will always be aware. Believe me—I can be much more effective that way."

"What about Darcy? You say he's not dead. Is he likely to be a threat in the future?"

Dominic answered, "The Secret Service has been informed of his involvement, and he has been taken into custody."

Diego turned again to the laptop and Richard. "And exactly what is it that you want of me?"

"We are not ready to discuss that with you just yet. But the time will come soon when we will be contacting you. Do you have any further questions for us at the moment?"

Diego considered and then asked, "Is there a way for me to contact you?"

"Dominic will be checking in with you on a regular basis, and you can communicate through him. But for now you cannot contact us directly. It's a matter of security—for both our sakes."

Diego had one more question. "How do I know you are who you say you are? And how can I find out more about your intentions?"

Richard smiled. "I would expect nothing less from you. You will have ample opportunity, in good time, to ask us as many questions as you like. But for now please be patient. Now I must say good-bye. Dominic, take good care of our friend, won't you?"

"It will be my pleasure."

The screen went blank as Richard logged off.

Diego stood. "I really must be going. I've been gone much longer than a normal shopping trip should take, and I'm sure my mother must be frantic with worry by now, with all that has happened recently."

Dominic rose and took Diego's hand. "I will keep in touch. And know that we will be looking out for your welfare."

"I appreciate that."

Carmella was quartered in one of the guest rooms in the private residence at the White House. It was more like an upscale hotel suite than one of your fancy well-known White House rooms like the Lincoln bedroom, and that was okay with her. She had work to do. She was attempting to keep up with her university work while she was a guest of her father. She'd had had her assignments emailed to her, and she was reading on her bed in the family quarters. It was about 11 p.m. It was very quiet. There was no radio in the room so she was listening to some music on her laptop. There was a knock at her door and Elena entered somewhat shyly.

"Are you terribly busy?" she asked.

Carmella closed her book and turned off the music. "I'm due for a break. What's up?"

Elena pulled a chair up to the bed, sitting with her hands folded in her lap for a moment before speaking.

"I understand from your father that you had a great summer at the lake."

Carmella's mood brightened at the topic. "Oh yes, it was lovely. Who knows, it might be the last lazy time I'll have for a long while. I graduate in June—and then it's out in the cold, cruel world or possibly graduate school. Haven't decided yet."

Elena smiled her number eight smile—carefully considered empathy. "Oh, I shouldn't worry about that if I were you. A bright young woman like you should have no trouble finding the right job. And, of course, there are your father's connections."

Carmella laughed. "I somehow don't believe his connections will work too well for me in my line of work."

"And why is that?" Elena asked.

"I'll be looking for environmental work."

"And what, your father doesn't like the environment?"

"Well, he likes destroying it." She laughed and reached over and patted Elena's hand. "I don't mean to be mean. But well, look at his record."

"But he likes oil. That's all natural, isn't it?"

Carmella laughed. "You are absolutely right—completely natural." She was not going to contest Elena's charming innocence.

There was an awkward silence. "Did you want to see me about something in particular?" Carmella asked.

"Well, yes, now that you ask..." She shuffled awkwardly in her chair. "As you know, I wasn't able to be up at the lake with you and your father and that lovely girl, what's her name?"

"Lia."

"Lia. Yes. Well, you see, I was wondering if your father and that...what's her name again?"

"Lia."

"Yes, Lia. I was wondering if they spent much time together...alone. If you see what I mean."

"Alone. You mean like alone, alone?"

"Yes alone, like fucking." She said in an even tone.

"Oh my...I have no idea." Carmella was genuinely startled. The thought had never crossed her mind before. But now that it was brought up, it was obvious to her that was exactly what was happening. How naive could she have been? "Yes, perhaps so."

Elena got up and paced the room. "Yes, exactly as I thought. I knew he was cheating on me with that little slut."

"Elena, she's my friend."

"Really? Well, some friend. And I suppose you set it up, no?"

Carmella got up off the bed and stood tall before Elena. "I beg your pardon. I knew nothing about this. Lia is my teacher, my friend, and remember, she also saved my life. Dad met her through me, yes, but I never facilitated any kind of a romantic connection between them. I think you would be better having this conversation with your husband. I don't think that I can help you anymore. Good night." She went to the door and opened it, standing aside to usher Elena out.

Elena stood up. She was smart enough to at least know she was not going to get any more information from Carmella.

Elena held her head high and strode regally out of the room. "Good night."

Carmella was agitated by the whole interaction. Was Lia really seeing her father? It made sense. And was she still seeing him? She had no way of knowing. And it certainly put a *very* different spin on her feelings for Lia. It was quite clear now that she could never speak to Lia about her own romantic aspirations.

☆☆☆

It was near the end of the week at Milly's lake house, and Diego had spent the entire time grieving for Brandon. He called Brandon's parents and had a long talk with them, which had been difficult. More difficult, though, was hearing that after the explosion there was nothing left of Brandon to bury. Don and Betty told him there would be a memorial service in a week in Cincinnati, if he wished to attend. He said he would love to but just couldn't because of the attempt on his life. He would need to be very careful for the foreseeable future. They told him they understood.

He spent his mornings meditating and his afternoons hiking around the lake. He was so shaken by his loss of Brandon that for the first time he really began to challenge his desire to go into politics. More and more, the spiritual life appealed to him. He saw the craziness of the world—the greed, the rapaciousness, the total insensitivity to the pain and suffering of the ordinary person. But he also asked himself if that insight did not demand that he do all he could to help alleviate that pain? These were concerns he could not resolve right now, he decided. It would take time and a great deal more contemplation before he could satisfactorily answer those questions for himself.

He'd taken great comfort in his mother who was working hard to comfort him. Milly had suppressed her natural tendency toward irony, sarcasm, and acerbity. She was motherly and attentive to Diego, allowing him lots of time alone and freeing him from any household responsibilities.

Most of his mornings, he meditated in a small, enclosed porch overlooking the lake. Wrapped in a blanket, he would perch himself on a couple of sofa pillows facing the windows when the morning sun was just peeking over the horizon. Today the sky was streaked with clouds of soft pink and yellow, and the sky was a baby blue. Milly came in softly, sat down next to him, and put her arm around Diego, meditating with him. When he had finished, he put his hand on her knee. She leaned in and rested her head against his shoulder.

"Was that nice?" she asked.

"Very," he barely whispered.

"Do you truly feel ready to go back to Chicago now?"

"Yes and no."

"No need to until you are quite certain."

"No, it's time."

"You never told me very much about your trip to Bhutan."

"I almost didn't come back. Life at the monastery was just remarkable. If it hadn't been for Brandon and Carmella...and you, of course, who knows?" He smiled shyly at Milly.

"Well, I'm glad you did." She studied him. "You going to be safe when you get back to Chicago?"

"I believe so. I have reason to believe that I will be well looked after." He had not told Milly about his encounter with the Franklin Society and their promises to him.

Milly inhaled sharply and let out a long sigh. "I didn't tell you, but your father called me all in a dither the other day while you were out hiking. He is just beside himself over concern for your safety now, and he wants you to have your Secret Service protection again as soon as possible. Of course, I told him you were perfectly capable of caring for yourself, but he just won't hear of it."

"I'll call him. I do owe him that." He rose from the pillows. "Hey, you haven't said anything about Mr. TV Personality lately. Are you two still an item?"

"Oh, my dear, he is *so* finished. Wifey found out about his little indiscretions and threatened Armageddon if he so much as peeked at another woman. And as he didn't have the foresight for a pre-nup...well, you can just imagine. And besides—let's just say he was lacking a certain...quality of intellect."

Diego laughed and then looked at her. No doubt Milly, too, was ready to go back into her super-charged world once again.

"And oh, my darling, there's this absolutely charming charity ball coming up which I know you will just adore..."

Crossing the Line

Day 331 of the president's term

The exhaust fumes from the rumbling engines were sickening in the stillness of the dark morning air as the army of tanks, trucks, and additional transport vehicles idled at the border crossing. General Santiago waved an official looking sheaf of documents at the flustered Guyana border guards. They were frantically trying to reach their supervisor on the phone, who was not responding, and they were visibly struggling with their own fear at the massive army parked just across from their flimsy wooden crossing gate. This did not bode well.

At this location on the Venezuela/Guyana border, there was little defense on the Guyana side. The two countries had been sleepy neighbors for many years, and these two greenhorn guards were only trained to issue passport stamps and check the odd traveler for illicit drugs. They generally did far more sleeping than guarding. Today they were paying the price for their lazy lives.

The General advanced toward the Guyana guards, accompanied by six heavily armed Special Forces soldiers with automatic assault weapons at the ready. He walked right up to the gate.

"I demand that you open this border crossing," he shouted. "We have legitimate international security concerns that need to be addressed immediately."

"I'm trying to reach our colonel. He's the only one who can deal with this," the frightened guard replied.

"We have no time," the general shouted. "Raise this gate immediately and let us pass or there will be consequences."

The first guard turned to the second, completely at a loss as to what to do. "Did you reach him yet?"

The second guard shook his head and started backing up toward the guards' office building. As he did so, he nervously reached for his side arm, but before he was able to take it out of the holster, he was gunned down by the soldiers accompanying the general. The first guard turned to run, but was quickly dispatched as well.

"Okay, take 'em on through," the general ordered. He got on his phone and called General Casados. "We're in. The enemy attacked us first, and we had to defend ourselves—just as you suggested."

"I'm so glad to hear that, General," Casados responded with a chuckle. "The republic of Guyana attacks the sovereign state of Venezuela, and we march forward to defend ourselves in moral victory. There's our headline. Now get your butts over to those oil and gas fields. Establish a perimeter and make sure they are well defended. Then head toward Georgetown. The Navy is right now shelling the capitol and enforcing an embargo. Any questions, General?"

"Sir, what about air cover? You promised us adequate support."

"And you shall have it. Not to worry. Proceed."

"Sir." General Santiago closed his phone, got into his jeep, and led the army victoriously across the border.

☆☆☆

The test result was exactly what she hoped for. She was pregnant. Sitting in her thesis advisor's office, the pain of her incumbent decision weighed heavily on Lia, but with what she knew was ahead, she would have to withdraw from the Institute, her thesis, and her teaching job.

Brent Carmichael, a young thirty-eight-year-old junior professor, looked across his desk at Lia who was sitting staunchly before him. He shook his head in sadness. "Lia, I just don't understand. Why would you give all this up right now? You're one of our top students, a brilliant teacher, and you have a very promising thesis. Can you tell me why?"

"I'm pregnant."

Brent paused and considered that. "All right, but that's no reason to give up everything. And don't forget you have a wonderful scholarship."

"Yes, I know."

"Why can't you do your work here, and have the baby too? Women

176

do it all the time."

"There are circumstances."

He looked baffled. "Can you tell me? Perhaps I can help."

Lia considered whether she wanted to share this just yet. "The father is the president."

Brent's brows furrowed in shock. "Of the university?"

"No, the United States."

Brent sat back in his chair, speechless.

"I'm going public with the information. And, as you can imagine, it is going to create a royal shit storm. I will be inundated with press and the media. I will have no regular life again—ever, I suspect."

Brent bowed his head. "If there is ever anything I can do…"

"I appreciate that." Lia rose to leave. "Here are the keys to my office. I shall be out of there by this afternoon." She was sad, but also determined and resolute as she left the office.

☆☆☆

Ed squinted in dazed confusion at the clock on his bedside table. It was three o'clock in the goddamn morning. Who the hell was knocking at his bedroom door?

"Mr. President, there's an urgent situation developing in Venezuela." He heard his head of the Secret Service say, as he opened the door. "You're needed in the Situation Room immediately."

"Huh? What?" Ed raised his sleepy head from the pillow.

Elena stirred and muttered, "Did you forget to take out the trash?"

Ed threw his legs over the side of the bed. "I'll be right there. Get me Martin and Madison and whoever the fuck else you can round up at this ungodly hour."

"Sir." the Director left and closed the door.

Ed continued muttering to himself as he put on his robe. "Goddamn if they're gonna sleep, if I can't." He stumbled over to the bathroom to take a quick shower.

Elena propped herself up on her elbow. "You can make your own damn coffee. It's way too early to get up." She collapsed back into her mound of pillows and was soon back asleep.

☆

"Now then, what's so fucking important that you have to get me out of bed at three in the fucking a. m.?"

The secretary of defense answered, "Venezuela just invaded Guyana."

"They invaded Africa?" Ed asked, slightly confused.

"No sir, Guyana is the country just to the east of Venezuela."

"Oh." He paused. "Well it sounds like some place in Africa."

The secretary of defense didn't comment on the blunder. "They're shelling Georgetown—the capital—and securing the Guyana oil and gas fields," he said instead.

"Why?"

"We don't know. But perhaps they want the gas and oil," State replied, with just a hint of sarcasm.

"So? What's that to us?" Ed couldn't see what he was getting at. "How is this our problem?

Defense spoke up. "Well, if you remember just a very short while ago Venezuela armed themselves with North Korean nuclear missiles. Remember that?"

Ed leaned on the table and scowled. "Don't be a dick. Of course I remember."

Defense continued, "And now they are attacking another country in our hemisphere, with which we have a defense treaty. Getting it now?"

"Ummm, how the fuck do we get ourselves into these situations?" Ed asked the room. "So, Guyana is going to expect us to defend them against a country armed with nukes, with a crazy son-of-a-bitch dictator who would not be shy about sending them our way? Does that sound about right?"

"Yep."

Ed considered that. "Then let's just nuke him first. Sounds pretty straight forward to me."

"Mr. President..." State spoke slowly but firmly. "Might I remind you that Venezuela also has defense agreements with countries like Russian, Iran, North Korea, and Pakistan? And need I spell out the havoc that could be unleashed by them if we struck Venezuela with a nuclear weapon? Not to mention the horror and outrage that our *friends* would heap upon us."

"And then there is also the possibility of nuclear fallout from our attack spreading to Florida and the southern states," the secretary of the interior interjected.

"I think we need to look at other options," Defense said.

Ed wished he was back at the oil fields where he felt at home, instead of dealing with this bullshit.

"We might—just might—be able to persuade Russia to intervene on our behalf," State added. "And then there is, of course, the UN."

"The UN is run by terrorists. They will certainly side with Venezuela." Ed said, dismissing that idea instantly. "What if we used conventional weapons?"

"That would demand a military commitment on our part. Boots on the ground—and I don't think the American people or Congress would approve that, coming after *two* very messy and prolonged wars."

"Yes, but this is much closer to home," Ed observed, studying the map of the conflict area.

"But they would see it as all about oil again," State commented.

"What about the markets this morning?" Ed asked, turning back to the advisors.

"Oh shit, oil's going to shoot through the roof," Interior said.

"There—that's a good enough reason for us to attack. We've got to preserve our economy."

Madison, who had joined them quietly a couple of minutes before, spoke up. "Sir, I don't believe there would be a great deal of credibility on your part, considering the role you played in raising the price of oil in the Brightgate incident."

"Humm. Yes. Perhaps best if we didn't go in that direction," Ed acknowledged, a bit sheepishly. He thought further for a moment. "Then let's issue a very strongly worded statement of commendation against Casados and insist he pull back. Let's fly our flag of indignation and threaten consequences if he doesn't comply. In the meantime, let's confer with our allies and see what they have to say."

"Very good, Mr. President. That will give us time to consider our next steps," State said.

"One more thought...," Defense said. "Might I suggest, Mr. President, that we send our fleet to shadow the Venezuelan Navy at Georgetown. Not close enough to engage, but ready if we need to."

"Good idea. Do it."

Diego received a long, heartfelt hug from Chester on his first day back at GreenPAC.

"Why are you back here so soon?" Chester asked as he released Diego.

"I meditated every day up at the lake. I relived Brandon's and my time together, and although it still cuts deep, I need to move on. After a time, it's just self-pity. I'm sure you can understand."

"Okay, bud." Chester gave Diego a punch on the arm. "Then we got a lot of work to do. Did you see the news about Venezuela invading Guyana this morning?"

"I sure did."

"The markets are already tumbling, and the price of oil is skyrocketing. Another great opportunity for us to advocate for green energy development."

"What about Geiger? Any idea what he's up to?"

"The FBI is dead silent. Every time I follow up with them, I get stonewalled. He is still walking around scot-free, I'm afraid."

"Hmmm. That's what I was afraid of," Diego said. "We both need to continue to be very careful. He might still feel he needs to try and eliminate us."

"Yeah, was thinking that too."

"But I've meditated on it, and I might just have come up with the perfect plan."

"Great. Do tell. Let's go into my office."

☆☆☆

Terrance was in a quandary. He had very successfully eliminated that bitch Salcido. He had spent far too much money in squelching the subsequent investigation by the Houston FBI. But he had succeeded there as well—at least for now.

However, he had been widely exposed in the media over the Brightway incident, and he was certainly being watched very carefully by the press for any further slipups. But his plan to eliminate Diego had failed. That agent, Darcy, had escaped the car blast and might yet spill his guts about being bribed by Terrance—he would be almost impossible to neutralize now. And the AmVista Board was very nervous about retaining Geiger as CEO. He had to tread very carefully, but he was still itching to get both Diego and Chester—preferably at the same time. He wanted them dead for the trouble they had caused him over Brightway and whatever else they might be up to. They were dangerous and needed to be eliminated as quickly as possible.

What scumbags were still at his disposal? he thought. That creep who masterminded the car explosion was a total loss. At least he got what was coming to him. It was almost worth losing his Mercedes.

Terrance surveyed his address book. He had a special section he thought of as his bruiser file—unsavory characters who could be called upon, when necessary, to perform discreet, nasty little tasks. He studied the entries. Oh yes, here was one—Crank—a truly despicable character, but brutal, reliable, and relatively cheap. He picked up the phone and called.

☆☆☆

"Mother, can you do lunch?" Diego asked Milly from his office phone.

"Of course. Tell me, do you have some wonderful surprise for me?"

"No, but I do need your help."

"Very well. I feel like lunching at Tadpole's today. Meet you there at twelve thirty?"

"Perfect." Diego hung up with a self-satisfied grin.

181

☆

They both arrived at the same time, and Milly insisted upon her regular table, which she, of course, got. She had every respectable restaurant maître-d' on speed-dial and *always* got the table she wanted as she was a most generous tipper.

Milly settled back in her chair and took a long look at Diego. "How is it to be back at work? Are you settling in? I am in a constant state of anxiety over your recovery. Why, only yesterday, I was saying to Margaret Woolworth how brave I thought you were and how well you seem to have recovered. She told me about her daughter, Melissa, who had been in some terrible automobile accident, poor dear, and had lost both of her front teeth..."

"Mother, you are rambling," Diego cautioned, taking her hand and softly stroking it. "Everything's going to be okay."

"Oh..." She stopped and looked at Diego for another long moment. Then she picked up the menu. "Oh my, soft shell crabs. Just imagine. This time of year? Can't be—must be frozen. But always a favorite, anyway. Have whatever you like, of course."

"Thank you. Just a burger."

"Darling, all that saturated fat..."

"A burger, if you please."

Milly raised her left eyebrow—a sign he long recognized as disapproval. "If you insist, my dear."

"Now then, that favor...," Diego proceeded.

"Of course, anything. Just ask." She rested her chin on her hands folded in front of her to show that she was listening with undivided attention.

"I know you are no longer seeing him, but I would very much like for you to set up a meeting for me with Mr. TV Personality."

"Dexter? Oh, I don't know about that." She abruptly leaned back.

"But you said—anything."

"Oh yes, dear, but Dexter... He's so...yesterday. I'm not sure I could bring myself to actually speak to him again. And then there's the wife... I wouldn't want to do anything to jeopardize their marriage."

"That didn't stop you before," Diego said with a smile.

"Well, yes, but that was before I found out that he was not all that good—" She sat forward again and whispered "—in bed."

Diego winced slightly. "TMI..."

"I beg your pardon?" Milly chided. "I do not speak initials."

"'Too Much Information.'" He enlightened her.

Milly absorbed the explanation with a quick nod of her head. "I see. I don't know why you didn't just come out and say *that*."

"Sorry, I forgot you were texting impaired."

Milly disregarded the remark and continued, "And why do you want to meet him, may I ask?"

"Chester and I have a little plan. A little exposé, if you will. We are pretty sure we know who was behind the bombing, and we have some evidence that could pretty well put that gentleman out of commission for good. And Mr. TV Personality could be just the one to do it on his show. And it would be a really big scoop for him as well. I feel certain that he would jump at the chance to air that little scandal."

"Well, that certainly is intriguing. Let me see what I can do. Fuck the wife."

Diego laughed. "Oh mother, you are just too much for words."

"Yes, I know. And it's such fun."

☆☆☆

Poor Ed. His presidency was not going very well. All his hopes. All his plans. It had been just one crisis after another. It was all he could do to put out one fire before the next two or three came roaring along.

If one took a snapshot of the present world situation one would see that the price of oil had climbed worldwide. All the major stock markets were tumbling. Unemployment had risen by two and a half points. The dollar had devalued by twenty-five percent against most world currencies and was still declining. There were riots and demonstrations in many of the major cities. The Republicans in Congress threatened to shut down the government if the president didn't invade Venezuela. The Democrats threatened to shut down the government if the president did invade Venezuela.

Russia had sided with Venezuela—claiming that Guyana had started the conflict and stating that Venezuela was just protecting its vital interests. North Korea, Iran, and Bolivia announced they were boycotting all goods from the United States and the European Union. China had blocked a US resolution in the Security Council condemning the Venezuelan invasion. General Casados threatened nuclear strikes on Washington DC, Atlanta, and Disney World if the US so much as launched a row boat against Venezuela.

And all of this was *before* Lia stepped forward.

☆☆☆

It wasn't the easiest decision he'd ever made, but Diego thought it was for the best: he was giving up the apartment he and Brandon had shared. He just couldn't live there anymore—having to see the ruined trees and sidewalk where the explosion had occurred. Instead, he moved back to the family home. It was large and empty, but at least there were some good memories there from when he was a child. And because there was a larger perimeter around the house, it was easier for the Secret Service to protect him.

Diego learned from one of Chester's many inside government sources that Agent Darcy had committed suicide. He was despondent over betraying his trust and duty, the source said, but apparently not enough to disclose the identity of who had hired him to kill Diego.

It was a Sunday morning. Diego was still in bed doing crosswords—but no Chiquita; no Brandon. He struggled to control his urge toward self-pity. His cell phone rang.

"Diego?" an unfamiliar voice asked.

"Yes, who's this?"

"Dominic."

"I wondered if you would ever get in touch again," Diego said, brightening.

"Didn't I say I would?"

"Yes you did, but well—you know. People don't always do what they say they're going to do."

Dominic chuckled and then paused for a moment. "You free? May I come over?"

"If you give me half an hour. I'm still in bed."

"Lazy boy…"

"Yeah, well it's Sunday… crosswords, you know."

"Do you have twenty-seven across yet?"

"Philanderer."

"Damn, you're good."

Diego laughed. He was beginning to like this guy. "You know I'm not at the apartment any longer."

"Of course I do. Remember we are keeping close tabs on you."

"Glad for that. Okay, then. See you in thirty." He hung up and jumped out of bed to shower and shave.

Dominic appeared at the front door holding a large bunch of tulips. Diego was surprised. "What? Is this a date, then?"

"No, a thank you."

"For what?"

"For…" Dominic tried to find a clever answer. "For being you. Sorry, that was really lame. I don't know. I just saw them and wanted you to have them. I think tulips are kind of special."

"Well, that's very nice. Come on in." Diego ushered him inside and headed for the kitchen to get water for the flowers. "I could make a fresh pot of coffee."

"Not for me, thanks."

"So what's the occasion? Why the visit?" Diego asked as he filled a vase with water at the sink.

Dominic sat in the chair at the kitchen table where Brandon had confessed his indiscretion in the men's room. This clouded Diego's thoughts for a moment, but he quickly recovered.

"Just wanted to check in. See if you had any further questions for me. It's been almost two weeks since we met at the lake."

Diego put the flowers on the table and sat opposite Dominic. "Well to be honest, I did do an Internet search on the Franklin Society but didn't come up with much. Just that there was a group by that name founded at Brown University sometime in the nineteenth century. Is that correct?"

"Yep. Got that part right. Find anything else?"

"No. Seems to have disappeared by the twentieth century. Not much out there at all."

Dominic smiled and nodded. "And we like to keep it that way."

Diego studied Dominic. He noticed for the first time what nice eyes the guy had—friendly, smiling, full of warmth. "So why me?" he finally asked. "And just who are you guys, anyway? What the fuck do you want with a schlub like me?"

"Hey, don't put yourself down. You've got a lot to offer."

"Yeah-h-h, sure." He leaned back in his chair, studying Dominic more, trying to get past the guarded exterior and get a sense of the guy.

Dominic suddenly leaned forward, arms on the table. "Okay, here's the deal. I probably shouldn't be telling you this yet, but I think you have a right to know. You are a Perez—son of the president but a polar opposite. You have a nationally recognized name because of your father and because of your own good work. You made quite a splash and a very positive impression when you revealed the Brightway scandal.

He briefly narrowed his eyes. "The country is in an existential crisis right now. Just look at what is happening out there. Many of us in the society believe your father is going to crash. He is very unlikely to serve his full term. Either he will be impeached or forced to resign. And if he does, we want to put you up as a presidential candidate for the next election."

Diego was speechless for a second until he managed to he sputter out an answer. "But that is years away. My dad is only finishing his first year. And if he does resign, he will be succeeded by the vice president—hardly much better in my estimation."

"We agree. But just think what we could do with three years of preparation."

"Wait, wait, wait. You know I'm gay. Do you really think that would fly with the American electorate?"

"That issue is rapidly changing. In three years, who knows? In any case, we believe you have the best chance to claim the new center—with our help, of course. You are bright, articulate, attractive"—Dominic lowered his voice—"and very, very sexy—and that can't hurt."

☆☆☆

Crank had checked into a non-descript hotel near the O'Hare airport, and the getaway car he had rented was a fast one. He got into the car and drove to the GreenPAC offices. He waited and watched. No explosives for him. They were too unreliable and were not as precise as he liked. With a name like Crank, one might expect to see a massive brute, but Crank was slight, cunning, and could escape from a crime scene virtually unnoticed.

He was planning a surgical strike on the two men. He had studied their pictures, their dossiers, and he felt he knew them intimately. But he wanted to take his time. He wanted to know every single available angle before he decided where to shoot from. His method was usually a long range, high-powered rifle. He studied the surrounding rooftops, considering which one would provide him the best shot. Now he just needed to find out where his two targets were located inside.

Crank was wearing a generic serviceman's uniform. He rummaged through his bag and pulled out a fire inspector's badge and a clipboard. He got out of the car and walked into the GreenPAC building.

"Fire Marshall. Here to inspect the premises." Crank flashed his badge at the reception desk. A security guard inspected it and gave his okay.

"Of course," the receptionist answered.

"Can you show me where you have the fire extinguishers? I need to check the tags."

The receptionist led him to the three extinguishers.

"Can you show me the emergency exits?" There was one that led to a fire escape. Crank checked the panic bar and noted how he could jimmy it if he needed to gain entry from the outside. He also noted that it was alarmed.

As he walked, he made a rough sketch of the office layout. He found Chester's office first. It would be an impossible shot, as it was in the interior, and his desk was out of sight from the outside. Diego's desk, on the other hand, which he identified next, offered a clean shot.

When he'd finished his sketches, he flipped some sheets back on the clipboard to cover them.

He headed back to the reception desk.

"Here's a list of the issues that need to be corrected. Those boxes in the hall by the kitchen are creating an exit hazard, and your fire extinguishers are about to expire. Need to get them taken care of. I'll be back in a few weeks to check it out again. Thank you." He smiled at the receptionist and guard who returned his smile as he left.

If he wanted to get both of these men at the same time, this might require a more complex plan, he thought. None of the roof perches across the street would allow clean shots at both men. But perhaps he could lure Chester to Diego's desk and get them both at the same time? Or he might need to come in by the fire escape and do a surgical strike inside the office. But that would trigger the alarm and might not give him enough time.

Or maybe he would need to go in a totally new direction. He would have to consider all his options.

☆☆☆

"Mr. Matthews will see you now, Mr. Perez." The male receptionist led Diego to Dexter's office—a scramble of books, proposals, DVDs, and periodicals covered every free surface of the room, particularly Dexter's desk and credenza.

With a broad smile, Dexter stood at his desk and waved for Diego to come in and sit down. But first he had to remove a pile of books from Diego's chair. He made a wry face as the receptionist left. "You should have seen the hot little number who used to be up front. Man, *she* was something else. Ass from here to Ashtabula. But the wife... She's been breaking my balls ever since she found out about me and your mother. But hey, your mom tells me you're some kind of a fairy. Guess you would rather have what's up there at the reception desk now, huh? I'm sure I could arrange something for you if you like."

Diego briefly closed his eyes to gather his patience. "I'm here strictly on business, Mr. Matthews. But thanks for the ever so generous offer."

"Hey, call me Dexter. So, what can I do for you today? Your mom said you might have something I might really like."

"I certainly hope so." Diego pulled out a DVD from his bag. "Got something I can play this on?"

Dexter reached for it and put it in the player at his multimedia center after moving another pile of proposals. "What we got here?" He pressed play on the video.

Diego laid out a quick summary of the events as they watched the DVD. He explained about Deborah's surveillance of Terrance and how that had led to her death. He went on to explain that the case had been languishing with the FBI in Houston—or it was being buried.

"I feel we need to jump-start this case. And your TV program would be the perfect venue to air this material to put pressure on the Feds to act. They couldn't ignore this shocking evidence any longer if it was broadcast on national television." Diego knew he was becoming excited and passionate, but he couldn't help himself.

Dexter was thoughtful when the DVD finished playing. "It certainly looks promising." But he looked concerned as the leaned forward to confront Diego. "However, I need to know what your source is for these videos before I can move forward with something this big."

"I'm afraid the source is the woman who was killed. She was also the one who gave us all the information about the Brightway scandal. I'm sure you know about that."

Dexter nodded. "I do. Very impressive. That sure shook up the establishment for a while. But like so many good scandals, it soon got bogged down in congressional bullshit and fizzled."

"Yes, I'm afraid you're right." Diego needed to press his point home. "And that's why now is the perfect time to strike again."

Dexter considered for a moment. "I agree. Except for one little issue."

"And what's that?" Diego asked.

"Well, your source is dead. It's almost impossible for me to verify your claim. And remember, that AmVista group is one big powerful motherfucker—their lawyers have lawyers. We need some protection here. Both of us. You understand?"

Diego took a deep breath, sighed, and nodded. "What kind of verification do you need?"

"Some kind of corroboration. Something to support the videos. Something from that Deborah woman that connects her personally to these videos. As they are now, anyone could have made them. They could be a hoax. Who knows? Is that something you think you could get?"

"I'll see what I can do." Diego was not very hopeful as he got up from his chair.

"Sorry, I've got to edit some cut-a-ways for this week's show. You get back to me if you come up with anything else. Nice meeting you though. Say hi to your mom." He removed the DVD from the player and handed it to Diego before leading him to the door.

☆☆☆

The US Navy had established its cordon around the Venezuelan ships. Nothing could move in or out. Even with all their bluster, the Venezuelans were vastly outnumbered by the US ships and guns. Unless Venezuela decided to go nuclear, the end was inevitable. The Americans could mop up the enemy fleet whenever it was decided it was time to act. But then there were still, of course, the nukes.

Casados was not particularly pleased with the way things were going. His land convoy and troops had bogged down long before they reached Georgetown. They were unable to back up the Navy the way they had planned. And now the damn *yanquis* were about to overwhelm his embargo. He had to come up with a plan.

He had been successful securing the Guyana oil and gas fields, and he was pretty certain the Guyana border with Brazil was as porous as a tart's fishnet stocking. That was it—he would invade Brazil. There was a new, almost untouched, oil field down there that was being exploited by AmVista. He chuckled. His old buddy Terrance Geiger would sure be pissed at what he was about to do. He was certain they had only minimal security, and his troops and ordinance could quickly overwhelm the few oil field guards.

He was delighted with his new idea and picked up the phone.

"Terrance Geiger, please. This is the President of Venezuela."

☆

Terrance cleared his throat before he picked up the call. Clear and confident—that's how he had to sound. He smiled so Benevito could hear it in his voice.

"Benevito Casados, you old scoundrel—you sure have been making one hell of a nuisance of yourself. What the fuck you up to? Naughty boy." Terrance decided to play the interaction playfully. The son of a bitch had nukes, for fuck's sake.

"Terr-ance, is that any way to treat an old buddy?" Casados laughed. "Boy, you sure got dragged over the coals in that capitol hearing, didn't you?"

"I held my own. All that shit is long gone. Sensational congressional hearings come and go here faster than popsicles in hell." Terrance was becoming nervous. He knew this was not a social call. Casados was up to something, and Terrance wanted to get to the point of it as soon as possible. "So what's up? You gonna invade Houston next? We got a few barrels of oil here, ya know."

Casados laughed. "Oh no, Houston's way too swampy. Wouldn't like that. I was thinking Brazil would be nice, though. I have my eye on a nice piece of property down there where they have this really unusual tree— the Baobab, I believe it's called."

Terrance was rendered silent as he took in the significance of what Benevito was saying. This was the tree that had become AmVista's green logo. This was the tree that was at the heart of their vast new oil fields in northern Brazil. And these fields were just below the Guyana border and with minimal protection. What the fuck was Casados planning?

☆☆☆

Lia had done her homework. She had prepared and packaged all of her evidence—DNA testing, photographs, and even some covert sound recordings she had made of Ed at the lake. And finally, she had the proof of her pregnancy. She sent all of this along with her announcement that

191

she was pregnant by the president via email to all the major media outlets, political blogs, and to the White House and Congressional leaders. Now all she had to do was sit back and wait for the firestorm to descend upon her. And she was ready—ready for the questions, the jeers, the accusations, and the flood of media demanding personal interviews. She would be the dragon lady for the conservative talk show hosts, and a precursor of the Second Coming for the progressive Rachel Maddow crowd.

☆

Martin threw Lia's email with all the damning attachments on the president's desk first thing in the morning. "I sure hope you had your coffee today, Mr. President, because you're going to have to be really wide awake when you read this. Or if you aren't, you soon will be."

Ed looked at the papers. He groaned and leaned forward, banging his head on top of the email. "Just go ahead and shoot me," he said rolling his head from side to side.

"Call in the firing squad, and take me out of my misery."

"Oh sir, you haven't even begun to know the misery yet," Martin said with a wry smile.

Ed sat up straight again. "Can we assassinate her? Can we wipe her out and destroy all of this in a fire?"

"I'm sure we could burn all of this. But what do you want to bet she has sent this to all the news media in the world as well? She is now as protected as a pontiff."

Ed looked really sad. "But I really liked her. And I thought she liked me. What do you suppose happened?"

"Oh Ed, who knows? Perhaps somebody paid her a lot of money to get at you. Maybe you pissed her off somehow. Maybe it's political, or she had a grudge of some kind. But you can be certain we'll probably find out when she speaks to the press."

"How do we contain this?" Ed asked.

"No way we can, right now. It's out there. But let me get with Madison and a few of the others and see how we might spin this. I'm going to have to get back to you on this."

Ed laughed slightly. "Oh, Elena's gonna love this. She has been looking for an excuse to barbeque my balls."

"Well sir, better get yourself a stainless steel jock strap then."

"Think I'll take a vacation. Maybe camel trekking in the Sahara, or solo sailing the Pacific in a skiff. Or how about living in a snow cave in Siberia?"

"Dream on..." Martin turned to leave the Oval Office and then stopped and turned back to the president. "And Sir, remember you've still got Venezuela."

"Oh for Christ's sake, I'll *always* have Venezuela."

☆☆☆

Diego was in bed with his laptop checking his emails just before turning out the bedside lamp when he spotted one he didn't recognize.

Probably spam, he figured. He was just about to delete it, but he paused and looked at the sender's address again—grasshut@entmail.com. Hum. He decided to open it.

Right at the top of the email in bright red letters it read: *You have 15 minutes to read this email. It cannot be copied, printed, traced, or saved. At the end of that time this email will self-erase and will be un-recoverable.*

"Oh yes..." Diego sat up straighter.

Diego—Greetings. This is a voice from the grave. Ha ha. I have an idea you probably know who this is and where I am. But will not go into the details. Suffice it to say, I did not expire in the explosion in Houston. Because of the monitoring I did of a certain fellow employee, I was able to determine what his plans were ahead of time, and I made a few plans of my own.

It was kind of gruesome, but I asked a favor of a buddy of mine in the Medical Examiner's office. Transients and homeless folk pass away all the time, and the bodies are either cremated or buried without ceremony or identification. I simply requested a female corpse about my height and shape from a friend. Easily accomplished, with the addition of a little extra cash, of course. It was delivered to my house the afternoon before the explosion, and I positioned the body so it would be mostly destroyed by the explosion. Everyone would conclude that the body in the house was mine. There would be no distinguishing details, no need for an autopsy or DNA testing, and the case would be written off as a terrible accident. The case would be closed, and I could conveniently disappear without a trace. And, of course, Terrance would believe he had accomplished his task. Pretty neat, huh?

And yes, now I am exactly where I wanted to be. I'm sure you remember where that is.

Now then, about our friend in high places who masterminded my demise. I shall be sending you, in a separate email, a video attachment which you can download that should be self-explanatory and should provide you with all the evidence you need to nail the nasty son of a bitch once and for all.

We shall most likely never meet again. All the very best to you and Chester. Thank you for your courageous work. And who knows, if you ever have a yen to construct grass huts, our paths might cross again.

A friend.

Diego took a deep breath. He was shocked, of course, but he was also greatly relieved, knowing Deborah was still alive. And now he had exactly the proof he needed to convince Dexter. He tried forwarding the email but it wouldn't allow that. What could he do to save this? Deborah had said the message couldn't be copied.

He got an idea. He opened his cell phone and took a couple of photos of the screen. He looked over them—they were readable.

He wanted to relate all of this to Chester and Dominic. He waited, intrigued, to see if the email would indeed self-destruct, and it did—in exactly 15 minutes. Poof—and it was gone. Diego didn't know such software even existed. Or maybe it was something Deborah had devised on her own. She was certainly knowledgeable enough about security operations, and she knew how to cover her tracks. Good girl!

Diego scanned the rest of his emails, searching for the promised one with the incriminating attachment. Ah...there—that must be it. It was attached to another email that had been forwarded any number of times, so it would be almost impossible to trace back to her. She sure knew what she was doing. With nervous anticipation, and with his fingers momentarily freezing up, he finally downloaded the video file and played it.

He recognized the style of video and the location immediately. It was from the same surveillance setup in Terrance's house that the other videos had come from. This must have been recorded about the same time as the others—probably shortly after the GreenPAC press conference. He watched in fascination as Terrance spoke with a man who identified himself as a Houston FBI agent about the news conference and its implications for Terrance and AmVista. Then, with the video still rolling, Terrance went to a wall safe, opened it, and took out a large amount of cash and gave it to the agent. The speech was somewhat indistinct, but Diego could just make out what Terrance was saying. He was instructing the agent to make sure everyone was taken care of at the FBI so this whole investigation would go away. Before the video ended, the agent smilingly assured Terrance that all would be well.

Diego closed the video file. He considered and decided that this was exactly what Dexter would need, along with his phone photos, as the confirmation needed to proceed with airing the TV show. Terrance was clearly identified, as well as the agent. They should be able to nail him on conspiracy to kill Deborah from the earlier video as well as bribing the FBI agent from this video.

But this brought up an interesting twist, he realized. The authorities would try to pin Deborah's supposed murder on Terrance, but of course, she was *not* dead. This could prove to be a dilemma because Diego knew she *was* still alive. If he revealed that, though, he might jeopardize her anonymity and her safety.

But then, he also remembered that Terrance was also responsible for both Brandon and Danberry's murder. So if Terrance got nailed for Deborah's murder, even if she wasn't dead, that would take care of his culpability in the other two murders. *Neat the way Karma works*, Diego thought.

☆☆☆

Casados didn't want to send in his Air Force to bomb the oil installations in Brazil because he didn't want to damage the wells. He would need them for his own use. His intelligence agency had determined that the AmVista oil fields were lightly guarded, and Brazil had almost no military presence anywhere nearby. Now all he needed was an excuse to invade and take over the oil rigs. He had justified his attack on Guyana as self-defense. He couldn't quite see how to do that with Brazil. He would have to come up with another compelling reason.

He was having dinner with his Foreign Minister and their two kids.

"No, no, no. Not at the table," Benevito scolded Carlito, who was tearing holes in a tortilla and covering his face with it like a mask, peeking out of the eye holes and making scary noises at his sister who started crying.

"What about drugs?" Benevito asked Hortencia.

"I don't understand."

"Well, if someone in Brazil was running drugs across our borders, we would be justified in attacking, no?"

She put down her fork and daintily wiped her mouth with her napkin. "I don't see how that would work. I mean we could just arrest them as they crossed over into our territory. That wouldn't provide an excuse to attack another country," she observed. "At least not enough to persuade the international community. I mean, look at Mexico and the US"

"Hmmm." Stymied. Benevito didn't like that.

Now his son took a leaf of spinach from the salad and pasted it over his eye like an eye patch. "Argh, Argh," Carlito growled, waving his table knife around like a sword.

Hortencia sighed loudly. "Now, stop playing with your food. How many times do I have to tell you?"

Carlito growled again, "Avast. You are a scurvy lot." He surveyed his family from his uncovered eye.

Benevito laughed and then laughed a little more when it dawned on him this was the solution he'd been searching for—pirates!

☆☆☆

Dinner was ready to be served, but Ed had made some lame excuse about a congressional delegation needing his immediate attention. So now, Elena sat in stony silence waiting for him in the White House dining room. He had told her to go ahead without him, but she was determined to have it out with him right now, so she waited.

She had seen Lia's news conference. She had studied all the supporting documents on the Internet. She had seen the gloating newscasters on the evening news. She had read the scathing emails from her supporters, as they blasted that bastard, Edward Perez. Finally, she had spent all day alone in the first lady's office in the East Wing, stewing and thinking about this whole situation. And she knew what she wanted to do and was determined to act on it tonight.

"I am *so* sorry. I hope you didn't wait." Ed breezed in and sat down at the other end of the dining table. He didn't look directly at her but signaled for the attendants to go ahead and serve dinner.

They ate their Montana grass-fed beef—medium rare—in utter silence. It was becoming increasingly uncomfortable. Finally, Elena looked up to find Ed glaring at her like she had snakes growing out of her head.

He blared out, "Okay, so you've seen the accusations that Lia made. And I suppose you want to discuss this."

Very slowly and lady-like, she took a sip of wine. "Discuss! Discuss? What is there to discuss, pray tell?"

"Well, you might want to hear my side of the story," Ed said in an attempt to defend himself.

"Oh boy, I bet that will be a fine fairytale," she said, laughing and dabbing at her mouth with her napkin.

"You could at least hear me out."

"Are you kidding? I have seen the evidence, Ed. Pretty smart—that little cookie. She sure covered all her bases. Don't think there's much you can say against the hard evidence she presented. Pun intended," she said, laughing.

"Oh, now, darling..."

"You must have really pissed her off for her to go after you like that. Pregnant! Pregnant! When did that happen? Michigan—I'll bet you anything. And me with a sick mother to attend to." She put both her hands flat on the table and glowered at Ed.

"Well, it wasn't like it meant anything. You know it's always been you I love."

"Oh, come on. You are more promiscuous than a sultan. Good God, why you're so famous Miss Piggy does infomercials about your dick. No. No. No. There is only one thing."

"And what is that, my darling?" Ed sighed.

"I want a divorce." She stood up to make her point.

Ed chuckled, "Oh my dear, you know that's not possible."

"Oh really? And why is that?"

"Well, I'm a sitting president. Divorce just doesn't happen in the White House. Never has. Never will. It would ruin my chances for re-election."

Elena threw her head back and laughed. "Huh. Well, that would be just a dandy side benefit for me, I can tell you."

"You don't mean that. I know how much you enjoy being the first lady."

"You think? The constant surveillance, the boring state dinners, the smiling and happy attitude no matter how I feel, the constant press coverage, the oh-so-dull trips to schools, hospitals, war memorials...and the list goes on and on. I can't tell you what a relief it would be to eat a doughnut in public or go to the store in curlers." She'd been waiting for months to say that.

"I'm so sorry you are disappointed. But there will be no divorce." He slapped the table.

"Well, we'll just see about that. Don't you dare underestimate me, Mr. Smarty-pants." Elena rose from her chair and, nose in the air, marched out of the dining room.

☆☆☆

Crank was a well-known threat. His ties to Terrance Geiger had been traced by the Franklyn Group. But the discovery was not enough to legally interrupt the planned assassination. Crank had to be caught in the execution of the act for the authorities to effectively prosecute both Crank and Geiger.

However, the Franklin security group knew the moment Crank landed in Chicago. Dominic was alerted, and he and several other society members had been tracking and documenting Crank's activities ever since he arrived.

Dominic knew everything about Crank's intentions; he knew that Crank was ready to strike soon. Dominic also knew who the targets were, and suspected what Crank was planning to do—but just not when. And while the society was secret, it was not violent. It held itself to the highest standards. If there was a danger, the society made sure the proper authorities were alerted so they alone could act to resolve the issue. And he was prepared to act quickly once he knew Crank's intentions and timing.

☆

Crank was feeling safe and secure in his shabby motel room. He was sure he had covered his tracks well and felt totally prepared for his mission. He had cleaned and oiled his two handguns for the second time and placed them in his briefcase. He then took apart his rifle and placed that it in his briefcase too. He was poised to strike. He picked up his phone and used his encryption device to make his call.

"Mr. Geiger—Crank. Our little surprise will take place tomorrow. Watch the news."

"Excellent."

"I won't be contacting you again. Make sure the money is deposited where we agreed."

"It will be. Not a problem."

Crank ended the call.

He carefully laid out his clothes for tomorrow—aligning them exactly, and smoothing the pants out so as not to muss the crease. He finally packed his bag, ready to leave quickly in the morning, and then he turned out the lights. He went to the bathroom window and looked out the back. He saw nothing. He went to the front window overlooking the motel parking lot and checked out that window.

There was a van parked in an odd way that looked suspicious. He did not like the look of that. Surveillance? Crank decided to go out and scope it out. He slipped out of his room and skirted the shadowed wall of the stairwell that led from the second floor of the motel to the parking lot.

He made his way between parked cars, carefully keeping out of sight. He approached the van from behind a hedge that bordered the street. As he neared, he caught the distinct aroma of stale marijuana smoke wafting out of the open windows. Definitely not a surveillance operation. But, just to be sure, he peeked in. There were four zonked-out adults and three kids, sleeping blissfully on the floor. No doubt crashing in the motel parking lot so the kids could use the pool and the pool house restrooms. *Bunch of goddamned hippies.* Crank returned back to his room, secure in the thought that he was still undetected.

☆

But Crank was mistaken. What he didn't know was that Dominic and a couple of Franklin Society associates had been shadowing him ever since he had arrived in Chicago. Between the three of them, someone was always right on Crank's tail.

Dominic was on duty when Crank first left the motel on the first day of his arrival. Dominic had followed him and was not at all surprised when Crank went to the GreenPAC offices. Dominic watched as Crank went inside the GreenPAC building dressed in the uniform of a fire inspector. He followed after him, in case Crank was planning to strike right then. But Dominic didn't think that would be the case as Crank would leave himself too exposed. Crank was a planner and an executioner who took his time and set up his hits so that he could save his own skin and make a clean get-away.

Indeed that was the case; Crank soon left the GreenPAC offices. Dominic followed and observed, from a safe distance, as Crank crossed the street and stood examining the rooftops from the sidewalk below.

All the buildings on the street were old, dark-brick office buildings of no more than three stories. Finally, Crank chose a building and went inside. Dominic followed closely behind, being careful not to be seen. Crank went to the top floor, found the exit to the roof, and went outside. Dominic slipped quietly outside too, concealing himself behind an air conditioning unit. As he observed, he saw Crank check the site lines of GreenPAC building across the street. He took out a rifle scope and trained it on the windows. He calibrated the distance and then turned to look around the rest of the roof.

Dominic peered from behind the AC to keep his eye on Crank. Crank went around the perimeter—obviously looking for his best escape route, Dominic decided.

Dominic kept himself well concealed. Crank was smart and organized. Dominic surmised that, after the shooting, Crank would choose not to go back down the building's main stairs. Indeed, as he watched, Crank found a fire escape that led to a first floor wing of the building that could be used to escape to neighboring buildings where he could become easily lost, which is exactly what he did now.

Damn it. Dominic would be too exposed if he tried to follow. Still, he knew Crank had come in a car. He would most likely end up back at the car, and Dominic could easily follow him from there.

Now Dominic felt certain he knew the method of the assassination, as well as the place—but not the exact time. From the intel the Franklin Society had gathered, Dominic knew Crank used an encrypted phone. The Franklin surveillance group had the software to unscramble any encrypted call Crank made. Eventually, Crank could be counted on to reveal his plan, through a phone call to Terrance, about when the hit would occur. Dominic was sure of it.

The Franklin surveillance group had members within the Chicago PD and the FBI. And when that last call to Terrance was finally made, revealing the day of the hit, Dominic would be waiting to intercept. He alerted both agencies to what was about to happen and turned the apprehension of Crank over to them.

But that did not relieve Dominic of his responsibility to cover Diego. He would remain forever vigilant.

☆

Diego and Chester were very pleased. They'd had a call from the Bennington Family Foundation, a major environmental funding group that wanted to meet to discuss the possibility of a major operational grant. Chester had set up a meeting for ten o'clock this morning. The Bennington director suggested a casual environment for the first meeting. Chester had just the place in mind—a cozy coffee shop, just down the street from their offices. That sounded delightful, the director said.

In the suggested café, Diego and Chester were eagerly awaiting the Bennington director. They had gone to the café early so as not to miss him on any account, but Diego was surprised to see Dominic walk into the café. He stood up and was about to go over and say hi, but Dominic shook his head and went to get a coffee. Diego sat back down. *How did Dominic know they would be here?* He pushed the thought out of his mind and turned to Chester.

"Did he give any indication of the grant amount they might be considering?" Diego asked, as they sat with their coffee and with a good view of anyone coming in looking for them.

"Not specifically, but it could be substantial. They have a track record of being unusually generous."

"That could help us so much." Diego smiled.

The café door opened, and an impeccably dressed gentleman of short stature and closely cropped salt-and-pepper hair appeared and looked around the café.

"That must be him," Chester nodded toward the gentleman. "Mr. Langer?" he called out.

The man turned and walked toward them. The two Secret Service agents stood. Diego turned to them and nodded that it was okay. The man came forward and placed his briefcase on a chair.

"Gentlemen, it's a real pleasure," Langer said, offering his hand. They shook.

"Can I get you a coffee? Croissant? Biscotti?" Chester offered.

"Thank you, I'm fine. Just came from a breakfast meeting. Went on far too long. Shall we?" He indicated they should sit. He remained standing as he opened his briefcase. "Now, gentlemen, I would like you to take a look at these papers. It will give us a basis for discussion." He reached into the briefcase, and to Diego's stunned surprise, swiftly removed two hand guns that he aimed at the two agents and shot them before they could stand up.

The man stared coldly at Diego and Chester. "Now, gentlemen, this is a little token of respect from Mr. Terrance Geiger," he said, aiming the two guns at Diego and Chester.

Diego held his breath in utter terror and waited for the end to come. But in the time it took the man to speak his sentence, Dominic had rushed up behind the shooter, grabbing him around his neck and pulling him backward. The man discharged both guns twice, the shots firing into the ceiling. The gunman twisted around and was able to free himself from Dominic's grasp. Dominic fell backward onto the floor and rolled away as quickly as he could, as the assassin aimed both guns at him.

With the killer's back turned, Diego and Chester seized their opportunity. In unspoken synchronicity, they rushed forward and struck Crank with body blows, sending him reeling toward the floor. But they weren't quick enough—he was able to discharge both guns again, hitting Dominic twice.

Three café patrons—a burly student and two young office workers—sprang into action, throwing themselves on top of the shooter as Diego wrested the guns from his hands.

As soon as Diego had the guns safely in his grip, the Chicago Police rushed in and began to secure the chaos of the scene, cuffing Langer and spreading out to attend to the fallen.

One of the officers came directly over to Diego, taking the guns from him.

"Diego Perez?" he asked.

"Yes, sir. I am."

"Are you injured?"

"No, but my Secret Service agents were shot." Diego pointed to the inert bodies stretched out behind him.

"We'll take care of that."

Diego couldn't understand how the police could have gotten there so quickly. He stopped one of the officers—a young guy with a stern air but a kind face.

"How did you know this was happening? You got here so fast."

The officer looked left to right and leaned forward to answer. "We were tipped off. We were staked out across the street to take this hotshot down. Our informant advised us he'd be shooting at your office from the rooftop across the street."

Diego nodded but was still in too much shock to be taking it all in.

"But he obviously changed his plans. When we heard the shots, we knew he'd acted."

Diego ears were ringing; he felt faint. The first shock was beginning to wear off. "Well thanks for getting here when you did."

"You sure you're okay?" The officer reached over and took hold of Diego's shoulder. "The medics will be here soon. Have them check you out."

Diego nodded.

The officer nodded once and turned to check out Chester.

Outside, Diego heard the scream of sirens as several ambulances arrived, and he turned to check on Dominic. From where he was standing, he could see Dominic was still breathing—alive but unconscious. The two agents hadn't fared so well.

There was blood everywhere. A couple of medics rushed in to work on Dominic, but he was unresponsive. It was impossible to tell where he had been wounded from where Diego stood.

Diego followed the gurney carrying Dominic out to the ambulance. He took Dominic's hand. "You're gonna be okay, buddy. They'll take good care of you."

He had to drop Dominic's hand as the EMTs loaded the gurney into the back of the ambulance. They slammed the doors shut, ready to speed off.

"Is he going to be okay?" Diego asked the chief EMT who was still outside the ambulance.

The man shook his head. "Won't know till we get a better look. But right now I would say he's probably got about a fifty-fifty chance."

Chester came up and put his arm around Diego as the ambulance sped away. "I hate to say this, my friend, but you sure seem to have a tough time keeping Secret Service agents. Bet they'll just be lining up to serve with you now."

Diego turned and scowled. "Not a good joke, Chester. Bad taste."

"Sorry, just trying to lighten things up a bit."

"I know." Diego put his arm around Chester and leaned his head against his shoulder. Now he would have to recover from yet another attack on his life.

☆☆☆

The troop carriers plowed down the dirt road toward the AmVista oil fields in Brazil, the tanks and artillery following closely behind. General Casados had given strict instructions not to damage the well heads. The Venezuelan military was to take the oil fields with as little disruption to the oil flow as possible.

General Santiago had deployed snipers in advance of the troop movement to pick off the security guards before they could respond in a meaningful way as the Venezuelan troops arrived. He had brought forward a single tank to lead the troops. It was symbolically menacing and could be called upon to strike terror amongst the oil field workers, who were not likely to be overly protective of the wells if their lives were at stake.

However, the General was surprised to find the oil fields fortified with a few artillery guns waiting for them.

Casados, on the other hand, shouldn't have been surprised. The minute Terrance had ended the call with the Venezuelan president; he'd called his Brazilian contacts. The Brazilian army had been able to move a few guns from the nearest post after the incursion into Brazil had first occurred. But Santiago definitely had the field advantage. He moved a few more tanks forward and began to blast the Brazilian guns. The snipers were able to pick off the gunners in short order, and the Brazilian guns fell silent.

However there was one surviving casualty. As the smoke cleared, the towering Baobab tree emerged from the haze of battle missing a few limbs. It had suffered a few direct hits, but it was still standing.

The Venezuelan troops moved forward, took the oil fields, and began supplying their own tankers with the pilfered crude from the AmVista fields.

☆☆☆

Ed was beyond exasperation talking on the phone to Diego, as he trolled the West Wing portico outside his office. "Son, I'm running outta Secret Service agents here. You are one expensive proposition to this nation. What the fuck is up with that? We've lost four agents because of you."

"Dad, you might want to ask your old buddy Terrance Geiger about that. He's still smarting because of the Brightway revelations. And I've got conclusive evidence that he conspired to murder Deborah Salcido because she helped us with the Brightway incident. I also suspect that he was responsible for Brandon and the first agent's murder. And now he has tried to take Chester and me out. He's a real menace. Is there nothing you can do about that?"

"Well, that's a sobering announcement to digest. But, as I see it, that's a law enforcement issue."

"We contacted the Houston FBI, and so far they have done absolutely nothing."

Ed paused. "But are you okay now? I've been fully informed about the incident in the café."

"Dad, I'm fine. I'm on the way to the hospital right now to visit a friend who was shot." He paused a moment. "I still miss Brandon a lot, but I'm sure that's no sweat off your balls."

Ed sighed. "Yeah, well I was sorry to hear about that. Really."

"And this injured friend was the one who saved us today. You oughta give him a medal or something."

"I doubt that's going to happen."

There was a pause at Diego's end. "So—I understand I'm about to have a new baby brother or sister."

"Yeah, well, shit happens."

"Is that really how you feel about it?"

Ed glanced around to see if anyone could overhear. "Little slut set me up. She's having a kid just to spite me and to give me a shit load of new grief. Let me tell you, this president business sure puts you in everybody's crosshairs. You gotta be a son-of-a-bitch to stand the heat up here."

"No one forced you..."

"I know. I know. But, Son, there are times when I would give just about anything to go back to my Texas days with just my truck and my crew. Those were good days."

Diego chuckled a little. "Dad, are you going soft and sentimental on me?"

"Not on your life. Just a moment of reflection is all."

"Okay Dad, I understand."

Ed headed back toward his office. "And try and keep your agents alive from now on, will ya?"

"I'll see what I can do. And hey, thanks for calling."

"Say hi to your mom. She won't talk to me any longer."

"Will do."

We Are So-o-o Fucked

Day 340 the president's term

"What the fuck do you mean they're all gone?" The president threw his hands up in the air in exasperation as he paced the Situation Room. This was just the latest in a long line of emergency meetings. "How can the entire Venezuelan naval fleet just disappear?"

"That's exactly what we are trying to figure out, sir," Defense shook his head. "When dawn came, our fleet was still there, but all of their ships were gone."

"Then how did they escape? Are there secret canals or some shit?" Ed asked, increasingly irritated. "Did they don disguises? Did they slip by our ships using smoke and mirrors? What?"

A very tired and rumpled defense secretary took off his glasses and rubbed his eyes. "The satellites didn't show any movement, sir. There were no other ways out of the blockade. They were trapped in a bay. They were simply there the night before, and gone the next morning. It was virtually impossible for their ships to slip by ours undetected. We have the most sophisticated and comprehensive navel and satellite detection in the world."

"Sir, you should probably see this. It was recorded earlier." A military aid brought up General Casados speaking on the Situation Room monitor.

"Our country will never stand for such bold aggression," Casados was ranting on Venezuelan TV. "In the interests of self-defense, our military forces shall be advancing on the country of Brazil immediately. Their act of piracy is totally unacceptable and shall be met with the vengeance of our glorious military might. People of Venezuela stand tall—stand strong. We shall prevail."

Ed stood for a moment trying to comprehend what he had just seen. "What the fuck was that? What is he talking about?"

The aide added, "Sir, his armed forces have crossed over into northern Brazil from Guyana."

"What? Is this guy insane? What was that about piracy? What was he talking about?"

The secretary of defense had been reading some urgent memos just handed to him. He looked up and spoke to the president. "Sir, Casados claims that Brazilian pirates just sank all of his navy ships, which he says were protecting Georgetown from US aggression."

"Pirates, what pirates?" Ed was becoming totally confused by all of this. He shook his head in disbelief.

Defense gave this question some consideration. "Sir, I think I see what's going on here."

"Then please enlighten me, if you can," Ed pleaded.

"I think the Venezuelans scuttled their own ships—which is why they disappeared—and are claiming Brazilian pirates attacked them."

"And why would the Venezuelans do such a dumb thing?"

"To have an excuse to invade Brazil."

"That's about the dumbest thing I have ever heard of. Is the man a complete psychopath?"

Defense, with a slight smile, nodded. "Very likely, sir."

The secretary of state dashed into the room. "We have a situation."

"Of course we do," Ed sighed. "What insanity now?"

"The president of Brazil just called. He says Venezuelan troops have crossed his northern border and have taken the AmVista oil fields. He would like to speak to you immediately."

Ed nodded and picked up the phone. He was starting to get a headache and rubbed his eyes. "Mr. President..."

"Mr. President," the Brazilian president said frantically. "We are under attack from Venezuela troops."

"Yes, I have just been informed."

"We have troops moving in to meet them now, but we do not have the air cover we need. I am asking you, under our mutual defense treaty, for air support. I understand that you have a carrier off the northern coast of Guyana. That is easily within striking distance of where the Venezuelan troops are now. Will you assist us?"

Ed looked to State and Defense. They shook their heads. "I'll have to get right back to you. I need to confer with my cabinet first."

"Please, I urge you to come to our aid as soon as possible."

"Before we get into a conflict, first let me see what I can do diplomatically. I'll get back to you shortly." Ed hung up the phone. "Get me Casados."

An aide immediately called, but this time Casados came through via video link, and it flashed up on the situation room screens.

On the screen, Ed could see Casados leaning back in his fine Corinthian leather desk chair and puffing at his cigar. "Ed, I thought I might be hearing from you. I was just having a friendly chat with the Iranian and Russian ambassadors. Their governments have been *so* supportive of our incursion into Brazil, after the terrible attack upon our Navy by those scurrilous Brazilian pirates. I'm sure these pirates acted in full cooperation with the Brazilian government. Are you calling to lend us your support as well?"

Ed jabbed his pointed finger toward Casados. "You know that is not the case, General. I am asking you to withdraw your troops immediately from Brazilian territory." Ed paused for a reaction, but there was none. "You have committed an act of war, sir. They have every right to defend themselves. And they have, in fact, called upon us to honor our mutual defense treaty with them and provide immediate air support against your invading troops."

"Oh, but Mr. President, it is in fact my country who is the wronged party here," Casados said in his most injured voice.

"Come on, General. That is a total ton of horseshit. You know it, and I know it. Pirates? Really? Who do you think you're kidding? I know for a fact that you scuttled your own ships to give credence to this fabricated pirate story."

"Why Mr. President, you wound me in the heart."

Ed laughed, "I sincerely doubt that, General—I'd be greatly surprised if you even had one. And you can tell your Russian and Iranian friends that the US protects this hemisphere, and that they can just keep their nasty little noses out of our business. Now I strongly urge you to recall your troops immediately, or there will be consequences."

"Mr. President, might I remind you that we now have nuclear weapons aimed right at your heartland. I truly doubt that you want to risk an unfortunate accident by damaging, in any way, my beloved country and forcing us to defend ourselves against naked *yanqui* aggression."

Ed was really huffing and ranting now. "And I would remind you, as well, that we too have an extensive nuclear arsenal, and we have the capability to wipe your insignificant little country off the map, no matter how many nukes you send our way. Are you sure *you* want to risk that?"

Casados was quiet. "And I, myself, am backed up by a few countries with extensive nuclear capacity. If you were to attack us, there would be substantial additional consequences for you as well. Remember, you are not the only one with mutual defense treaties." Casados laughed. "I think this is what might be called a stalemate. Don't you agree?"

Ed was sobered into silence and disconnected the video link.

☆☆☆

Diego sat at Dominic's bedside in the hospital—this hospital visitation routine was getting to be too much of a habit. Dominic was still unconscious, but at least he looked more presentable once he was cleaned up, even though he was still pale and ghostly looking.

Milly and Carmella had ferreted out Diego in the hospital to invite him for lunch at Carmella's favorite rib joint. Carmella was staying with Milly over the Christmas holiday.

"So who is this new friend of yours?" Carmella asked.

"Don't know a lot about him. We just met recently. But it was he who saved Chester and me by taking down the shooter."

"My darling, you really *do* need to get over these extravagant life threatening incidents." Milly said, tapping her apple-colored nails on the plastic arm of what she'd loudly announced was the *most* uncomfortable chair. "It's starting to affect my social calendar. Do you have any idea how many functions I've had to cancel or postpone on account of your run-ins with the criminal element?"

"Mother, how lapse of me. I shall be sure to schedule all further attempts at my demise around your schedule. Please email me your calendar in advance so that I can be sure to comply."

Milly and Diego looked at each other and burst out laughing.

Carmella looked at them both with a slight sneer. "You two... Mother, are you sure you're not gay? I do believe you are a gay man in a woman's body."

"Yes, I expect that is quite correct," Milly agreed. "I do find gay porn most stimulating."

Carmella cringed. "How did I ever get born into this family?"

"Little dumpling, you are definitely one of us," Diego added. "You are an Oz munchkin of the first order. I do believe the spirit of our Dorothy resides within you, too. Perhaps it's just not been awakened yet."

"Yes... Well, we'll have to talk about that at another time, Carmella answered with a shy smile."

Diego nodded to Milly. "You've said absolutely nothing about Dad's latest peccadillo." He turned to Carmella. "Seems we're about to have a new sibling." Carmella blushed. "Isn't she your teacher? And isn't she the one who saved you from the fiery car?"

"Yes and yes. I had no idea they were carrying on right under my nose at the lake house this past summer. It's all very embarrassing. I introduced them at the White House reception. I feel somehow responsible."

"My dear, I don't see how. It wasn't your prick playing hide and seek." Milly may have been trying to reassure Carmella, but it only succeeded in embarrassing her even more.

Carmella buried her face in her hands. "Mother, stop, please."

"Are you sure you're my daughter? You seem to lack the capacity to appreciate the finer points of the truly absurd. It really is such fun. Perhaps your brother can give you lessons. He's quite good at it. But never mind. Maybe it's a quality that ripens with age. There may be hope for you yet."

Carmella glanced at Dominic. "Should we be talking like this in front of your friend...?"

"Oh, he can't hear anything. He's been in and out of consciousness since they brought him in," Diego answered, then considered. "So does that make Lia our stepmother?" Diego asked.

"Only if they marry, I believe," Milly answered. "Oh my, the poor Elena must be having a fit of historic proportions right about now."

"Yes, Dad does seem to get himself into some fine situations. It's a wonder he ever became president."

"Cleaners and scrubbers—he employs the very best scandal relief team in politics." Milly looked restless; she started rummaging in her handbag. "This young man friend of yours is not very interesting company. My dears, I suggest we go for a nice long two or three martini lunch." She gathered her bags together in preparation for leaving.

Diego said, "You two go on. There's no reason for you to be here. But I'm not ready to leave him just yet."

Milly looked askance at Diego. "Do I detect the hint of a new budding romance?"

"Mother... Not now."

"Very well, my dear, we shall leave you alone to play out romantic scenes from *The English Patient*. Come beloved," she instructed Carmella. "Lunch. There's nothing quite as fetching as you tearing into a giant plate of sloppy ribs." As they were leaving, Milly turned back to Diego. "We shall be at *Como's Ribs and Things* if you suddenly feel peckish. Would love for you to join us."

After the two had finally departed, Diego turned his attention back to Dominic. He took his hand. He stared at Dominic's drawn face.

"I can't believe your mother is trying to fix us up," Dominic spoke softly with his eyes still closed.

Startled, Diego dropped Dominic's hand.

Dominic slowly opened his eyes. "Yes, I heard it all, but couldn't bring myself to join in the family gossip."

"Well, at least you know now what I have to deal with on an almost weekly basis," he laughed.

"Thank you for being here." Dominic smiled. His lips were cracked and pale.

"How do you feel?" Diego leaned in to examine Dominic more

closely.

"Like elephant shit."

"They say you're going to be okay."

"Bet I'll have a limp, though. Got me in the leg and shoulder, you know."

Diego nodded. "Physical therapy will take care of that."

"That's okay. Just happy to be here...and to have you here." He frowned. "Sorry that guy wasn't your big donor—the creep."

"We'll survive. Oh, Chester wanted me to thank you, too—for saving us."

"Ah, do it every day." Dominic tried joking, but started coughing. "Want a nurse?"

Dominic shook his head. He took Diego's hand again. "Why don't you go have lunch with your family? Those ribs sound awfully good. I'll be okay. And I need to sleep some more."

"Okay then, see ya," Diego replied, rising to leave.

Dominic nodded. "Keep safe."

"I'll try. But I haven't got you backing me up any longer."

"Not to worry. There are others."

☆☆☆

"Good shot, Mr. President," Norman Wilson, the head of the Republican National Committee congratulated Ed as he teed off at the third hole at the Boca Raton Resort.

"This Florida weather sure beats the crap out of that winter mess up in DC," Ed said, as he picked up his tee and handed the driver to his caddy.

The convoy of golf carts, Secret Service agents, and other members of the president's golf party headed out to find their respective balls. It had been planned ahead that each interested party would have a moment alone with the president to discuss their particular concerns. Pressure was building on the president in Washington. And it seemed like this golfing excursion would be a good way to confront the president on the many issues without it seeming as if they were all ganging up on him at once.

It was Norman's turn with Ed. "I suppose you've seen the numbers?"

"Yeah—tanking."

"I hate to say this, but you're killing the party, Ed. Christ almighty, your personal life is in the toilet."

Ed glowered at Norman.

"Is the first lady really going through with the divorce?"

"She thinks she is, but I'll take care of that."

The cart had come to where the balls had fallen.

"Three iron," Ed requested of his caddy. "Have you tried the new Gordon putter?" Ed asked Norman.

"Got one of the first."

"Sweet."

"What about the girl...what's her name? Tia?" Norman continued in an urgent tone.

"Lia," Ed corrected. "Hell, I don't know how the girl became pregnant anyway. I was always very careful to use protection. She says she can prove it's my baby, but how do I know it's really mine? I think all she has is circumstantial evidence." Ed swung and his ball landed just short of the green.

"DNA is not circumstantial, Mr. President."

"Eh..." Ed waved Norman's concerns away. "I've got a slush fund that I'm sure can persuade her to go away." He handed his iron to the caddy.

"I'm afraid it's a little late for that strategy, Mr. President. She's already all over the news everywhere. The damage is already done."

Norman played his ball, and it landed softly on the green.

"Ah, trust me—it will all blow over within a month. You know how these news cycles go. Ask the average Joe in six months who this Lia gal is, and he won't have a clue. I just need to give the public something really strong to rally behind. Been thinking of sending in special forces to take out the Venezuelan nukes. That should give my ratings a huge spike. Hey, great boost with that six iron. Never tried that from this distance."

"Little trick I learned from Tiger."

Ed tilted his head in admiration. "Ya don't say."

"Look Ed, all I'm saying is that I don't think this mess is going to go away as quickly as you might think. Those congressional impeachment hearings are really heating up. Remember, Nixon thought he was untouchable too. Just saying..."

"Ah...it's only the end of my first year. This will all blow over by midterm. You just wait and see."

"What about an address to the nation? You know, talk to the people. Address all these issues. Eat a little humble pie. Tout your achievements, and address this Venezuelan mess head on. Rally the American people around the flag. That sort of thing."

They got back into the golf cart and Ed drove it forward.

"Maybe."

"Well, ya gotta do something, Ed. I'm getting calls from the grassroots wanting to know if we can field a challenger for next term."

Ed looked at him. "You gotta be kidding me."

They arrived at the green.

"Let's see you play that with the Gordon putter," Ed challenged. Norman took his putt. "Nice. Nice. Let me give it a try." Norman handed him the putter and Ed landed his ball in just two shots. "Gonna get me one of these."

"Take it. My little gift, Mr. President."

"Why, thank you." He swung it several times to get the feel of it. "Nice action."

Now it was State's turn with the president. He came over as they walked to the next tee.

"That's the new Gordon, isn't it?" the secretary commented, swinging his driver in a practice shot.

"Sure is."

"Can I have a go with it at the next green?"

"You bet." Ed took the first swing, the ball traveling about halfway to the next green with a definite slice. "Ouch."

"Mr. President, I'm getting a shit load of grief from some of our major allies. They're concerned about China, Russia, and Iran's stance with regard to the Brazil and Guyana incursions. They underscore that we don't have the security council votes. And this whole nuke business has them really scared, too. We've got to stabilize this situation and fast."

"Working on it."

"What does that mean?" State asked with an edge of sarcasm.

"It means that I'm waiting for you guys and gals to come up with some solutions. I can't operate without knowing what all my options are."

"Sir, the markets are going crazy, and the dollar needs stabilizing too. We can't go on like this for much longer. Treasury, Defense, and us, we're all working full-out to give you what you need."

"Need to replace that divot." Ed pointed out to State.

"Oh yeah, sorry."

"Gotta keep our fairways green."

☆☆☆

"It's going to be a doozy of a show, boys and girls," Dexter said, addressing his staff in his preshow meeting on the set of *Confidential Confessions*. "Can you believe we have Lia Braga, the woman who has been fucking the president? *And* we have Diego Perez, the president's son. Who could have dreamed of a better lineup? Just wait till the share numbers come in tomorrow. We are gonna soar."

Diego had persuaded Dexter to run the videos of Terrance paying off the FBI agent and setting up Deborah's assassination. Deborah's email had done the trick of convincing Dexter that it was genuine. He felt his ass was now covered. Now there could be no excuse for the FBI not to round up the sucker.

At the same time, Dexter, seeing a grand opportunity to see sparks fly, had approached Lia with a proposal to present her evidence about Ed on national TV. And neither knew the other was to be a guest on the show. Dexter couldn't believe his good luck. Each guest would not only be good television by themselves, but he planned to bring the two together face to face and let them duke it out—Lia accusing the president; Diego defending the president.

As Diego was having makeup applied by a stylist in the studio green room, he turned and looked at the woman who'd just sat down beside him as they waited for the show to start. She looked very familiar.

"Don't I know you?" Diego asked Lia.

She turned to him. "Carmella's brother—David, right?"

Diego laughed. "No, Diego. And yes, Carmella's brother."

"Sorry, it has been a rough couple of months. Memory's not as sharp as I would like these days." She sighed. The stylist turned to work on Lia.

"Yeah. How do you happen to be here?" he asked, beginning to have an inkling that something fishy might be up.

She suddenly looked very embarrassed. "Oh dear, very awkward. I'm here to present my evidence against your father." She laughed. "You are about to have a baby brother, you know."

"A brother, huh? Great. Now we can go hunt some bear together," he said in his mountain man voice.

Lia laughed. "Might be a little while before that is possible."

"Like never." Diego laughed, too. "I'm not the hunting type, I'm afraid."

"Oh yeah, the big environmentalist, I seem to remember."

"Exactly."

"You're all ready," the stylist said, "They'll come and get you when it's time."

"Thanks," they both said.

Lia assumed a mock hurt attitude. "Hey, we were supposed to have a drink together at the White House reception, and you stood me up."

"Oh yeah, my dear father had just arranged to have my partner seduced by one of his FBI agents. I was not in a mood to socialize, I seem to remember."

Lia nodded. "Sorry about that. And why are *you* here today?"

"Ah yes, well, you might have heard about the attempt on my life a few weeks back." She nodded. "I've got evidence against the man who planned it—huge big gun at AmVista. The group I revealed as being behind the Brightway scandal, along with my father and that bozo Casados. It's gonna blow my dad right outta the water."

"You're kidding—AmVista?"

"Not at all."

Lia suddenly became very animated. "AmVista is the company that

219

bought up my family's land in Brazil and arranged the takeover of our farm which resulted in all of my family, except for one sister and me, being killed."

"Oh yes, I know about that. My God, I am *so* sorry."

"That's why I'm going after your father. Son-of-a-bitch was supported by AmVista—and they helped him get elected. He's a major part of the corrupt system."

"You got that right."

"And as you can see, we are united by more than just your father." Lia nodded.

"You know, I am really so glad to see you again." Diego smiled. He was beginning to genuinely like her.

"Yeah." Lia nodded and smiled, too. "I remember liking you when we met. Wish it could have been under better circumstances—for both of us."

Diego thought for a moment. "You know, it can't be a coincidence that we're both on this show at the same time. I'll bet anything Dexter is planning to pit us against one another at some point in the show. You know how these guys love the drama."

"Hadn't considered that, but you could be right."

"Hey, I have an idea if he tries that. You willing to play along?"

"Could be. What you got in mind?"

☆

Diego was called to the stage first; Lia was to follow after. After presenting each guest's evidence separately, Dexter called them both to sit with him so he could interview them together.

Diego found the studio lights unmercifully glaring and hot. It was impossible to even see the audience, though they could certainly be heard—stirred up into hoots, cheers, and loud applause.

Dexter, in his sincerest voice said, "Thank you both. Thank you both so very much for your stunning insights. I know a few houses of power whose foundations will be shaking this evening because of your presentations. Nothing like people with a mighty broom to sweep out a dirty house. Am I right, audience?" he said turning to the audience. The crowd cheered even louder. Dexter certainly knew how to work up an audience.

Dexter turned back to Lia and Diego. "Well, well, what an interesting meeting for you two. You must be ready to scratch each other's eyes out. Lia, you with your accusations against the president— and Diego, you the president's son. Now there's a match made in heaven. A boxing match, I mean." He turned to the audience again for the appreciation of their laughter.

Dexter turned back to them. "Diego, what have you got to say about Lia's accusations? Anything you want to say to her in defense of your father?"

Diego was enjoying this. He paused thoughtfully and then said, "Well Dexter, an odd thing happened while we were waiting just now in the green room to come out here."

"Oh really, and what was that?"

Lia took Diego's hand. "Tell him, darling."

"Darling?" Dexter exclaimed with surprise.

"Yes, Dexter. It was a kind of miracle, really. We met and talked and fell in love. I have asked Lia to be my wife, and she has agreed."

Dexter was flummoxed. "But a...I ah... But aren't you gay?" Dexter asked.

"Oh yes, Dexter, I was. But the love of a good woman has changed all that. We mean to marry as soon as possible. And just think—as her husband, I will soon be able to raise my own son—who is also my brother. My father will have two sons and a son-in-law and a mistress and a daughter-in-law all in the same nuclear family. What a treat that will be!"

☆☆☆

Terrance cleared Cayman Islands immigration and customs without a hitch. He paid the taxi driver in cash to drive him to a friend's residence where he was to stay. He couldn't risk having any of his credit cards traced to a hotel, and paying in cash at a hotel would also raise suspicions.

After Diego's revelation on the Dexter Matthews show, there was no way the Houston FBI could put off the apprehension of Terrance Geiger. But what they could do was alert him to the fact that they were on their way. He had already prepared for such a development. He always held an open ticket to the Cayman Islands under the assumed name of Thomas Gunderson and a fake passport in that name as well—just in case. Now was the "in case."

He asked the taxi to wait as he left his suitcases and greeted his hosts, and then he went directly to the Cayman Security Bank where he held his secret accounts. These, too, were under his assumed name, and he quickly dealt with Sir Neville, closed his account, and had a shipment of gold consigned to a clearing house in Thailand. Sir Neville said that Margaret McPherson would send Terrance all the codes to claim the gold to his secure email account once the codes were generated. It would take about three days.

Terrance wasn't quite ready to retire just yet, but he would now have to set up life as an eccentric expat somewhere near an exotic welcoming coast that did not have an extradition treaty with the US His wife and daughters were already provided for and were shielded from any consequences of his illicit behavior. But he didn't blame anyone else for his misfortunes. He knew full well what he was getting into when he hatched his various nefarious schemes. But he had planned well and was now about to embark on his new adventures as Thomas Gunderson—he was tickled by the convenience of the pseudonym; using the same initials as his own, he wouldn't have to change the monograms on his luggage or custom-made shirts.

Terrance hadn't gone as undetected as he thought. The moment he came out of the bank, he was observed by a man waiting in a car across the street. Terrance hailed a taxi and headed back to his friend's house where he would stay for one night and depart for Asia the next morning.

"He's gone into the residence." The man watching in the car told his colleague in the Franklin Society by phone. "My guess is that he won't be coming out again until he is ready to depart Cayman tomorrow morning."

"What do you suggest?" the voice on the phone asked.

"He'll call for a taxi when he's ready to depart for the airport. We know which flight he's scheduled on. Our friends in the police force have access to his calls, and I have acquired a taxi and will be the one to pick him up."

"Excellent. Proceed as planned."

The next morning, the Franklin Society man was just around the corner in a taxi ready to pick up Terrance when he called for his ride. Terrance would have to leave in the next fifteen minutes if he was going to make his flight. The man watched closely and awaited word from the police when Thomas requested a taxi.

The man wasn't prepared to see a car come from the residence when it did. As the car passed, the man could see Terrance inside. *Shit!* Terrance wasn't taking a taxi; he was being driven to the airport by his friend. The man had to scramble. There was nothing to do now except follow the car.

He pulled out his phone and dialed as he drove. "He didn't call for a taxi. I'm following him to the airport now. We have to abort our plan. Do you have a Plan B?"

"Is our plane ready?"

"Yes, sir, ready and standing by."

"We've got to get him on that plane. I'll call our backup team at the airport. You keep on Geiger's tail, and someone will contact you as soon as you get to the airport. Good luck."

He pulled in at the airport just as Terrance got out of his host's car. Terrance checked his bags curbside and went to the ticket line. The Franklin man abandoned the taxi at the curb and followed Terrance inside.

He had to move quickly. He didn't have a ticket, and he couldn't t go through the immigration and the security checkpoints without one. The backup team would need to contact him quickly; Terrance, a first class ticket holder, was already being processed and would soon be heading toward security.

Terrance finished at the ticket counter in just a couple of minutes. The Franklin man was beginning to panic. He frantically searched for his backup team, but before he could find them, Terrance changed course and headed for the men's room. He went inside.

The Franklin man searched the surrounding terminal for his colleagues. He didn't know if he should go into the men's room or wait outside. He decided to wait, as Terrance would soon be coming back out.

Two men came up to the now panicked Franklin man. "Sorry, took us a while to find you. Where's Geiger?"

"Men's room."

"How long has he been in there?" one of the two new men asked.

"About five minutes."

"Shit. Come on. There's a second exit."

The three Franklin men rushed into the men's room. Terrance was gone. They dashed out the second exit, and then they spotted him: Terrance was headed toward security.

His first tail rushed to the courtesy phone on the nearest wall and grabbed it quickly. He spoke to a representative and sighed in relief as he heard the loudspeaker announcement a moment later.

"Paging Thomas Gunderson. Paging Mr. Thomas Gunderson. Please pick up the nearest courtesy telephone. Thomas Gunderson, please pick up the nearest courtesy phone."

The three men saw Terrance pause. He then turned and walked toward the nearest phone.

"Now!"

The three raced toward Terrance as he picked up the phone. "Hello, this is Thomas Gunderson."

He was too distracted by the call to see the men advance on him. Two of the men provided body shields as the third man administered a shot in Terrance's neck, knocking him unconscious almost immediately with little struggle.

"Time for your beauty nap, Mr. Geiger," the man with the needle whispered in Terrance's ear as he collapsed in the other men's arms. A service door was nearby, and the men slung Geiger's arms around their shoulders, dragging Terrance, like a man overfortified with booze for his flight, to and through the service door with little notice from other passengers rushing to their flights.

A private plane was waiting to whisk Mr. Geiger back to Houston and into the arms of the FBI, but the men had to get Terrance onto the plane without going through immigration.

Ten minutes later the men were wheeling a coffin, previously delivered to them from the Society's modest-sized private jet, back toward the plane. A customs official came over as they were just about to load the coffin into the cabin.

"Gentlemen, may I see the papers for the body, please?"

"Certainly." One of them handed the papers to the official.

He examined the paperwork. "Hum. I need to see inside."

"Oh sir, I don't think you want to do that."

"Oh really?" The official stood taller and stiffened. "And why not?"

"Industrial accident. Very messy."

"Open it," he instructed again.

"Are you sure? It's really gross."

"Open." The agent was becoming impatient.

"Okay. It's your call." Two of the men opened the top of the coffin. Inside was a body, horribly mangled and already decomposing. The stench was horrific.

"Oh my God," the agent stepped back. "Close it up immediately." He signed the papers and rushed back to the terminal.

The Franklin taxi man was the only one of the three men to accompany the coffin on the trip. The plane soon took off and headed toward Houston. The man enjoyed a glass of a good burgundy served by a charming flight attendant. He checked his watch, and when it was time for the sedative to wear off, he went to the coffin which had been placed at the back of the lounge area and opened a panel at the bottom where Terrance was hidden. Terrance was still groggy from the sedative but functional. The Franklin man escorted Terrance out of his hiding place, safe in the knowledge that he was secured with handcuffs and leg restraints. The Franklin man offered him a drink, which Terrance readily accepted.

"And where exactly are we headed?" Terrance finally asked.

"Back home. And into the welcoming embrace of the FBI. You have been majorly punked."

"And who are you?"

"Citizens who care about correcting the disastrous course in which our country is headed."

"Oh great, a bunch of radicals."

"Not at all. Centrists who believe that politics must be purged of corporate conquest and corruption. Is that too radical?"

Terrance just shook his head. He leaned his head back in the seat, took a sip of the wine, and closed his eyes. Finally, he opened his eyes and spoke again, "How much would it take to drop me off in Mexico?"

☆☆☆

The stealth helicopters sped low across the waters from the American carrier, the Alexander Hamilton, headed toward the Venezuelan military bases where the North Korean nuclear missiles were positioned to strike the southern US Elite Special Forces teams were prepped and ready to strike. Their specific instructions were to disable the warheads and bring them back if at all possible.

The president's security team was in place in the Situation Room, watching the action unfold live on the giant media screens. The Special Forces teams were equipped with cameras in their helmets that transmitted the action in real time. There was the deathly stillness of anticipation as the security team waited for the special forces to land and begin their mission.

There were three destinations. The three copters split up as they neared the Venezuelan coast. It was timed so that the three teams would land simultaneously. That would maximize the element of surprise— with no opportunity for one base to alert the others of the attack.

The teams were almost at their destinations. The stealth helicopters set down quietly near the perimeters of the three bases containing the poised nuclear missiles. The three teams swiftly disembarked from the aircraft and then expertly breeched the outer perimeter fences and headed toward the more imposing inner barriers.

The president's emergency telephone rang. Defense answered. "Sir, it's Casados."

Ed grabbed the phone. "Yes?"

Cascades clicked his tongue. "Mr. President, naughty, naughty, naughty. Did you really think we wouldn't be watching? Or that we would be unprepared?"

"General..."

"I did warn you," Casados said ominously, "and now you will reap the consequences. Boom, boom, boom." Casados hung up.

The Situation Room screens lit up. Search lights flooded the areas where the special forces were trying to breech the military bases. Massive firepower erupted, forcing the teams to retreat or risk immediate annihilation. The teams did their best to evade the Venezuelan troops, but they were vastly outnumbered. The teams returned to the helicopters, but they too were under fire. Direct hits destroyed two of the aircraft. The third managed to take off, but a surface-to-air missile struck, and it plummeted into the sea.

Ed watched it all play out without a word. What was there to say?

The Venezuelans soon rounded up the remaining US soldiers but not without a fierce battle. Soon after, all transmissions from the special forces ceased.

There was deathly silence in the Situation Room.

"Mr. President, Venezuela has just launched their nuclear missiles."

"Everyone in the West Wing to the bunkers!" the president shouted, and a loud emergency alarm blared to warn the West Wing staff to seek immediate shelter.

Elena had resisted all of Ed's entreaties to delay the divorce, at least until after the midterm.

"Ha!" she emphasized. "Double fat chance. Ha!"

She had gathered together all of her gowns, her good shoes, and her jewelry and was packing to go. She paused. Where would she go? Certainly not to Mama's in Alabama. Back to Chicago? No, too many memories. Maybe California. She had always fancied herself in a seaside villa—Malibu perhaps. And just how was she going to pay for that? She had no money of her own. And the divorce and distribution of any settlement could take a good long while. And then there was the pre-nup. Maybe there wouldn't be anything. Oh my. She sat on the edge of the bed.

What to do? She frowned her baby-doll pout. Then she got it. Oh yes. The tabloids, online blogs, newspapers, and TV would all pay handsomely for her lurid story of sex, betrayal, and abandonment.

But how to go about that? She didn't know any talent agents or how to contact them. She thought some more, and then a big smile graced her face. The intern in the West Wing. He was educated. He mixed with the powers that be. He had said that if she ever needed anything... She bet he would know exactly who to contact.

She smoothed out her dress, after standing up from the bed, and went out to the hallway in the private residence and headed directly for the cutie's desk. As she approached the West Wing, she could hear some sort of shrill alarm. She was surprised to find the halls so quiet on a weekday. She passed through to the West Wing and stopped. All the lights were on, but no one was about. The alarm continued sounding. Oh, there must be a fire drill, she surmised. That was probably it. *Bother*.

She peeked into a number of offices, but all were empty. She pouted again and headed back to finish her packing. She would have to come back after the drill was over.

☆

The first missile to reach the United States was headed toward Atlanta. It whistled and hummed as it headed for its target—Centennial Olympic Park. The missile landed in a hog field thirty miles east of Atlanta. Death toll—1 sow, 3 piglets and a slightly damaged hay port.

The second missile headed for DC, splashed into the Potomac, and disappeared immediately into the depths of the river without a trace. Death toll—none. A fisherman on the Arlington Memorial Bridge thought he might have seen a jumper and called police from his cell phone. An investigation was launched, but no body was found.

The third missile—destination New Orleans—suddenly changed course and headed back toward Venezuela. That sure had the Venezuelan brass going for a moment. But it landed in a swamp and was immediately attacked by a crocodile, thinking it was a cow.

General Casados stood at his military monitors. There were no explosions. He turned slightly green. "Those fuckin' Koreans sent us a shipload of duds."

☆☆☆

"Mr. Geiger, there is a slight problem," Terrance's attorney, Milton Greenberg, said candidly as he sat facing Terrance sitting on his prison cell bed.

"Oh? And what might that be?" Terrance asked, feeling confident that he could fix almost anything.

Milton was a stern, pasty-faced law partner, who'd probably seen an hour and a half of direct sunlight in his entire life. "We need a substantial retainer, and you have been unable to provide us with that so far."

Terrance laughed. "Mr. Greenberg, you know I'm good for whatever you need. However, my funds are in transit from the Caymans to Thailand. It's just a matter of a few days before I will have access to those funds. You see, I was not planning on coming back to Texas."

"I understand. However, we require immediate ready cash if you wish us to proceed with your defense."

"Well, there's my house. I'll take out a quick second on that for a short time."

"You seem to forget, Mr. Geiger, you turned the house over to your wife and daughters before you left."

"Well, that's not a problem. Just give Dorothy a call, and tell her what you need. She'll take care of it."

"We did that, and she wanted us to relay you a message."

"Yes?"

"She said, and I quote—tell the fuckin' son-of-a bitch he can go straight to hell and to please hurry—or words to that effect."

Terrance was silent for a moment as he assimilated that. "I'm sure she was just kidding."

"I assure you, sir, she was not."

"I'll tell you what..." Terrance scribbled out an email address and a password. "This is where the bank is sending me the codes to claim my gold in Thailand. You take this, and go ahead and take possession of the gold, and transfer whatever you need into cash as my retainer. Oh, and you will also need my thumbprint as final verification. You can get that from the FBI. Milton, I really can't stay here much longer. What about bail?"

Milton was skeptical, but he took the email address. "I will confer with my partners about this. You might need to sign some papers before we can do this."

"Of course. Anything."

"And as for bail, well, you might remember the judge considers you too great a flight risk. So, no bail for now."

"Then please hurry. This place is driving me crazy."

☆☆☆

Diego was having tea in his mother's conservatory. She rested in the shade under a tall Fatsia japonica, fanning herself with one of its plucked leaves.

"My darling, it seems I am to have grandchildren after all," Milly reported, with just a twinge of irony.

Diego chuckled and was ready for her. "Why, is Carmella pregnant?" he exclaimed with mock shock.

"No, my dear. I saw Dexter's show. Quite impressive, your little presentation about that gentleman in Houston. Did they catch the scoundrel?"

"I believe they did, but not before he fled the country. However, some resourceful chaps brought him back. Very comforting."

She fussed with her silk wrap. "Now then, what about this proposed marriage business with Lia? You can't be serious, surely."

"Of course not—we did it to ruffle Dexter's feathers. He was being such a pill."

"I am *so* glad. You can't imagine the fright it gave me to think that you might have suddenly joined the ranks of the conventional."

"Oh, Mother—ye of little faith."

She gave a great sigh. "Well, I received numerous calls of congratulations—which annoyed me to no end. I just had to check and make sure you were still my darling, unsullied Diego."

"Yes, Mother. Nothing to fret about. Your darling baby is still a faggot."

"Oh. I am so relieved." She poured Diego another cup of tea.

☆☆☆

"Will I have to wear a veil or a burqa?" Hortencia asked Benevito.

"How should I know?" he snapped, in a surly mood. "Are the kids packed?"

"I'm working on it." She rushed back to the kids' room.

Only yesterday Casados was still General Casados. How quickly things can change. Now he was packing up his family to live in exile in Iran. The other military brass had not taken too kindly to Casados's failed missile attempt and the now aborted military excursions into Guyana and Brazil—not to mention the scuttling of three-quarters of the Venezuelan Navy. As soon as the Americans saw that the bombs were duds, their Air Force pummeled the Venezuelan forces until they retreated back to home base from both Guyana *and* Brazil.

And the allies who had defense treaties with Venezuela soon found half-a-dozen loopholes to avoid having to commit any resources to Venezuela's defense once it became clear that Venezuela did *not* have any working nuclear capacity and was retreating with its tail between its legs in the face of fierce US firepower. No one wants to back a loser.

Actually, the general was lucky to still be alive. The coup that followed relieved the general and his wife of their positions, and the new rulers demanded that Casados and his family leave the country to live in perpetual exile. The only country that would accept them, however, was Iran. The general was already growing out his beard. But it was a whole lot better than having your head displayed in public on a post.

"Oh *querido...*" Mrs. Colonel exclaimed. She was the wife of the newest and latest Honorable Leader for Life, Colonel Javier Quintana—now General, and head of the coup that deposed Casados. "We absolutely must change that color in the dining room. What were they thinking?" She was unaware that the former occupants of the presidential palace were still there. But it was doubtful she would have cared even if she had known. They were previewing the palace for their own immediate occupation.

Hortencia heard this, of course, but kept her thoughts and feelings to herself. As Benevito had reminded her repeatedly, they were fortunate to be walking away with their lives, if not their possessions. But it was not all *that* dire, as the good General had privately squirreled away a couple of billion dollars in a Belize tax haven—thanks to the good citizens and the oil of Venezuela, of course.

Carlito was not as astute as his mother when it came to the subtleties of disposed dictator protocol, and he rushed toward the bedroom door to beat back the invaders. Hortencia was quicker, however, and snatched the child before he could cause his family to face a firing squad.

Mrs. Colonel continued to survey her new domain and could be heard exclaiming to her husband, "We need to expand the kitchen. This just won't do." She then migrated out the kitchen door to the pool and garden area. "Oh my, that bougainvillea is so messy. Certainly we can cut that back. No, on second thought, let's just yank it out. I think a Venus de Milo would look very tasteful there, don't you? You know, I was thinking that perhaps we might take a shopping trip to New York City. Caracas just doesn't have the same quality of shops."

Hortencia saw the new owners' exploration of the outside patio as the perfect opportunity for the family to flee. She corralled Carlito and their daughter, grabbed Benevito, and hefting as many bags as she could carry, lumbered to the car that was to whisk them to the airport and their new life in exile.

☆☆☆

There were just a little less than two months to go before the birth of her baby boy. Lia sat in a comfortable chair in the waiting room of the *OWN* network with her hands on her burgeoning belly, feeling the child moving. Was he going to be an athlete? He sure could be, the way he liked to move about in there.

Lia's passion and outrage over her family's demise was subsiding. Little Cala was being well cared for by her aunt in Brazil, and she seemed to be happy in her new school. And no doubt Lia's pregnancy was mellowing her as well. She was no longer obsessed with revenge, and her terrorist inclinations had all but disappeared. But she was restless and didn't feel like going back to the Institute just now. With a new child on the way, what would her life be like in the months and years ahead? Where did she want to set her sights?

She had been surprised by how much reaction there had been to her appearance on the Dexter Matthews show. She was seen as a heroine to many young women, and her Facebook page was swamped with "friend" requests. And then she had received a call from Oprah Winfrey's *OWN* network. A producer there was developing a new talk show about issues concerning young women and wanted to interview Lia for a position on the show in New York City.

This was the morning of that interview. Lia was in the comfortable chair, contemplating the new child about to emerge and how changed her life was now from just a few short months ago. Fondly, Cran crossed her mind for a brief moment, but she had dismissed him so out of hand, she felt he must certainly resent her. She would need to move on and not look back.

"Ms. Abadi will see you now," the receptionist announced. Lia began to pry her pregnant body from the low chair as Ms. Abadi appeared at the door leading to the offices.

"Lia, what a pleasure! Can I get you something to drink?"

Lia laughed. "No, but I do need to pee like crazy—the pregnancy."

"Down the hall to the left. My office is right over there. See you in a minute."

After relieving herself, Lia walked back to the office. When she stepped inside, she was ushered to a sofa.

"I'm Tanya." Ms. Abadi offered her hand. Lia shook it. "Now then, let's discuss your future here at *OWN* network."

☆☆☆

"So where are we? Did you get your retainer?" Terrance asked, as he rose eagerly from his sagging bed, anticipating a joyous outcome to his request.

Milton hesitated.

"What? Now what?" Terrance pushed.

Milton couldn't look Terrance in the eyes. "I'm afraid there's been a slight glitch."

"No. No. Don't tell me that."

"Yes, well, it seems your email account has been hacked."

"You're killing me..." Terrance collapsed back onto the bed.

"When our agents went to retrieve the gold at the clearing house they were told that someone had already come forward with all the required documentation, and the gold had been transferred out of the country at their request."

Terrance was too stunned to even respond.

"It appears that someone hacked your email account and downloaded all the codes before we got there."

"But it also required my thumb print as final verification. How could that not have stopped the transaction?" He got up and began to pace the cell, combing nervously through his hair with his hands.

"Don't ask me how, but whoever did this had your thumb print too."

Terrance was angry now, looking for someone to blame—other than himself. "This is totally unacceptable. Your office must have screwed this up in some terrible way. How do I know you don't already have all the gold for yourself?"

Milton stood up from his chair. "No, that accusation is what is unacceptable. I believe my visit is done here, Mr. Geiger. I will be saying good-bye now." Milton turned to leave.

"No, wait, wait, wait. I'm sorry. I didn't mean that. It's just that I'm so agitated. I'm sure you can understand that."

"Mr. Geiger, there is nothing more we can do for you. I'm sorry. If you are somehow able to raise the required funds, then we can speak again. However, I can recommend a fairly decent public defender. He has about a thirty percent success rate—but hey, that's something. Good day."

Oh No You Don't

Day 392 of the president's term

Of the three Brightway participants, two had suffered rather fatal setbacks and—some might add—their appropriate comeuppance and just rewards. The third, Ed Perez, had certainly suffered some severe hardships, but he was still holding his own and continued to fight for his political life.

The US triumph in routing the advancing Venezuelan armies in Guyana and Brazil and sending them scurrying back home played well with the American public. But Ed's approval ratings rose only modestly as the American public still remembered the stink over the Brightway scandal with the inflated gas prices and the unexpected defeat of the US Special Forces—with American military prisoners being paraded down the streets of Caracas.

The fact that nuclear missiles had been fired at the US, despite being duds, was never widely known. Only the top military brass and a few in Congress had been appraised of that situation. However, a pig farmer in Georgia insisted that he had been attacked by a North Korean missile. Even the tabloid *National Enquirer* wouldn't touch that despite the vivid photographs. It was so obviously a hoax.

Meanwhile, Congress was excited with its *new* impeachment hearings, examining in endless and sordid detail the newly developing scandal around the president's impregnation of that Brazilian girl who had so bravely saved his daughter from the fiery crash. Of course, the president had denied it, but the DNA evidence was incontrovertible. And who could doubt such a sweet-faced heroine?

"We need a new issue. Something positive. Something big. Something to distract the public from these endless goddamned

235

impeachment hearings. What have we got?" Ed asked his senior advisors in the White House Cabinet room. The advisors looked at one another, desperately searching for an issue. "Come on, somebody must have something," Ed was urging.

Transportation responded. "Sir, how about a massive road and bridge improvement program? Infrastructure is crumbling around the country. It would create jobs and goodwill in cities across the land."

Ed considered. "Too expensive. Congress would never give us the funding. Next."

"How about we invigorate the space program? We could do a partnership with the travel industry and develop some vacation retreat resorts on Mars. Would be a very hot ticket," Interior blithely encouraged.

Ed just scowled. "Come on guys, I need something real here."

Energy raised his hand.

"David, whatcha got for us?"

"Mr. President, I recently had an, as yet unconfirmed, report that there has been a massive uranium deposit discovered out west."

"That's good. I like that. We could build a whole new energy initiative around that. American's answer to Mideast oil. We could spur a new drive to become energy self-sufficient with nuclear power. So where is this uranium find? Where?"

"In Arizona."

"Okay, still good. They are a mining-friendly state."

"Yes, but there might be one small problem."

"And that is?"

"It's at the bottom of the Grand Canyon, and it runs about three miles long on both sides of the most scenic stretch."

"Okay, and that's a problem because...?"

"Well sir, it would probably destroy the Grand Canyon, pollute all the waters of the Colorado River, disrupt water supplies in three or four states, and desecrate an American icon."

Ed paused but a brief moment. "Now then, how can we spin that?" Ed asked, looking to his advisors around the room.

☆☆☆

Two things were happening simultaneously at GreenPAC. Chester was checking the organization's bank balance online, and Diego was checking his email. Both men let out whoops of surprise and dismay. Chester discovered that there had been a ten million dollar deposit in their account overnight that could not be explained. And Diego had received an email from Grasshut once again. It read:

Surprise! Surprise! Bet you didn't think you'd hear from me again. However, now that a certain mutual friend of ours is behind bars, it frees me up to contact you again without the fear that I might be knifed in my sleep.

To start, if you check GreenPAC's bank account this morning, you will find a nice little donation—indirectly courtesy of Mr. Terrance Geiger himself, although he may not know that quite yet. But really it is from me as a donation on your website. (And I won't be needing the tax write-off as on paper I have absolutely no money at all. I'm dead, remember. Isn't that nice?)

And now a nice little tale as to how this all came about. A certain Big Bad Wolf huffed and puffed, and before he knew it, he blew his own house down. He fled the country and transferred all his wealth in gold to Thailand where he planned to claim the loot all for himself. However, he forgot to count on a very formidable adversary—me.

With my many skills and abilities, I was able to hack his email account, download the codes needed to claim the gold, and I had a latex thumb print of the dude, from the days when I still worked with him—always and ever resourceful and thinking ahead, if I do say so myself. The thumb print was the last identifying element needed to claim the gold. I simply attached his latex thumb print to my own thumb and voilà—I walked away with twenty million—you see, you got half. (I mean, how much does one need to maintain a grass hut?)

Now, I wish you two boys the very best. And please, use the money wisely and well.

Your ardent admirer.

This email Diego was able to print out. He rushed to Chester's office and placed it in front of Chester who was sitting in shock.

"You might want to take a look at this," Diego said.

Chester read the email. "So *that's* where it came from."

Diego could hardly bring himself to speak it, but he said, "We can't accept this, of course. It's stolen money."

"But how can we give it back? We don't even know where she is. And we certainly aren't going to give it back to Geiger."

"Maybe we could trace it back to the bank that sent it."

Chester considered the situation for a moment. "Diego, I absolutely love and admire your sterling ethics, but if we were to scrutinize every single donation and examine where that money came from, we would probably not be able to accept a single penny. You know as well as I do that most big money comes from the exploitation of something or someone, somewhere. If the wealthy feel guilty and want to assuage their conscience by donating their blood money to a worthy cause, who are we to judge? If we did that, we would be broke and unable to do any good at all. And besides, Geiger did donate five hundred dollars to us once before. Think of this ten million as an add-on to that donation—an expression of his sincere interest in our cause."

Diego had to smile, but he also nodded, neither agreeing nor disagreeing. "I guess it's not for me to say, in any case. After all, you are the head of GreenPAC, and I'm just a worker here."

"But you are also my friend, and I do value your input."

"Thanks."

"Now, let me call your attention to this, if you haven't seen it already." Chester passed Diego a press release from the White House. It outlined the president's new energy initiative for extracting massive amounts of uranium from the Grand Canyon to be used in an accelerated program of nuclear reactor construction. "The president's new solution to solve the energy crisis," Chester continued. "I think we are going to have a major campaign ahead of us, and I need you to be the face of the opposition."

Diego considered that a moment, and had a thought. "But not me alone. I have an idea I want to explore, and I'll get right back to you."

✩✩✩

Dominic was already in physical therapy. He was walking, but he still had difficulty with the arm where the bullet hit his shoulder.

"Ouch!" he exclaimed as his therapist made him rotate his arm and stretch it to increase its range.

"You're good for a break now," the therapist allowed after Dominic had worked his shoulder for a good half hour.

Dominic limped over to where Diego was sitting and waiting for him.

"Looks painful," Diego said.

Dominic collapsed in the chair next to Diego. "You have no idea." He leaned back and put a damp towel over his forehead and eyes.

"I would ask how you're getting on, but I think I know."

"It's going to be a while, I'm afraid."

Diego considered whether he really wanted to do this or not, but decided he did. "I hate to bother you with this just now, but I really need to contact Richard Buller. Do you think you could help me do that?"

"Actually, Richard was asking me how he could reach you." Dominic removed the damp towel. "Come on, the laptop's in my room. We can contact him now, if you like."

"Great."

They headed for Dominic's hospital room.

"Don't you need a crutch or a cane?" Diego asked Dominic as he limped his way to the room, his hand on Diego's shoulder for support.

"I need to work through this. The injury to the leg was a lot less severe than the shoulder. That's what really hurts the most and is gonna take the longest to heal."

They reached the room and Dominic limped forward to open his laptop. He turned it on and logged in to chat with Richard.

"I'm so glad to see you again, Diego," Richard greeted from the screen.

Diego sat next to Dominic, leaning in, so he could be seen on camera. "And you, sir."

"Diego, let me get right to the point. We are very concerned with what we see happening in the White House: this scandal with the mistress; the divorce; the debacle with Brightway; the business with Venezuela; and now your father proposing this massive energy program causing the destruction of the Grand Canyon; and his unrelenting effort to construct seemingly unlimited nuclear facilities, completely disregarding the lessons learned from the Japanese tsunami."

Diego had to laugh. "Yes, sir, I am aware of all these things."

"It is most important now that we have a credible opponent in this Grand Canyon matter. If this moves forward, it will so polarize our nation that we will become functionally incapacitated as a country."

"And sir, that is why I wanted to speak to you as well."

Richard seemed eager to hear his response. "Go ahead."

"GreenPAC is going to take this issue on. We have received a large donation and are preparing to launch our defense of the Canyon. They want me to be the face of the campaign, and I have agreed to do that. But I feel we need more. I feel very strongly that we also need a powerful and persuasive woman to join us in this effort."

"A woman. Interesting," Dominic commented, turning to Diego.

Diego asked Richard, "Do you know of anyone who could help us? I know of several women in the environmental movement, but none are quite right for this project. Either they are too extreme for the general public, or they are not strong enough as public figures."

Richard considered this request for a moment. "I may have just the person for you. Let me confer with her, and I will have her contact you directly if she is interested and available."

☆☆☆

Lia considered for a long while before she picked up the phone.

"Cran, it's Lia."

"Well, well..." he answered rather snidely.

"I'm sorry."

"For what?" His tone was brusque.

"For the way I treated you. I was in a terrible state."

Cran appeared to ease up a little. "Yes, I realized that. And that is why I offered to help you."

Lia was nearing the conclusion of her pregnancy. She didn't want to have her baby completely alone. It was, of course, impossible to expect anything from Ed, not that she would want anything from him anyway. Her family—or what was left of it—was still in Brazil. And Cran had been out of her life for so long, would he be open to re-engaging with her?

Lia answered. "I wasn't able to accept your help at the time. I am truly sorry."

Cran hesitated and then said, "You've been in the news a lot lately."

"Yes, I have." She chuckled briefly.

"Fucking the fuckin' president?" he commented with an edge. "Wait, sorry. That was inappropriate."

"Can we meet? There's a lot to explain...and Cran, I miss you."

There was a long pause. "I guess so."

Lia started to cry. "Thank you. You're not seeing anyone?"

"No," he said after a beat. "How about at our old coffee shop? In half an hour?"

"Yes. See you there." She hung up, and as she walked over to her apartment window to stare out at the gusty clouds, she made another call. "Carmella?"

"Hello. Is that Lia?"

"Yes, sweetie. Sorry I haven't been in touch. There has been a lot going on."

Carmella laughed. "Ya think?"

That set Lia to laughing too. "I miss you."

"Yeah, me too."

"You back at the university? Will you be able to graduate with your class like you wanted?"

"Yep. Gonna have good grades too. And I've been accepted into the institute's graduate program. Was thinking to take a year off to travel, but my dad won't let me do that—sitting president's daughter and all that— even though he *promised* I could after he became president."

Lia paused. "I'm sorry."

"What for?"

"Where do I start?" She laughed. "How 'bout having a baby with your dad, for a start."

"Oh yeah, that..."

"And then, I was not too nice to you at the end there. I guess you can imagine why."

"Well, I was not completely blameless, either," Carmella admitted.

"Oh, and how is that?"

"Well, I sort of had a crush on you, and I couldn't bring myself to say it."

Lia was truly surprised. "Really? Guess I missed that."

"You're telling me... But I'm over that now. Not to worry."

"Thanks for letting me know. Very flattering." But Lia wanted to get right to the point of her call. "But the reason I called is because I need a girlfriend...well, not *that* kind of a girlfriend."

Carmella laughed. "I know. And besides, I've got one of my own now. We met at a lesbian mixer at the university. Great Jewish girl from Brooklyn."

"That should make your dad really happy." They had a good laugh at that. "No, what I wanted to ask you was if you would be my coach when I give birth. The kid will be your brother, after all."

Carmella gasped. "Oh my gosh. I would love to. That would be so cool. Thanks for thinking of me. How soon?"

"Days. Any day now."

"Well, do we need to practice or something?"

"Probably a good idea. Got any time tomorrow morning?"

"Sure."

"My place at ten?"

"See you then."

☆☆☆

The House of Representatives passed the articles of impeachment against Edward Perez. It was mostly along party lines, but a number of socially conservative Republicans joined the Democrats to protest the president's disgraceful behavior with that Brazilian girl. Of all the issues that came up in the committee, the only one that was valid for impeachment was that the president had exceeded the constitutional bounds of the powers of his office by going to war against Venezuela without the authorization of Congress, though a few of the members in the know pointed out privately that Venezuela had sent three missiles against us, and an attack was therefore justified. A few more pointed out that the two missiles that actually did strike us were totally ineffective, and in fact, the third missile had turned around and struck Venezuela.

But everyone knew that the *real* motive behind the impeachment was the president's outrageous behavior in the Brightway scandal, the embarrassment of having a child out of wedlock as a sitting president, and the disgrace of a divorce.

Now the case would go to trial in the Senate. Ed would have to appear in his own defense, and his bevy of attorneys were worried as Ed did not have the best control of his temper in a challenging situation and was prone to unruly verbal behavior.

"Son of a fucking, Christ-pounding, mother-rutting son of a fucking bitch," Ed commented upon learning of the Senate trial. "What are we going to do here?" he asked his senior attorney.

"I would suggest some coaching. And you might want to consider approaching the trial in a more—how shall I put this—with a more subdued demeanor."

"Oh, go fuck yourself."

☆☆☆

After the divorce—which did happen, even against the president's wishes—Elena moved out of the White House. She took an apartment in New York City with the money she made from spilling her guts to a number of trashy tabloids—both print and TV. She was heady from the attention paid to her by the press, and feeling that she could do almost anything, she embarked upon an acting career.

She appeared as "the mountain" in an experimental off-off-Broadway production of "The Magic Mountain." It ran for three performances to a total audience of twelve. It only lasted that long because Elena put some of her own money into the production, extending the run in order to let it "find its natural audience." They must have lived elsewhere because they never appeared. That used up a considerable amount of Elena's reserves, and she began to search for additional income.

She thought she might pen her memoirs, but after shopping a number of agents and publishers, discovered that because of the sensational tabloid exposure there was nothing shocking left to reveal, and they all thanked her and suggested she try television. That appealed to her greatly, and she secured an agent from an ad in the trades. His office was located in a walk-up office building on Tenth Avenue, and he demanded a retainer before he would even pick up the phone. That required the last of her tabloid money. And after hearing nothing from him for two weeks and suffering endless unreturned phone calls, she went back to the office to find it vacated with no forwarding address.

In desperation, she called her brother and pleaded for him to send enough cash for her to get back to Alabama, which he reluctantly sent. And her last day in New York City was spent at the bus terminal, bags in hand, crying and wondering if Burt of Burt's Diner and Tiki Lounge would take her back as a cocktail waitress.

When she got back to Selma, Burt was happy to see her again and renamed the Tiki Lounge the First Lady Lounge and set her up as hostess. To celebrate the occasion, Burt hired the Ben Livingston Combo for entertainment on the weekends. If especially urged, and if she was drunk enough, she might be persuaded to sing a few choruses of "The Lady is a Tramp" late on a Saturday night.

☆☆☆

Diego was meeting Libby Darra at the Knoxville, Tennessee airport. He had flown in from Chicago just an hour before. Libby had telephoned him two days earlier to say she was interested in supporting GreenPAC's campaign against the Grand Canyon mining project. He was looking forward to meeting Libby—or to give her her full title, Senator Libby Darra, Independent from Rhode Island. As an independent, she was fiercely centrist. She sometimes voted with the Republicans and sometimes with the Democrats. She was a tireless advocate for compromise and spent endless hours trying to negotiate agreements between the Republicans and the Democrats—something almost unheard of in today's Congress.

Diego was waiting for her at a table in the cocktail lounge, overlooking the runways. He was nursing a Perrier as he tapped away at his laptop, working on a press release to be handed out at the upcoming GreenPAC press conference where they would launch their initiative to ban mining in the Grand Canyon.

"Mr. Diego Perez, I recognize you."

Diego looked up. Senator Darra beamed with a radiant smile. She was a large, heavy-set lady—a real Ganesha—but she slid into her seat with the grace of a gazelle. "I've seen your picture with your family at the White House. You have a charming sister too, I believe." She extended her hand. "Hi, I'm Libby."

"Senator, it's a real pleasure," Diego replied, shaking her hand.

"No, no...just Libby." She leaned forward, both arms crossed on the table. "It's really nice to meet you, too. I'm so sorry you have had to come all this way. But I just couldn't get up to Chicago this week."

"Don't mind at all. I was pleased to get your call."

"The Environment and Public Works Committee is taking a look at the TVA, and I was here to check them out." She gave a big belly laugh. "There is lots of talk these days about dismantling dams—taking the corsets off the rivers and letting them flow free. Sounds kinda nice to me, don't it?"

Diego was really liking this lady—so unassuming and down to earth. He believed they might work really well together. "Yes. I like the way you think. You will lend a lot of prestige to GreenPAC and our cause. I hope you've had time to read what I sent you. My father is going way overboard on this mining business. And with his plan to ramp up nuclear energy, there are just too many unconsidered consequences."

Libby reached over and pinched Diego's cheek. "You are just s-o-o cute and s-o-o earnest." He was surprised and withdrew. Libby laughed again. "Yes, yes, yes. I know. Out to save the world. Right all the wrongs. Reverse the clock, and go back to the good old days."

"Well, I..."

"Let me tell you, the 'good old days' are only the 'good old days' in retrospect and to those who never lived through them. There were a lot of people who suffered and struggled to make things better for themselves and their families. What you might think of as exploitation of the resources now, they might think of as progress."

"But there are so many more of us today. And the strain on the resources and the planet needs to be re-examined."

"Yes, and there I agree with you, young man. But look what we have become. We no longer examine anything dispassionately. We rush to our corners and shout. There is no discourse anymore. No thoughtful examination of the issues. The left and the right are all beholden to their sacred cows. They can't break free of their crusty world views formed decades ago and never thoughtfully reviewed or adjusted."

Diego considered her argument. He nodded. "Yes, I understand where you're coming from. And I look forward to working with you, sharing your passion, and learning from your vision."

"Hey, me too, honey. Look, I gotta run. Back to DC and the bubbling cauldron of government inaction."

Diego stood up and offered his hand. "Will you be able to join us for the Press Conference? We will arrange it around your schedule. It's really important for you to be there for that."

"Wouldn't miss it. Send me a selection of proposed dates, and I'll check my schedule." She gave him her card. "My private number. Will get you past all my screens. Feel free to call me whenever. And that's my email. Keep me in the loop. And if you need anything from me, just holler."

She started to leave but stopped and turned back. "Oh, by the way, not so sure you're right about stopping the nuclear power plants. Energy *is* a really big issue for this country. You might want to take a look to see if you, too, might have a crusty world view. Bye, sweetie."

☆☆☆

"Oh shi-i-i-t!"

"Breathe, Lia, breathe." Carmella huffed rapidly to get Lia breathing again.

"I'm dying."

"No you aren't. Come on now, not much longer."

True to Carmella's word, Lia did not die. Instead she delivered a charming, and quite healthy, baby boy with all his fingers and toes, a nice willy, and a head of curly, black hair that made him look like an orange Muppet until he gained his natural post-birth coloring.

Back in Lia's hospital room after the delivery, Carmella babbled on about how brave Lia had been, how cute the baby looked, and how Carmella and her partner were already talking about having children of their own.

Exhausted, Lia reached over and put her hand on Carmella's arm. "I need to rest, honey. Do you mind?"

"Oh, sorry. Just get a bit excited. Guess I babble too much. Huh?"

"That's okay."

"What are you going to call him?" Carmella couldn't stop herself.

"Tomas, after my father."

"Ah, that's nice." Carmella leaned over and looked closely at the new little face. "He's got your coloring. Looks like a little caramel drop. Do you think Dad will want to see him?"

Lia could see that Carmella was not going to shut up, so she just settled into the conversation. And she had something she wanted to say, so this seemed to be the time to do it. "Honey, sit down a moment. I have something I want to tell you."

Carmella sat close to the bed and leaned in to hear what Lia had to say. In the hospital room, with baby Tomas close by, Lia told Carmella the story about her family's destruction, how Ed had been connected to the group that took her family's land, how she had sought revenge on Ed after she met him through Carmella, how she had seduced the president and collected the evidence to implicate him, how she had compromised the condom, hoping she would become pregnant, and how she had used all of that evidence to embarrass her father, if not destroy his presidency.

"You did all that?" Carmella was shocked, but also in awe. "Wow— *that* took some guts."

"Are you angry with me?" Lia asked.

Carmella considered. "I don't think so. Hell, I would have done the same thing, if I was brave enough. But I don't think I am."

"I hope you still want to be friends."

"Are you kidding...?"

"Knock, knock. I hear there's a new arrival." Cran came into the room with a huge bunch of flowers. He came over and kissed Lia. "Let me see." He leaned over and examined Tomas. "Looks like the real thing. Can he play catch yet? I've already got the mitt."

The ladies laughed. "I think you might have to wait a few more years for that," Lia cautioned. "Do mitts keep?"

"I believe so. Just have to keep them well oiled."

There was another knock at the door and in popped Milly.

"Mother, what are you doing here?" Carmella exclaimed as she bounded up and rushed over to give her a hug.

"Well, I heard my daughter was going to be a champion birthing coach so I just had to come and shower salutations and gifts on the newborn infant." She deposited bags with gifts for the baby beside the bed. "And besides, I was craving a little jaunt to New York."

"Milly..." Lia opened her arms to give and receive hugs.

"Adorable...," Milly commented, after examining the infant. "Just like his father. Oops. Perhaps I shouldn't have said that. Indiscreet. So sorry." She turned to Cran. "And so who are you? The beard?"

"Oh, Mother, do shut up," Carmella said. "You are such a scandal."

But no one seemed to mind.

☆☆☆

At the reception after the GreenPAC news conference, Diego and Libby were in a heated conversation with a conservative Illinois Senator.

"Yeah, we know all your arguments, Senator: Jobs; energy independence; national security; blah, blah, blah. But come on—the Grand Canyon? Really? You want to bulldoze the Grand Canyon?" Libby was having such fun.

"Well, mock me if you must, but *we* shall see who shall prevail in this matter. My committee shall see to that." The Senator turned in a huff and marched off, enlivened with self-righteousness.

Libby snorted. "Oh dear, now I'm going to have to send him a fruit basket. But the poor old dear won't even remember we had this conversation after his third Scotch. Never mind." Libby turned to Diego and pinched his cheek again. (She seemed to have a penchant for cheek pinching.) "Are we having fun yet?"

Diego leaned in and gave Libby a hug. "I'll let you know when this is all over," he said as he released her. "I'm a wreck. I don't think I've slept all week. Burning the midnight oil working on all the charts and graphs for the PowerPoint presentation."

"Well, you did a splendid job, my lad. If I didn't believe in your project before, I certainly would now."

Diego tilted his head. "Are you patronizing me?"

"Oh..." Libby waved her hand in the air. "Well, maybe just a little. Come, I want to introduce you to someone." She grabbed his hand and led him across the room to where an older gentleman was standing with his back to them. Libby put her hand on the gentleman's shoulder. "Richard, have you met..."

The man turned before she could complete her introduction. It was Richard Buller.

"We have, but only online." Richard offered his hand.

"Finally... It's a real pleasure." Diego took Richard's hand.

"That was a splendid presentation you three did. I've not met Chester before. You must introduce us. Libby, you were magnificent as always. You always lend such a grand presence to any occasion."

"Yes, I know. I've been meaning to go on a diet, but with all the receptions and dinners and fund-raising events..."

"That isn't what I meant, and you know it." They both laughed heartily.

"You must let me steal you away for a moment, young man," Richard insisted. "I need a word with you. You'll excuse us, Libby."

"Oh yes, and I have other fields to plow as well. I never let an opportunity go by to wreak havoc with other people's minds."

Richard led Diego to a quiet corner. "I believe Dom has already advised you as to our plans for you. Have you given it any serious thought? It looks as though your father is either going to be tried—and most likely convicted on the impeachment charges—or he will be forced to resign. In either case, we need you to step forward now if we are to build you into a credible candidate for the next election."

Diego thought carefully before he answered. "I really appreciate your interest in me, Richard. I certainly understand your desire to build a centrist coalition. And I would probably join it as a voter, but I don't think I'm your man. I'm just too committed to my own particular causes—and I am probably too far left to be your credible centrist candidate. And being gay, I believe, would be too many strikes against me with the American electorate at this time. And, you understand, I won't go into the closet."

"Yes, I do," Richard responded, but with a trace of disappointment.

"But the most important issue of all for me is that I just don't have the stomach for politics, Richard. I have been critically traumatized by all that has happened to me these past months. And I don't think public life is for me too much longer. I'm too private a person. And though I am willing to put myself out there occasionally for my causes, the thought of the constant glare and demands of a campaign are just too much for me, and when all is said and done, the whole process simply appalls me."

"I appreciate what you say Diego, but you are just *so* perfect for this," Richard pleaded. "Is there nothing that I can do to persuade you otherwise?"

Diego leaned in closer to Richard. "Listen, I think you are missing a great opportunity here."

"Oh really, and what is that?"

"I think you have the ideal candidate right here in this room, and you don't even realize it."

Richard scanned the reception. "Really, who?"

"Why Libby, of course. She's bright; she's funny; she's personable. She's independent. She can raise money, and the nation is ready for a woman president."

Richard turned his gaze toward her. She was surrounded by a large group, laughing and listening to her every word. He studied her thoughtfully. He turned to Diego and nodded and smiled. "You might just be right. Then how about you for vice president?"

Diego laughed. "You just never give up, do you?"

"Never."

Dominic came limping over. "Hey, you two. Am I interrupting?"

"Not at all," Richard replied. "But your boy here just turned us down as a presidential candidate. But he did give me an excellent alternative suggestion."

"I can't wait to hear about that."

"It'll have to wait. I need to talk to the prospective candidate myself first. If you two will excuse me..." Richard wound his way through the crowd toward Libby.

"You look better," Diego said after examining Dominic.

"Much. Thanks. I'll always have a slight limp and diminished rotation in my shoulder and arm, but I'm hanging in there—guess there go my chances as a pitcher in the major leagues."

"Well, you can pitch on my team anytime you like."

Dominic hesitated briefly. "Oh, there's any number of ways I could interpret that."

Diego smiled slyly. "I'm sure there are, and they would all be right."

Chester came up just in time to save Dominic from further embarrassment.

Diego turned to Chester. "Where have you been? The party needs its leader."

"Oh man, the phone has been ringing off the hook. We've been getting calls of support from everywhere since the press conference. Organizations and individuals have been flooding the phone lines from all over the country and even abroad. And donations on the web have been pouring in."

Diego took Chester's shoulder. "That's terrific. You deserve this."

"We all do. We're a great team."

Diego's phone buzzed. He checked the caller ID. "Oh, it's my dad. Better take this. I have been a *very* bad boy, and I'm sure to get a spanking. Excuse me." He walked aside. "Dad. I think I know why you're calling. Let me guess. Does it have something to do with uranium in the Grand Canyon?"

"Are you trying to kill me?" Ed shouted.

"Well, not you personally, but your project—yes."

There was a strained silence. "I'm gonna cut your little faggot ass to pieces."

"Really? And just how is that going to happen? Gonna send in the storm troopers?"

"Don't be a snotty little brat with me, Diego. I'm your father and the president of the United States, remember?"

"I don't want to argue with you, Dad. You know I am only doing what I have to do for the good of the country."

"You can't say that," Ed retorted. "That's my line." Diego laughed—and Ed too. He couldn't help himself. "I know, son. But I'm in some deep shit here. I'm sure you're aware of my situation."

"Of course I am. And, Dad, I'm sorry about your divorce from Elena. Can't have been easy for you—both personally and professionally."

"Little tart..."

"Dad, you can't call her that. That's mom's line."

Ed laughed at that. "How is Milly? She won't speak to me anymore, you know, unless there's an emergency, like with Carmella."

"Milly's great. She dated this TV guy for a while, but she was way too smart for him. Or maybe he was way too dumb for her. Either way, that ended in less than a month."

"Oh, son, I know I called to give you shit. But I'm really hurting here. My only chance to survive this mess is to put this big energy project through. Don't thwart me on this. Hear me?"

"I do understand. But I don't believe you're doing the right thing. And I *am* going to fight you on this. Sorry."

"Then heaven help me." Ed hung up.

Diego felt really bad for his father. Despite everything, he was sorry he couldn't keep his dad from sorrow, but he also knew he couldn't compromise his own beliefs on this matter. There was nothing he could do but stand with GreenPAC and go forward in defense of the Grand Canyon.

Dominic came up to Diego after the call. "You look a little ruffled. Tough call?"

Diego nodded. "There's nothing I can do for him. The two of us are on an irreversible collision course, and there's no way to avoid it. One of us is going to be creamed."

Dominic took Diego's arm. "How about we ditch all of this and go get some dinner? Some nice little quiet place. You need to decompress."

"Sounds good. But not quite yet. I can't leave Chester right now. Do you mind waiting a few minutes more?"

"Not at all. Come find me when you're ready to leave."

Diego wandered over to the crowd around Libby. She was holding court and thriving. Richard caught Diego's eye and gave him a thumbs up. Diego nodded and smiled. Libby saw Diego, broke free of her admirers, and came over to him, pulling him aside.

"Well, well, well... Quite a day for you and yours."

"Thank *you* for *your* presence and help. Chester tells me support is just pouring in."

"I'm glad. I know we still have a major fight ahead of us with the energy groups and corporations supporting the president. But just you wait—the people will be behind you on this. It's amazing, but sometimes the people will surprise you, and once again one gets a glimpse of what democracy is all about. It's always messy, never predictable, and *occasionally* even successful."

"Did Richard have an opportunity to speak with you about his plans for the future?" Diego asked.

"He did indeed."

"And?"

"I said I would consider his outrageous request."

"It's not outrageous to me—very sensible, in fact."

Libby nodded, smiled, and gave him a big hug.

☆☆☆

Atop the north rim of the Grand Canyon, far from the tourist activity, a group of Hopi elders danced. The sun had not yet risen over the horizon. The last stars were fading, and the sliver crescent of the waning moon was winking to the dancers, with their rattles and ankle bells the only sounds breaking the morning silence, except for the cry of a bald eagle, circling, circling—an omen of certain success for the dancers. As the top edge of the sun peeked over the horizon, the rays caught the soft-pink tufts of the Apache plume, and a rabbit burrowed deep in its den to hide from predators in the searing heat of the day to come.

In Washington DC, letters, emails, phone calls, and urgent pleas flooded the congressional mailboxes and those of the White House. There certainly was some support for the uranium mining, but those letters were usually printed out on expensive stationary with extravagantly designed logos and letterheads. But by far the majority of the mail came on postcards, lined school notebook paper, third grade block letters in crayon, and chicken scrawl on pieces of paper carefully cut from brown paper grocery bags.

Someone got the idea to send a single pebble to the White House as a sign of protest against the mining. That person posted her idea on Facebook and Twitter and made a crude cell phone video which she posted on You Tube. All went viral, and before long, hundreds of thousands of pebbles, rocks, and stones started arriving at the White House. The news media picked it up, and the story ran for over a week. By the time the pebble campaign—called "Stone the White House"—was finished, ten dump trucks filled with gravel had to be hauled to a DC construction site.

The energy lobbyists were working it hard on the Hill, but the tide was against them, and the Energy Committees in both the House and Senate tabled legislation designed to extract the uranium in Arizona. President Perez bowed to the overwhelming public pressure and withdrew his "suggestion" for the mining. That left Ed with no credible energy policy other than more drilling for oil, natural gas, and the increased importation of foreign oil. He had never embraced alternative energies, and he had no idea how to even begin to develop such projects.

Diego, Chester, and Libby on the other hand—the symbols of GreenPAC—reaped homage and praise for spearheading the campaign to stop the mining. Diego appeared on countless interview shows. Chester was increasing the size of GreenPAC and beginning new projects aimed at developing and funding new alternative energy sources. He had been invited to serve on several university and foundation boards, and had been honored with numerous environmental awards.

Libby was the new star of the Senate. She had been asked to chair the Environment and Public Works Committee, and was seriously being considered as the Senate Majority Leader even though she was an

Independent, as the current leader was elderly, ill, and soon to retire. And even without Franklin Society intervention, there was increasing talk of Libby as a serious presidential contender.

Meanwhile, the Franklin Society *was* coming forward and into the public discussion with their centrist agenda. They were coalescing their support around Libby and actively establishing grass-root organizations in preparation for her candidacy.

☆☆☆

"Mr. President—five, four, three"—the rest of the countdown was signaled by hand by the White House television floor manager.

Ed sat at the presidential desk in the Oval Office. His face was drawn, and his thinning hair was considerably grayer than when he took office. He lacked sleep, and his face showed it. This was not a man at the top of his game.

It was less than a year and a half since he had been sworn in, and yet here he was about to speak to the nation.

"My fellow citizens of this great American Republic, it is with heartache and profound regret that I address you this evening. I have been beset by many personal and professional misfortunes in these past few months. I take full responsibility for my actions and place the blame on no one but myself.

"There cannot be one of you who does not know the nature of my many misfortunes. However, the greatest and most pressing is the Senate impeachment trial now in progress. I will not comment on its possible outcome, but to spare the American people any further time or treasure, I wish this evening to submit my resignation as President of the United States, effective tomorrow at twelve noon. My able Vice President, Malcolm Danzer, shall be sworn in, and will take command as the new president at that time. You may be assured of a smooth transition with the new commander in chief ready and prepared to act decisively in the event of any emergency. I am certain that he will serve this nation well, and you can be confident of your new president.

"As for myself, I have been proud to serve this great country and take leave now with a heavy heart. I am, indeed, reminded of something my son, Diego, once said to me as he faced the rigors of his bar exam. He said to me, 'Dad, a man is not measured by how he handles triumph. A man is measured by how he handles defeat.' I have taken his advice to heart and pray that you find me not wanting in the action I am now taking."

"So, in this, my final evening as president, I bid you all peace, prosperity, and happiness in all your endeavors. Good evening, farewell, and God bless the United States of America."

☆

Diego and Milly sat silently in her dim apartment as the commentators dissected the president's speech and speculated on the possible success of the new president.

Diego finally broke the silence. "Guess I'll need to get my own apartment again. I'm not sharing the family manse with him in brooding defeat."

Milly reached over and put her hand on Diego's arm. "The old bastard didn't do too bad. For a moment there, I almost believed him."

"Yeah, I need to give him a break. At least he went out with some dignity."

"Nice little touch there, quoting you."

"His scriptwriter must have gotten that from some book of quotes. I never said any such thing. I always knew I would pass my bar exams."

☆☆☆

It was the first Thanksgiving dinner since Ed left office. Milly was hosting the family this year. Diego had invited Dominic to join them, as his family lived in Boston, and he couldn't get home. Carmella was in from New York with her girlfriend, Rebecca, and Chester came with his wife and two twin daughters. The young girls were running around the apartment, with flying pinwheels, screaming like jet engines.

Diego and Dominic had taken over most of the responsibility for the dinner, as Carmella was helpless, except at chopping, and Milly had to entertain the guests. For her, that meant pouring endless champagne, and commenting on the tight ends' tight asses as the football game progressed on the TV with no sound. Hardly anyone paid her any attention.

Chester came into the kitchen looking for Diego. "My man, that sure looks good," he said, picking at the crispy skin of the resting turkey, steaming under a tent of aluminum foil, on the carving board.

Diego slapped his hand. "Not yet."

Chester slid his arm around Diego's shoulder. "Hey, just wanted to let you know I'm so glad you're getting away for a while. You really deserve it after all the shit you've been through these past few months."

"Thanks." He smiled at his friend. "Yeah, need to do some major meditation. There's a lot I need to figure out about my future."

"I hope GreenPAC is still included in that future."

Diego turned and looked at Chester. "We'll see. I've been approached by a publisher to do a book about all of this. Think I would like to try my hand at some writing, but I haven't decided on any one thing just yet. That's the major reason I want to get away. Need to clear my head to see if I can find my next direction."

"Well, you always have a place with us, whatever you decide."

Diego smiled and nodded.

Chester swiped another piece of crispy skin and escaped the kitchen before Diego could come after him with a cleaver.

"We're going to miss you," Dominic said as he began scooping the dressing out of the turkey.

"I invited you to come with me, remember?" Diego replied.

"I know, but it's not in the cards for me right now. Richard has been piling me up with new responsibilities, and I just can't get away."

"Don't think I'll be gone longer than a month or six weeks."

"Machu Picchu—man, that is so cool."

"Yeah, I've always wanted to meditate there at sunrise. And then on to the Amazon—double cool."

"Don't get your head shrunk by the head hunters."

Diego laughed. "That's not my usual problem. Most people think I got too big a head as it is."

Milly popped into the kitchen. Diego was now carving the turkey.

"Surprise guests. Can we seat two more?"

"Don't see why not. Who is it?" Diego asked.

Before she could answer, she popped out again, and Ed came into the kitchen with his date. "Hi gang," he greeted. "Sure is great to see the whole family again. Didn't know our Carmella was a beaver muncher now. What is it with the gay gene in this family? Must come from your mother's side."

Diego winced. "Dad, that is *so not* appropriate."

"Hi there. I'm Bambi," Ed's date announced.

"Oh Sorry. Kids, I want you to meet my date. This is Bambi Badino. She sells cell phones, don't you sweetie?" Bambi nestled in close to Ed. She was an Elena clone to be sure, except shorter and with green streaks in her hair. "Bambi, this is the gang."

"Diego," he introduced himself, as he sliced the turkey breast.

"Dominic," Dom raised his hand.

"Yes, you're the one who took the bullets for my son. Have to thank you for that," Ed acknowledged.

"He would have done the same for me."

"Hey, Dad—and I have to thank you as well," Diego said.

"Yeah, what for?"

"For no longer being president. Can't tell you how nice it is not to have the Secret Service dudes shadowing me every moment."

"I wish I could say the same. Will have them for the rest of my life, they tell me. But at least I don't have to be awakened at 3:00 a.m. with some horrible emergency—unless I want to be, of course." He playfully rubbed noses with Bambi. She chirped and blushed.

Milly came back into the kitchen. "How's that dinner coming? I'm starving, and if we don't get to the table soon, I cannot be held responsible. I'm just about to chuck those two rowdy girls over the balcony. Someone *must* restrain me."

If their lives were a movie, this is when the camera would draw back, and the audience would see the happy family joyously celebrating the holiday with goodwill and bonhomie. The music would swell, and the credits would roll. But this is not a movie, and this is not a Hallmark family. Let's just say the conversation was lively and occasionally fierce.

It may not be the typical American family, but it was still a real American family.

Epilogue

Six Years Later

Lia was now a very successful television producer specializing in shows of interest to women with a secondary focus on environmental issues. But she had also been approached again by the company she had been working with on the monkey bread fruit project when it was still her thesis. Together they were developing a whole new line of products for the health food market and as a tool for fighting hunger in third world countries. Cran, now her husband, had assumed the CEO position of their new company, as Lia was still busy producing television shows, and she wanted to continue that focus—for at least a while longer.

So Lia was very surprised one day to get a letter from an attorney stating that the AmVista drilling had ended on the family property in Brazil. They had removed all of their equipment, and a clause in the original contract of the sale for the land stated that, when AmVista was done with the oil production, the property would revert back to the family—which consisted now of Lia, Cran, her son, Tomas, and Cala.

They flew out the autumn after the letter arrived. The land was so quiet, Lia realized in surprise. No wells, no heavy machinery, no buzzing pipelines. Just the stillness of the jungle, the distant sound of the river, and the footsteps of the four walking toward the tall Baobab tree through the fallen forest leaves. Already the jungle was beginning to reclaim the land lost to the drilling.

Cran walked next to Lia. Lia held Tomas' hand. Cala, now thirteen, followed next to her. They were silent. For Lia and Cala it was a tumultuous moment. They were thrilled to have the family farm back again, but they were also awash with memories, both sweet and horrific of the time before and during the ordeal when the land was wrested from them.

The old tree rose before them, sturdy, weathered, and damaged—but stately and alive. Lia kneeled down before it. She put her arm around Tomas.

"Tomas, this is our land. And this land is part of your history. You already know your biological father's people came from Spain long ago, and it is very likely they mixed with the Inca or the Mayan people. And my people came from Africa and our family is also part Portuguese and probably part Indian, too. We come from many races—you might call us rainbow people."

"Like in the sky?" Tomas asked eagerly.

"Yes, my dear."

Cala knelt down beside him. "You see this big tree?"

"Like a skyscraper," Tomas said in some awe.

"It is," Cala agreed. "And the very first man in our family, who came from Africa, brought the seed that became this tree. It was many, many years ago, and now we are back home, and this tree is ours again. It is old but also still alive and strong like our family."

"Come," Lia said and went up to the tree and put her arms around it as far as she could reach, but she could not encircle its circumference. Cala came up and took Lia's hand and stretched her arms farther around the tree, but they could still not encircle it. Then Tomas and Cran came forward and joined them, but still the tree could not be fully embraced.

Then Lia spoke again. "You see, even now, we cannot all of us hug this tree. It is too big. But as our family grows, more and more will join us, and one day we shall all of us embrace this tree."

It was getting near evening, the time when Lia used to come out from the house, while her mother was making dinner, and sit with her back to the tree, taking in its energy as she watched the sun set and listened to the gentle humming murmur of the river as it flowed toward the ocean. And that is exactly what the four of them did just now. And for this moment, all the ancestors were at peace.

About the Author

Jon McDonald lives in Santa Fe, New Mexico. He has seven published novels, a memoir, and three children's books. His short stories have appeared in a number of prestigious publications. He considers himself a genre-bending author—he loves to take an established literary genre, play with it, and turn it on its head. He has lived abroad and traveled extensively.

Email: jonauthor@gmail.com
Website: www.jonmcdonaldauthor.com
Facebook: https://www.facebook.com/Jon-McDonald-146587072143639

Also by Jon McDonald

Gotta Dance with the One Who Brung Ya

NineStar Press, LLC

www.ninestarpress.com

www.ingramcontent.com/pod-product-compliance
Lightning Source LLC
Chambersburg PA
CBHW021955170626
46808CB00001B/162